'Your plight is desperate, is it not?' he asked roughly.

'Not desperate enough to forget my honour,' she responded, her sapphire eyes flashing with challenge. 'I am ashamed that I did not stop you sooner.'

At the coldness of her tone, his eyes narrowed. Then he checked himself, amusement overriding his anger. Many women in her position would have offered themselves to win his protection. 'I meant no insult,' he drawled, disconcerted by the levelness of her stare. Few men eyed him with such defiance. 'Will you allow me, then, to help you?'

'I cannot deny that I need a champion.' There was obstinacy and pride in the set of her chin, and a sad smile touched her lips. 'But my plight is such that only the king can help me.'

'You aim high,' he said harshly. 'Do you wish me to speak with my kinsman, the Earl of Trevowan? He has some favour with his Majesty.'

'Oh no!' Alynna looked taken aback. 'Why should the Earl interest himself in my case? I doubt that he even knew my father.'

The instant she had spoken, all colour drained from her face. His curiosity was aroused at her independent nature, and he again wondered what she was hiding. Did she truly not know who he was?

For as long as Pauline Bentley can remember, she has been captivated by history. She finds reliving the excitement of the battle of Crecy or a medieval tournament more exciting than the current news of the day. Born in Essex she was trained as a legal secretary, but always came away from visiting castles or manor houses with the desire to write about them. She now lives in Sussex and finds inspiration and relaxation during long walks over the South Downs with the family and dogs. She is married and has two children and a growing menagerie of pets. *Lure of Trevowan* is her second Masquerade Historical Romance.

LURE OF TREVOWAN
Pauline Bentley

MILLS & BOON LIMITED
ETON HOUSE 18–24 PARADISE ROAD
RICHMOND SURREY TW9 1SR

*First published in Great Britain 1988
by Mills & Boon Limited*

© Pauline Bentley 1988

*Australian copyright 1988
Philippine copyright 1988
This edition 1988*

ISBN 0 263 76041 3

*Set in 10 on 10 pt Linotron Times
04–0488–80,900*

*Photoset by Rowland Phototypesetting Limited
Bury St Edmunds, Suffolk
Made and printed in Great Britain by
Cox & Wyman Limited, Reading*

HISTORICAL NOTE

The Lollards (the word means 'mumblers of prayers') were followers of the priest John Wyclif, who preached that no homage was owed to kings, popes or prelates and denied the Church's right to lavish possessions. Forbidden to preach in churches, they went out into towns and villages, spreading a new mode of rebelliousness among those who had for so long been told to be meek and submissive. In 1414 an attempted rising failed, and the leaders were put to death. When in July 1415 the Lollards were implicated in a plot to assassinate Henry V, the persecutions against them or anyone suspected of sympathising with them increased.

CHAPTER ONE

As ALYNNA FRESTON and her mounted escort pounded over the rise of a hill, she saw a straggling line of people some way ahead. At that moment her palfrey stumbled on the frost-hardened track, and the long suppressed anger at the punishing pace enforced by the captain of the guard flared through her.

Pushing back a tendril of deep chestnut hair that had fallen across her face, she was appalled to see how fast her party were closing on the group of wayfarers, who were only just beginning to move aside. She glanced anxiously at the captain of the men-at-arms riding in front of her. When he gave no signal to slow their pace, her throat tightened in alarm. Surely he did not intend to run the travellers down?

'Halt!' she commanded, reining in the sweating mare.

The captain hauled his horse to a rearing stop. He rode back to Alynna's side, his heavy brows creasing into a scowl beneath the rim of his domed helmet as he snarled, 'What have you stopped for?' Before she could rebuke him for his impudence, he reached over, grabbed her palfrey's bridle, and with a cruel jerk dragged the tired mare onwards.

'Take your hand from my reins, Captain!' Alynna's blue eyes blazed at the man. He was a stranger to her, as were all his men, their snorting, sweating horses a confused mêlée around her. When the captain did not release her bridle and her mare was forced into a canter, Alynna's patience snapped. In all her seventeen years, no one had ever treated her with such insolence before. As the eldest daughter of Sir Robert Freston, all the servants and villeins at her home at Higham Mote treated her with deference and respect, but during the last hour —since these men had been sent to replace her original escort— she had begun to feel like a hounded prisoner.

'I ordered you to remove your hand!' she fumed.

When the captain ignored her command, unease prickled her spine. The guards' actions puzzled her, for there was something sinister about these rough-looking men, but she pushed the notion aside as absurd. Were they not her father's retainers?

On the track ahead, several of the crippled travellers were hobbling too slowly to reach to safety of the ditch, and fury replaced Alynna's annoyance. She would not allow those people to be run down. Knowing that any order from her would be ignored as before, she brought her riding-whip down across the captain's arm well above the protective steel plates of his gauntlet, at the same time pulling her lathered mare to a standstill.

An oath broke from the captain's lips that shocked her by its profanity. Turning away from him in disgust, she was relieved to discover that the road ahead was almost clear. One of the walkers, a tall dark-cloaked figure who moved with fluid, almost regal grace, was helping the last of the group, a man with bandaged eyes, to safety. Her attention caught, she saw they all carried long wooden staffs, and guessed that they were pilgrims on their way to Becket's shrine at Canterbury.

Alynna looked contemptuously at the captain, her tone icy. 'Take your hand from my horse this instant! We will continue our journey at a more leisurely pace, Captain. You almost ran those pilgrims down.'

'My orders were to return to Barkhurst by noon.' He removed his hand from her bridle and regarded Alynna sourly. 'You were expected yesterday.'

From behind her, Alynna heard her maid gasp at the man's rudeness.

'You will show your respect by addressing me as "my lady", as is befitting.' Alynna bristled, her level gaze unflinching beneath his hostile glare. 'I will not have the lives of other travellers endangered. Is that clear, Captain?'

His eyes narrowed, their glittering hardness menacing, and his tone was deliberately mocking. 'Yes, *my lady*.'

The escort closed in on Alynna, and for the first time she felt threatened by their presence. These men acted like mercenaries, yet her father despised the brutality of such men and had sworn never to use them among his guards. She studied the riders surrounding her, noting with disquiet the shabbiness of their cloaks stained with the rust from their armour. Sir Robert abhorred slovenliness. His men-at-arms took pride in their weapons. Why had he sent these men to replace her original escort?

Alynna pulled her sable-lined cloak tighter about her chilled body and quashed her growing disquiet. What could she possibly have to fear from her father's men? A week of travelling had left her weary and prone to fancy. Within an hour she would be warming herself by the fire at Barkhurst, reunited with her father. How they would laugh together at her strange notions, Sir Robert's booming voice chiding her for a faint-heart as he drew her closer. Yet into her reflections came the scornful voice of her mother marring the pleasure of the moment. If only this Christmas of 1415 could be different, and her mother would spare them one of her jealous rages. Alynna frowned, for it was so long since her parents had lived in peace and harmony, and now this summons for her to visit Barkhurst Manor puzzled her.

Seeking to cast off her unease, her gaze travelled over the pilgrim band, and the sight of their figures hunched against the biting wind aroused her compassion. Their hoods were pulled down against the cold; some leaned wearily upon their staffs, others upon crutches, and several wore medals pinned to their cloaks showing the shrines they had previously visited. They huddled together for warmth, or stamped their feet against the cold, many muttering their discontent at being forced off the road, all except for one pilgrim.

The tall dark-cloaked figure she had noticed earlier had detached himself from his companions and stood some distance away. There was something about his stance which captured her attention. It was proud, and he held his pilgrim's staff erect like a standard.

Shoulders squared and legs braced with his cloak billowing about him, he faced the icy wind. It was as though he challenged the elements themselves to defy him in his purpose.

She felt a twinge of disappointment that his hood obscured his features. There was something indomitable, almost mystifying, about his manner. She would have liked to have seen his face, if only to assure herself this self-possessed figure was human, for he stood solid and implacable as a rock. That he did not even glance at her party as they neared sharpened her interest. This was no ordinary pilgrim. There was a quality about him—an aloofness, a tangible air of authority—which set him apart from his companions. He might travel in humble guise, but there was nothing humble about that forbidding, arrogant figure.

Now, as her escort bore down upon him, Alynna's heartbeat quickened in dread. He showed no sign of stepping aside, and the captain seemed intent on running him down.

'Stand back, sir,' she warned.

Whether he heard her or not, the pilgrim did not move. Then, at the very last moment, he stepped back, but in a manner so proud and disdainful that Alynna had the impression he was merely condescending to allow her party to pass.

The pilgrim's eyes narrowed as he moved out of the riders' path and watched them ride on. A quick assessment of the troop had been enough to his experienced eye to know their type. The woman rode as though she had been born in the saddle, and from her rich dress was obviously of high birth, although he had been unable to see her face to recognise her. Neither did the troop wear insignia to identify the nobleman they served. He compressed his lips into a bleak line. Undisciplined and uncaring, the soldiers were unmistakably mercenaries. Since Henry V had returned to England following the victory over the French at Agincourt, such men, made restless by the prospect of months without fighting and plunder, had left the king's army to snatch what they could from the land. It was time they were stopped. Dear God, did he not know to his own sorrow what destruction those men wrought?

The unceasing remorse of the past weeks twisted like a knife into him. His hand closed over his staff, and he wished he were holding instead his double-edged sword, which he had discarded for the duration of his pilgrimage. His fingers itched to be revenged upon the brigands who had brought devastation to his family. When he returned to King Henry's court, he would counsel his Majesty to enforce strict laws against the mercenaries. Yet whatever laws were imposed, they would come too late to save those he loved most dear.

With an angry tug he pulled his hood further over his face. The pain that had been with him since he had learned of the events of that fateful day at Trevowan was unrelenting, grinding ever deeper. Would he ever know peace from this torment and guilt?

Alynna jerked her thoughts away from the lingering impression of the tall pilgrim. The unease that had been with her since she had been commanded by her mother, Lady Joan, to travel to Kent for the Christmas festivities intensified. The summons was unexpected and uncharacteristic. Always, to Alynna's puzzlement and distress, Lady Joan excluded her from any visit to Barkhurst, although her younger daughters frequently accompanied her. If Lady Joan showed little natural affection towards her eldest daughter, Sir Robert treated Alynna more like a son and, when Lady Joan was away, they became inseparable. That was why she could not understand her father's change of plan. She had already begun the preparations for the Yuletide feasts at Higham Mote and had had to leave their completion in the hands of the steward. The messenger, when questioned, had implied that her presence was needed urgently at Barkhurst—yet there was nearly a month to Christmas and all its festivities.

At a cry from her maid, Alynna looked anxiously over her shoulder. To her dismay she saw that she was now some distance behind, surrounded by four men-at-arms, while another bent over the foreleg of her horse. Alynna tried to slow her own mare, but the escort was so tightly packed round and behind her that she could not draw to a halt without injuring her palfrey, and she was forced on.

'Captain! Stop!' she commanded. 'My maid's horse appears to have pulled up lame.'

'Lady Joan expects you,' the captain grunted. 'There's been delay enough. The maid will be looked after by my men.'

Far from reassured, Alynna glanced back and was horrified to see that they had already lost sight of the others beyond the curve in the track. Enraged by her own treatment by her escort, she tried to draw level with the captain. 'I demand we halt! Stop at once, or Sir Robert will hear of this.'

A coarse laugh from the captain greeted her order. 'Sir Robert isn't in a position to hear anything!'

'What do you mean by that?' she asked, her body chilling with mounting fear.

He grinned insolently. 'You will learn soon enough.'

With that, he whipped his horse to a faster pace, clearly impatient to reach Barkhurst. Even as Alynna struggled to pull up her mare, anxious that her maid was left so far behind, her bridle was grabbed by one of the guards and her escort broke into a dangerously fast gallop. Because she was concerned that her mount would stumble again and break a leg on the frosty ground, Alynna stopped trying to slow her pace. Her maid would have to manage as best she could. She refused to admit she was frightened, but cold sweat stung her back, stemming from something deeper than her anger or humiliation at the way she was being treated like a prisoner.

Her throat went dry as the captain's words pounded through her mind. She had thought it strange earlier that her escort had suddenly been changed so close to her destination. After days of travelling, the men who had come with her from Higham Mote in Suffolk were tired, yet they had been dismissed and ordered to return at once. It was unlike Sir Robert to be so callous and uncaring of the welfare of his men. Had something happened to him?

She mastered her panic. She was being foolish. Nothing could have happened to her father. At five and thirty he was in the prime of his life—strong, virile, her adored hero, a golden giant. Yet since Henry V's army had first ridden out to France a change had come over him. The sadness, which he guarded so well, but which she sometimes glimpsed, had shadowed his eyes. He never spoke of why the king had not accepted his service to fight in France, and although he had stayed at Court to serve the king's brother, who had been appointed Regent in his Majesty's absence, she knew that it was more than disappointment that had robbed her father of his usual sparkle.

Throughout the remainder of her journey she could not entirely shake the sense of foreboding hanging over her. She had missed her father's witty companionship and their lengthy talks when he would discuss his plans for the estate or explain the king's policies in amassing his army for a war with France. Although she enjoyed her role of managing the household, the constant company of women, and their idle chatter, irked her. Her troubled thoughts followed the rhythm of the horses' pounding hooves. She had hoped this visit might be a sign of a reconciliation between her estranged parents. For, until then, Sir Robert had planned to return from the celebrations in London surrounding his Majesty's homecoming after Agincourt to spend the twelve days of Christmas in Suffolk. Yet in her heart she knew that a reconciliation was unlikely, as she could not remember a time when her parents had been less than icily civil in each other's company.

The escort's pace was unrelenting, her tired, aching body making it impossible to think. At last her party turned off the main track, slowing as they approached a river, where there was no bridge but only a large flat wooden ferry set between two ropes. While the captain ordered his men to dismount and lead the horses on to the wooden raft, Alynna hoped for a sight of her maid back along the track. The road, however, was disturbingly empty, leaving her with a feeling of isolation.

She remained mounted as her palfrey was led on to the raft. At a hoarse shout from the captain, a burly, bearded figure shambled out of a nearby ramshackle hut. To her surprise, he approached the captain and spoke to him for some time. She saw the captain nod and shout an order for six of the men to take their horses back on shore. When the ferryman strode on to the raft and picked up his pole to propel the vessel across the river, Alynna eyed the captain suspiciously.

'Is anything amiss?' she asked.

The soldier looked taken aback, then his customary scowl returned to his coarse face. 'Seems a servant due for a whipping has run away from the manor. He stole some silver. The men are to join in the hunt for him.'

Alynna hid her shock. No servants were ever whipped at Higham Mote. And stealing! It was unheard-of—the servants were always too well looked after there. How different from her own home Barkhurst began to seem, but this was Lady Joan's domain. Even at Higham, the atmosphere was colder and the servants sullen when her mother was in residence. She shivered. Everything was so strange and out of place here, and her eyes darkened to deep sapphire and she unconsciously pushed a stray tendril of dark hair into place beneath her jewelled cap.

Once on the far bank, the remainder of her escort remounted, and moments later they rode through a deserted-looking village. When a flock of untended honking geese scurried from their path, anxiety again knotted her stomach. It was midday. Why were the villeins not at work on the land or tending the livestock? And why were the shutters barred at the windows of all the simple wooden houses?

Alynna conquered her misgivings as they approached the bleak grey walls of a moated manor house. So this was Barkhurst. How different the neglected-looking dwelling was from the red-painted castle of Higham.

Like the village, it looked far from welcoming. And so remote, cut off as it was by the river. Her glance rose to the standard pole on the tower, her heart contracting in dismay when she saw no standard flying. Was Sir Robert not here?

The escort halted by a cluster of timber buildings to one side of the moat. A page wearing her father's green and gold livery ran forward to speak with the captain. With a curt nod to Alynna to follow him, the captain rode over the narrow drawbridge into the small court-yard of the Manor. Two grooms appeared to take the horses, but otherwise the place was devoid of servants. It was unnaturally quiet.

Alynna dismounted, and inhaling deeply to dispel her growing apprehension, she glanced around the court-yard. After the accustomed size and bustle she was used to at the efficiently run castle at Higham, the timbered Manor looked gloomy, cramped and uninviting.

'This way!' The captain fell into step beside her and led her to the gatehouse.

Although expecting to be taken to the solar of the main building, Alynna made no protest. Perhaps Lady Joan was closeted with the bailiff and had ordered her to be brought direct to her presence. Besides, her hands and feet were numb with cold and she was past question-ing any more. She followed the captain up the winding stone stairs, moving past him when he stood aside for her to enter a dingy chamber. Little light penetrated the arrow-slits which were all that passed for windows, and her nose wrinkled at the acrid stench filling the room from a nearby midden. More disturbing still, the room was empty.

Puzzled, she swung round to demand an explanation, but the captain's heavy footsteps were fading as he disappeared downstairs. Alynna shivered and drew her cloak tighter about her. What was happening? A frisson of fear sped down her spine. If Lady Joan was not here, why had she been brought to the gatehouse and not to her mother's private apartments? And where were the servants?

An ominous silence hung over the house. Alynna's heart thudded and she drew a steadying breath, mentally scolding herself for her weakness. The captain was an ignorant fool! He must have mistaken his orders. She moved towards the door, determined to find her own way to Lady Joan's chambers.

With a sound of rustling silk from the stairwell, a short, stout woman came into view. Recognising her mother, Alynna stepped back into the room and curtsied.

'So you've arrived at last!' Lady Joan snapped, her wide horned headdress forcing her to step sideways through the narrow doorway.

Startled by her mother's tone, Alynna threw back the hood of her cloak and rose to her full height. Lady Joan stood in a shaft of light from the arrow-slits. The hostility in her eyes was like a dagger thrust straight at Alynna's breast, and instantly she was on her guard, her long lashes hiding her pain at her mother's attitude. During her childhood, Lady Joan's coldness towards her, in contrast to her devotion to her younger sisters, had wounded Alynna, but that pain had been eased by the affection of her father. In later years she guessed that some of Lady Joan's resentment stemmed from the special relationship which existed between her husband and his firstborn.

It was that very closeness which had left Alynna unwed at seventeen. Every day, weather permitting, Sir Robert and Alynna went hawking together, much to the disapprobation of Lady Joan. Whenever the subject of her marriage was mentioned, Sir Robert always deferred it for another year, declaring that he would not be deprived of his brightest jewel.

Her puzzlement growing at her mother's manner, Alynna asked, 'Is Sir Robert not here? His standard does not fly from the tower.'

Lady Joan looked away, her voice devoid of emotion. 'Sir Robert is dead!'

Alynna swayed, a pain more agonising than a mace-blow crushing her chest. 'My father dead! How can that be?' she choked out. 'How did he die?'

'While out hunting a week ago, he was killed by an arrow,' Lady Joan stated, equally flatly. 'It was thought he was struck down by outlaws. The woods have been searched, but whoever was responsible has disappeared.'

The bare walls of the chamber dipped and swayed around Alynna and she leaned on the wall for support. How could her father be dead? Why should he be attacked by outlaws on his own land? It could not be true! Yet, as she met the full force of the hatred in Lady Joan's gaze, she knew it was true. If he was alive, Lady Joan would as usual be at pains to conceal her dislike for Alynna.

'The news is a shock to you,' Lady Joan said with unexpected sympathy, her expression hidden by the immense horns of her headdress as she bent to pick up a goblet, already filled with wine, that had been left on a dusty coffer. She pressed the cup into Alynna's trembling hands. 'Drink this!'

Still dazed, Alynna sipped it but, disliking the bitter taste, lowered it from her lips.

'I said, drink it,' Lady Joan snapped. 'It will ease the shock.'

Alynna ignored her mother's command. An icy numbness had settled over her, making it difficult to think clearly.

'W-where is Sir Robert's body? I would pay my respects,' she managed to force out through her heartache.

'Sir Robert was buried six days ago in the chapel vault.'

Outrage replaced Alynna's initial shock. 'Dead for a week, and I knew nothing of this!' she gasped, forgetful of the respect due to her mother. She knew that her parents argued frequently, and Sir Robert was noticeably more relaxed and content when Lady Joan was away at Barkhurst. But this! This hasty burial in such an isolated manor was an insult to Sir Robert's memory.

'Why was no messenger sent to tell me? Sir Robert

should be buried at Higham Mote, and with due ceremony. My father . . .'

'Insolent whelp!' Lady Joan shrilled. 'How dare you
question me! Always it was you and Sir Robert . . .
while I, his wife, was cast aside.'

A blush stung Alynna's cheeks at the sharpness of the
rebuke. Was it grief which made her mother act so?
Surely now they should be drawn closer to each other,
but why did she continue to look on her with such
loathing?

'Drink your wine,' Lady Joan stormed, her hands
fluttering nervously. 'Even now you are set on defying
me! For heaven's sake, girl, drink the wine.'

Alynna's hand was grabbed and urged towards her
mouth. As the goblet struck her teeth, she jerked it
away, astonished by her mother's behaviour. Somehow
it fell to the floor, its contents spilling across the flag-
stones. Lady Joan stared at the liquid disappearing into
the cracks, her face twisting with fury. The cup was
dented, and she supposed that was the reason for her
anger. Used to her mother's violent rages when anything
was damaged and had to be replaced, she paid little heed
to the incident, for, like her father, she despised Lady
Joan's miserly ways. Also, her mind and limbs felt heavy
and it was difficult to think.

'You forget your place, girl!' Lady Joan screeched.
'Your father's fault—he always allowed you too much
freedom. When I think of the years I have borne the
insult of watching Sir Robert dote on you . . . But no
more! Not for another hour will I acknowledge a baseborn brat as my own.'

Momentarily stunned, Alynna gazed dumbly at
Lady Joan, her dulled mind trying to understand. The
light from the arrow-slits falling across the older
woman's face revealed the glittering hardness in her
eyes.

'What are you saying?' she challenged, her tongue
oddly thick. 'How can I be baseborn? I am Sir Robert's
daughter!'

'You may be his daughter, but you are no child of

mine!' Flinging out an accusing arm in Alynna's direction, Lady Joan continued her tirade. 'You are the cause of my shame, yet you were treated like a princess by Sir Robert. He squandered a fortune on jewels for you. You had private tutors and were educated like a son. Only the finest Arab mare was good enough for you when you rode at his side in the hunting field. Well, that time is past. I disown you! Get you gone from my house and lands!'

Obviously her mother was distraught. She must be out of her mind with grief, and did not know what she was saying. The story was too absurd! Alynna acknowledged that she had never loved her as she did her two younger daughters, and was fiercely possessive. Too often she had witnessed her jealous ravings that Sir Robert neglected her. Reaching out, dazed and shocked, Alynna touched Lady Joan's arm, but her hold was flung aside.

'Do not touch me! I have borne your presence long enough. Go, before I summon the guards!' Lady Joan's hand whipped up to snatch at the jewelled cap on Alynna's head. 'You will take nothing of value with you. Nothing!'

The pain of the pins being wrenched free from her hair as the cap was pulled off stung Alynna into retaliation. Forgetful of her years of training to show respect to her elders, she demanded, 'What have I done to deserve this? You are upset—you do not know what you are saying, my lady mother.'

'Do not call me that!'

Fire shot along Alynna's cheek and her head snapped backwards, her ears ringing from the violence of the slap.

'Do you still not understand?' Lady Joan raged. 'I am *not* your mother. For sixteen years I have been humiliated by your presence in my home. I loved Sir Robert, but he never cared for me—as he never loved the two daughters I gave him. Always it was that trollop . . . She was never from his thoughts . . . his unattainable love. And you are her image . . . damn you!'

A cruel gleam brightened Lady Joan's eyes. 'You are

a bastard! Did you never wonder why, unlike your sisters, you were not sent to serve as a waiting woman in some noble household, or taken to Court, even though your father's position took him there often? Isn't it obvious why a husband had not been found for you? What nobleman would want to marry the bastard daughter of a knight? From this moment you will cease to exist as my daughter. Should you be discovered on any of your father's estates, you will be hounded from them like a felon!'

Through the agony of her grief and shock, Alynna strove against the numbing lethargy overtaking her and tried to make sense of it all. If Lady Joan spoke the truth, it explained the unanswered questions that had arisen over the years. Did not her appearance alone set her apart from her sisters? Both of them, like Lady Joan, were short and plump. Hitherto, she had always believed she had inherited her tall slender figure from her father, but no other member of her family had her sapphire and violet flecked eyes or dark chestnut hair.

An image of Sir Robert came to Alynna's mind. In the cold winter evenings she would sit at his feet as they played at chess or backgammon. Often he would look at her intently and his eyes glazed as he spoke of his years as a young knight at Court. Occasionally, when he had drunk deeper than usual of the potent Burgundy wines, he would speak of her likeness to her mother. Until now that had always puzzled her.

'Who was my mother?' she asked, as Lady Joan moved across to a coffer covered in an old woollen cloak.

'You are the daughter of a serving-wench who caught Sir Robert's eye,' Lady Joan scoffed, picking up the cloak. 'The woman died giving birth to you.' She spun round and flung the cloak at Alynna's feet. A swirl of dust flew up from the stale rushes as the garment settled on the floor. 'You may keep the travelling gown you are wearing, but you will leave behind your jewels and sable cloak.'

Defiantly Alynna's hand covered the jewelled belt about her hips. 'My jewels are all gifts from my father.

Even if what you say is true, and I am not your daughter,' Alynna tossed back her head proudly, 'I am still his child. You shame his memory by your deeds this day.'

'Be content that for seventeen years you have lived upon his bounty!' Lady Joan jeered.

Pride reared through Alynna's sorrow and pain. She might be baseborn, but she was still her father's daughter. A chivalrous, just man, true to his knightly vows, he had taught her the meaning of honour, of the need to strive to overcome adversity. Unflinching, she met the hatred in Lady Joan's eyes, but to her alarm her voice seemed to come from a great distance outside herself as a wave of dizziness returned. 'The disgrace of this day is yours alone, my lady. I want nothing from you, except what is mine by right.'

A flush of angry colour stained Lady Joan's fleshy cheeks. 'You will leave my house at once, as ordered. Do you think I have kept you away from my servants here, for you to flaunt your bastardy now? Go! Whether you leave on your own accord, or are dragged away by my guards, is your choice.'

Alynna stood her ground, anger burning through that heaviness of mind and limb. What she believed to be her birthright, her rank as a gentlewoman, even part of her identity, had been stripped from her. But she would not relinquish her right to honour her father's memory. 'I will not leave until I have paid homage to Sir Robert's tomb.'

For a moment the woman's mouth worked, but no words came, fury robbing her of speech. 'Guards!' Lady Joan finally choked out. Then, more strongly, 'Here, guards!'

Alynna heard the sound of running footsteps on the stairs, and the chink of chain mail against armour. Undeterred, she persisted as the first of the guards clattered into the room, 'I demand to see Sir Robert's steward. He must have attended the funeral.'

'You will demand nothing, wench! The steward here has no time for vagabonds such as you. All who attended Sir Robert on his arrival have left Barkhurst.'

'Sir Robert would not have cast me penniless from his home. He loved me. This is your doing.'

'Guards!' Lady Joan's body shook with the force of her rage.

Alynna shrugged off the mailed hand laid upon her shoulder, the exertion sending the room spiralling around her. 'The matter will not end here,' she gasped. 'I demand justice!'

Rough hands jerked Alynna backwards. She kicked out when an arm clamped about her waist, but her movements were strangely slow and ineffectual. The wine—had Lady Joan drugged the wine to make it easier to get rid of her?

Her eyes smarting with outrage, she was dragged towards the stairs. 'I shall petition the king . . .' Her parting challenge was cut short by a cry of pain, agony searing through her temple from a hard blow to her head. Splashes of light swam before her eyes, then the image of Lady Joan blurred. The room faded into blackness, the floor rushing towards her face. Vainly she fought to retain her consciousness, but she kept falling . . . down, down into a seemingly unending void.

Arrowheads of pain shot down Alynna's skull and neck as consciousness slowly returned. Her leaden eyelids refused to open. She was dimly aware of the swaying movement of her body, of the smell of horses and drumming of hooves. Gradually she reasoned that the painful chafing against her side was caused by the high pommel of a saddle, and that she was draped across a man's legs.

'This is far enough from the Manor.' A gruff voice penetrated her stupor. 'Throw her into the ditch.'

A groan broke from her lips as she was dragged from the horse, and she tried to rouse herself to fight, but her senses reeled sickeningly. Her head thudded against the hard ground, and as consciousness again slipped from her, she heard the horses ride off.

When next she stirred, she was aware first of the

freezing cold and that she was lying on the ground. All of a sudden dawning realisation came to her, and her flesh cringed with revulsion. Calloused hands were pulling her kirtle up over her thighs! Her eyes flew open, starting with horror. Above her, outlined by the dark grey sky, two bearded faces leered down. Dear God, they were going to rape her! Summoning her scattered wits, she began to struggle, and a cracked scream rose from her throat.

'She's coming round, Wat,' the larger of the two men wheezed, and as her wits cleared, she recognised him as the ferryman.

The acrid stench—like wild garlic and rotting fish—rising from his body almost robbed her of breath as her full senses returned. Terror set the blood churning through her veins, and she struck out at her attackers, despite the stiffness of limbs made sluggish with cold. She refused to submit, even though her heart beat so fast it seemed likely to burst. Although the weight crushing her body was overpowering her weakened efforts, fear gave her the strength she needed and she fought like a vixen, clawing and biting. Her screams were smothered by the hem of her kirtle stuffed into her mouth, and her throat grazed raw with the force of her muffled cries, while she twisted and arched her body to escape the repugnant touch of the man's hands upon her naked flesh.

'She's a lively piece,' a coarse voice behind her sniggered with lust. 'Hold the she-wolf still!'

Alynna lashed out, gritting her teeth against the agony shafting through her head as she raked at his face with her fingers. Her hands were wrenched aside and pinned to the ground by her attacker's companion, but her struggles had freed the hem of her kirtle from her mouth. Breathing heavily, she glared at the ferryman hovering above her.

'Release me at once, you filthy lout!' she shouted.

'High and mighty, ain't she?' Wat bleated behind her. 'Must be a new serving-wench from the Manor, aping her betters.'

'No!' Aylnna ground out, her voice shrill with fury. 'I'm no serving-maid. Get your vile hands off me!'

'Shut 'er up, Hugh!' Wat whined. 'Or else we'd better drag her off the Canterbury road. She'll 'ave those damned pilgrims coming back to see what all the screaming is about.'

'I doubt it,' Hugh sneered, as he eased back to fumble with his rough woollen hose. 'They ain't interested in nothing but their own salvation.'

Above her the bearded face ran with sweat, and Hugh grinned lewdly, sensing that her strength was failing fast. Merciful St Winifred, she prayed, would no one save her from this horror! Fury swept through her at this final humiliation. The ferryman came from the Barkhurst estate, so had Lady Joan planned this? Nausea rose to her throat as rough fingers dug into the soft flesh of her inner thigh. Screaming desperately, she arched her body, at the same time bringing up her knee to ram her assailant's groin. With a howl of pain, his hold slackened, but not enough for her to get free.

'Holy Mother, save me!' she screamed, her voice hoarse with terror. There was a loud pounding in her ears and her mind seemed to be on fire. Her strength was almost gone—it was useless. Her terror mounted when a third figure appeared behind Hugh.

'Whoresons!' the man bellowed, as he slammed a large stick against her assailant's head.

Hugh rolled off Alynna. Snarling with rage, he clambered to his feet to face his attacker.

'Keep hold of the wench!' he shouted back at Wat. 'I'll deal with this little rat.'

Belatedly Alynna recognised the bald pate and stunted wiry figure of her rescuer. What was Joel, her father's jester, doing here? Even as the thought raced through her mind, she twisted round on to her knees to escape from Wat's tenacious hold. She had to get free! Joel, for all his valiant heart, was no match for these two ruffians, and already he was being overpowered. She winced at hearing the vicious punches Hugh was slamming into his body.

Somehow she found new reserves of strength to fight on. Though shorter than Hugh, Wat was thick set, and the cruel gleam in his eyes warned her he was not about to loose his prize. Scratching at his face, her nails broke as they gouged his cheek and she managed to stagger to her feet, shaking the loosened mass of her hair from her face.

'Bitch!' he grunted, his hand raised to strike her. It froze in mid-air as he stared over her head.

'Release the wench!' a deep voice thundered its warning.

Alynna felt Wat stiffen, his arm closed around her waist, and uttering a curse, he jerked her against him. She turned her head to see who had spoken, and saw the tall dark-cloaked pilgrim she had noticed on the road to Barkhurst.

CHAPTER TWO

THE PILGRIM had already dealt with the ferryman, who was now sprawled unconscious on the ground beside Joel's gasping figure, and he paused. His hand resting negligently on his staff, he stood like a dark statue.

'So you want the maid for yourself, do you, pilgrim?' Wat jeered. 'We can all 'ave a share in 'er.'

'Then fight if you want her!' the pilgrim challenged, gripping the staff in both hands and testing its balance.

A tremor of fear went through Wat, but before Alynna could pull away, the sharp point of his dagger pressed against her ribs making her throat cramp with returning terror.

Round-eyed, she stared at the pilgrim. He had pushed back his hood, revealing a lean, strikingly handsome face and cropped black hair. Although he looked no older than the late twenties, he looked so assured and masterful that, when his full lips curved into a smile, showing white even teeth, a quivering sensation seized her heart. He was her champion—like those in the tournaments her father had so often described to her. He stood poised, balanced on the balls of his feet, ready to fight in a manner that showed he had been trained to knighthood. There was an arrogant thrust to his chin, and the dark stubble of several days' growth of beard, no doubt because of a vow he would have taken not to shave for the duration of his pilgrimage, accentuated the forbidding set of his jaw. But it was his eyes, grey and threatening as stormclouds, which made the deepest impression on her. Even though he did not speak, his presence dominated the track, a tangible menace as he waited, with predatory stillness, for his prey to make his move.

Alynna could smell Wat's fear, and her blood ran

cold. To try and save his own life, he would not hesitate to kill her.

'Stand bank, pilgrim,' Wat growled, 'or the wench dies!'

The pilgrim's grey eyes flashed like tempered steel, then, swifter than a striking hawk, his staff whirled, his arm a blur as he sprang forward. There was a rush of air across Alynna's face as the staff struck Wat's head. The dagger fell to the ground. Wat, screaming in pain, released Alynna and staggered backwards, his hands clutching at his bloodied, broken nose.

Shakily Alynna picked up the fallen weapon. With it in her hand, she no longer felt threatened, but when she made to thrust it into her jewelled belt, her anger flared at finding that gone. Gone also were the rest of her jewels and her sable cloak. Self-consciously she pulled the edges of the plain homespun cloak—the one Lady Joan had flung at her—across her crumpled mud-stained skirts. Her rage mounted. Lady Joan had left her nothing to betray her status. She pushed the mass of dark tresses back under her hood, ashamed that she had not even a plain wimple to cover her hair modestly.

On hearing a groan from Joel, who was staggering to his feet, she ignored her own discomfort and ran to his side.

'My lady, I . . .' Joel croaked.

She put a warning finger to her lips, silencing him. It was no good bewailing her fate. Lady Joan would never allow her to return, and she must make the best of it. But one day, she silently vowed, she would demand back her father's gifts—not because their value would allow her to live comfortably for some years, but because they had been given in love and as such were irreplaceable.

'No titles, Joel,' she whispered. 'It appears I no longer have the right.'

Concerned that the pilgrim might have overheard, she glanced in his direction, but his back was to her as he bent over the ferryman. Wat was already stumbling over the rutted track in his haste to be gone.

Turning back to Joel, she saw from the sadness in his

eyes that he knew something of her bastardy. Unwilling
to discuss the matter before the pilgrim, she handed the
dagger to the jester for safe-keeping and examined the
cut on his head, where the blood was beginning to
congeal. He winced, and she put out a hand to steady his
swaying figure.

'Are you all right?'

'Don't you worry about me!' Joel's eyes clouded with
anxiety. 'It's you we have to take care of.'

A lump rose to her throat at the jester's concern. He
had discarded his fool's parti-hose, and in a brown tunic
and hood he looked wizened, very different from the
jaunty character who was always ready with a quip or a
song. Once she had assured herself that Joel was not
badly injured, she curbed her curiosity as to how he
came to be here and glanced at the man who had saved
her.

The pilgrim was not even breathing heavily as he
ordered Hugh to his feet. 'If you value your hide,' he
said coldly, 'get yourself out of my sight. A sore head is
scant justice for the way you forced yourself on this
woman.'

Scowling, Hugh got up, his meaty fists clenched. For a
moment he seemed to consider taking up the fight. 'I
don't take orders from no pilgrim!'

'Then prepare to die, knave,' the deep, cultured voice
proclaimed.

Alynna held her breath, fearful lest the pilgrim should
be harmed on her account, but as the ferryman looked
into the face of his antagonist, whatever he saw there
made him change his mind. His hands fell to his sides.

'She's only a serving-wench,' he sneered, 'and most
probably a thief, from the clothes she's wearing. You
can have her, pilgrim.'

Turning his back on them, Hugh lurched into an
ungainly run to catch up with his fleeing companion. The
pilgrim pulled his hood over his head and moved away,
about to depart.

'Good sir!' Alynna called out, appalled that he would
leave before she could thank him. He glanced sidelong

at her as she walked towards him. 'You saved my honour and most likely my life. I am indebted to you, sir.'

Beneath the shadow of the hood she saw his lips tighten, and she was aware of his piercing grey stare. 'Your voice and gold-edged gown are not those of a servant,' he said harshly. 'What are you doing without suitable escort on the highway?'

A rush of heat burned Alynna's cheeks and she looked away, unable to hold the man's searching gaze.

Seeing the stain of colour across the woman's high cheekbones, the pilgrim, despite his inclination to return to his fellow travellers, found himself studying her more closely, held by the clear sapphire blue of her eyes. Why had her stare, which until that moment had been open and forthright, shuttered at his question?

'I thank you for your help, sir,' she continued, the faintest tremor still apparent in her soft voice.

It was that tremor, which she was so obviously trying to control, that sharpened his interest. The pallor of her oval face made her eyes glow like polished jewels, and the way she caught her trembling lower lip between her teeth and proudly raised her chin at him showed defiance at the circumstances in which she found herself. Noble qualities: she was courageous and beautiful. The delicate lines of her slim upturned nose and high cheekbones were both ethereal and sensual—a provocative combination. And the tendrils of dark chestnut hair clinging damply to her wide brow displayed a colour rarely seen. From the way the man accompanying her hung back, he was clearly her servant.

The pilgrim recalled the image of how he had first seen her—her long, slender legs kicking beneath the bulk of her assailant and her eyes wide with terror. The cold, implacable rage he had felt at seeing those two knaves about to rape her rekindled his own anguish, and he swallowed convulsively. It was not the flashing-eyed woman he saw now in his mind, but his sister. Was that how Meraud had looked when those brigands . . .?

He crushed the image of his sister being raped by drunken mercenaries, but the remorse gnawing at him

remained. He should have been at Trevowan protecting
his loved ones on that Godforsaken day. Instead, with
the victory over the French at Agincourt still pulsing
through his veins, he had dallied at Henry V's side while
London welcomed their hero sovereign. Fêted and
acclaimed by people and monarch alike for his own
valour on the battlefield and the number of French
noblemen he had captured for ransom, he had been
delayed in returning to Cornwall because the king demanded his presence at the celebrations. The guilt
stabbed deeper. How hollow was that praise to him now!
His courage had not saved his sister's innocence or his
mother's life that day, he reflected savagely. He had
failed them.

Instinctively his hand moved to his hip, and he felt
naked without the accustomed weight of his sword at his
side. He had been powerless to act against those
brigands. Although his men had scoured the west of
England, the mercenaries had fled, escaping his wrath.
He could never forgive himself for not being present to
defend his family. It was not for himself that he had
forsaken all comforts to make this humble pilgrimage—but for Meraud. Dear God, let him not fail his
sister a second time!

Already he had tarried too long in returning to his
companions, but intrigued by the air of mystery surrounding the woman he had rescued, he still hesitated.
Had he not heard her screams, her fate would have been
the same as Meraud's, and, in a strange way, he felt
protective towards her.

'You were fortunate to escape harm, madame. The
highways are dangerous for a woman to travel as you
do,' he said, more gruffly than he intended, the memories of his sister still haunting him. 'There's a track to a
hamlet a short distance back from here. Barkhurst, I
believe the place is called.'

Had he drawn a sword to strike her, she could not
have shown a more violent reaction. All colour drained
from her face and a shudder passed through her slim
figure.

'No!' Her denial was impassioned. 'I cannot go there!'

The servant moved forward, his face haggard as he looked at his mistress, saying heavily, 'Ay, we must move on. It's not safe here. Yet where are we to go? Do you know of a priory near here, sir, where we could take shelter?'

She threw him a sharp look. 'The pilgrim has delayed his journey too long because of us, Joel. We shall find shelter.'

Again he was struck by her quiet dignity. She asked or expected nothing from him, but then she would see him as a simple pilgrim, not . . . He crushed his bitterness before it formed. This woman was different—life at Court had made him cynical—too many people had intrigued to win his help. Even though she looked dazedly about her, there was no sign of fear on her face; just bewilderment and uncertainty. He was impressed by her courage. There was defiance in her voice and the way she straightened her back, but when she looked up, her eyes had dimmed with sorrow. Much as he would have liked to help her, he was committed by the vows he had taken to continue his pilgrimage.

'Were you set upon by thieves?' he asked, his curiosity aroused.

'We were robbed, certainly!' the servant cut in bitterly, and received a reproving glare from his mistress.

Clearly, whatever had happened to them was too distressing for her to speak of it. Understanding their wish for privacy, he respected it, and had circumstances been otherwise, he might have been able to help them. For the first time since starting out on this pilgrimage, he regretted his vow of anonymity.

'There is a priory a few miles from here. If you must travel these dangerous roads, you should join the company of others for protection,' he reasoned. 'Why not join our band?'

Alynna stared blankly at him. Her mind was too numbed by the news of her father's death and her own bastardy to think clearly.

Joel touched her arm. 'Mistress, the pilgrim speaks the truth,' he said in a low voice that would not reach him. 'I can guess something of what happened to you at Barkhurst, so would it not be best to join the pilgrims until we reach the next village, at least?'

She looked across at the pilgrim, who seemed impatient to rejoin his companions. A stay at a priory would be no real solution to her problem, but there was another way.

'Thank you for your advice, sir. I shall travel with your party, but as a pilgrim to Becket's shrine.'

The decision made, she felt easier. Becket's shrine was a place Sir Robert visited often, and it would be a link with him. The effort it was costing her to reason, when all she could think of was that her father was dead, made her head pound. She would need time to come to terms with her new life. At Canterbury, she would pray for her father's soul and seek guidance for her future. Somehow, she had to find an intermediary to petition the king on her behalf.

With a curt nod, the pilgrim spun on his heel and with long, loose-legged strides marched down the track. Joel dashed into the thick of the trees and returned carrying a bundle of possessions wrapped in sackcloth. Through a hole in its side, Alynna saw the bright red and yellow of his jester's parti-hose.

He grinned at her. 'I shall not desert you, my lady.'

'You are a fine jester! Lord Saxby has been trying to get you away from Sir Robert for years,' she said breathlessly, as they were forced to break into a half-run to keep up with the pilgrim walking ahead of them. 'What can I offer you but hardship?'

The other pilgrims were already in sight, and Joel halted and bowed to her with mock solemnity, pulling a wry face to ease the tension of the moment. 'I was more than Sir Robert's jester—I was honoured to be considered his friend. I shall not desert you while you have need of me.'

She was cheered and moved by his loyalty. Joel, both likeable and trustworthy, had been part of her world since childhood—always ready to amuse and tease her. She knew that while he outwardly played the fool to amuse Sir Robert's guests, his wits were quick and his eyes sharp.

'Sir Robert died in my arms on the hunting field,' Joel said more soberly as they joined the back of the pilgrim band, lowering his voice as several of the group nodded to them in silent greeting. 'I vowed to him that I would watch over you. I'm ashamed to say I almost broke my oath.' He looked away, his voice gruff with emotion. 'I'll serve you, my lady, with the devotion I served Sir Robert.'

Realising she was ill prepared for a world outside her father's houses, Alynna acknowledged that she would need Joel's help. 'I would be honoured by your companionship, but there must be no more "my lady". It is plain "Mistress Freston" now.' She glanced cautiously ahead to where the tall pilgrim walked apart from the others, preoccupied and preferring his own company. 'Are you sure you wish to travel to Canterbury, Joel?'

He nodded. 'Since December marks the anniversary of Becket's death, there will be many pilgrims visiting his shrine, despite the bad weather. Perhaps one will provide the answer for our future.'

'I fear the chances of that are remote—for me, at least,' she spoke out honestly. 'What use is it to me now that I can read and write, or even speak four languages? I can debate any point of our island's history or politics, yet no man would employ me as a scribe. What am I to do? I have been trained to run a castle household and manage two manors and a dozen outlying villages, but how can that avail me now?'

'Ay, you were never one to sit plying a needle, if it meant missing the hunt,' Joel quipped. 'And I doubt any woman would have you in her household—not when every man therein would become a slave to your beauty. Never fear I have no faith in the future! It will not come to that.'

To take her mind from the bleak prospect ahead, Alynna's eyes sought the man who had rescued her. He was talking to a friar who appeared to be the leader of the group, but it was to him that the friar was showing deference, not the other way round as she would have expected. Who could he be? But however much of an enigma her rescuer might be, soon the weight of her grief banished all other thoughts.

By mid-afternoon they had covered only a few miles, the cripples among the group being unable to walk long without resting. Alynna, weary from the exertion of unaccustomed walking and the long ride from Suffolk also having taken its toll upon her, welcomed the slow pace. At her side Joel had long since fallen silent; he seemed brooding and troubled. But then, in the circumstances, was that not natural?

The sound of advancing hoofbeats jerked her back to the present. Joel looked nervously over his shoulder, his face pale and anxious. Suddenly it occurred to her that he was the servant the soldiers at the ferry had been ordered to search for, but what had he done to earn himself a whipping? There was no time to question him now. The pilgrims were shuffling off the road and seeking the safety of the trees, and guiltily she remembered how her own party had almost ridden these travellers down. When a lame woman ahead of her slipped on the frosty track, Alynna hurried to her help. Raising her up, she helped her to the roadside.

'God bless you, sweet child,' the woman said, peering up at Alynna.

Alynna hid her shock and momentary revulsion as she saw the horribly scarred face. The woman looked as though she had been burned in a fire: one eyelid was grotesquely swollen and drawn down, the puckered skin of her cheek turning her face into a gruesome mask.

'You do not flinch from this devil's-face?' The woman took Alynna's hand and drew her closer. 'For that I thank you. I am Hester. I shall pray that the good Lord may grant you peace from the burden you carry.'

'God go with you too, Hester.' Alynna smiled at the woman, embarrassed by her reaction to a simple act of kindness.

The riders were almost upon them and, fearful lest they were the mercenaries from Barkhurst, Alynna moved further into the trees. For the first time in her life she felt vulnerable and wary of strangers. As the riders approached, she noted from the bells on their reins that they, too, were pilgrims, but unlike her own solemn band, they laughed and joked and were dressed in velvets and furs. To them, the visit to the saint's shrine was a time of revelry. They were noblemen, perhaps newly returned from France, who journeyed to Canterbury to give thanks for their success and riches won in battle. They travelled with every comfort, even their own beds, she saw, as the laden baggage-carts drew near.

Then she became aware that the tall pilgrim was also standing back in the shadows of the trees. Even through the stupor which had settled over her, she was somehow conscious of every movement of the stranger who had saved her. Although his action was not furtive, he seemed not so much to wish to hide as to remain inconspicuous. Did he know the travellers? If so, why did he not want to be recognised?

Her curiosity aroused by the pilgrim, Alynna stepped forward to peer at the party of approaching noblemen, but with a gasp, Joel drew her back.

'What's amiss?' she asked, puzzled by his act.

'It's best our whereabouts are not noted by too many,' he answered darkly.

'Why not?' Alynna was astonished by the sinister warning behind Joel's words.

Joel shifted uncomfortably, his usually cheerful face creasing with worry. 'It's a feeling I have, my lady . . . I mean mistress,' he hastily corrected. 'I can guess at what happened at the Manor. I know Lady Joan—she's jealous and vindictive. She wants what is yours for her own daughters.'

'But I have nothing.' Alynna looked at her half-frozen, bare fingers. 'Lady Joan—or her guards—took my jewels.'

Joel glanced anxiously towards the highway, where

the mounted pilgrims were noisily passing them. 'Whatever she told you, you are not a pauper—far from it. Sir Robert loved you, as he never stopped loving your mother. There is a large dowry set aside for you, and if he died while you remained unwed, you were to become a ward of the king.'

'But that cannot be!' She shook her head in disbelief. 'My father was but a humble knight. Why should the king take an interest in me?' Joel hesitated, prompting her to ask the question that had been plaguing her all day. 'Who was my mother?'

The jester sighed. 'Sir Robert confided many things to me, but never that. I have my suspicions, but now is not the time to dwell upon them. Of one thing I am certain: your mother was highly born.'

Alynna drew a shaky breath. If Sir Robert had loved her mother, why had they not married? Would she ever learn the truth, now that her father was dead? Grief tugged at her heart, and with an effort she pulled herself together. He would have expected her to be brave.

'If what you say is true, then I must fight for what is mine.' Alynna lowered her voice as the rumbling of the baggage-carts grew fainter. Already the pilgrims were reassembling on the road. Her curiosity aroused, she looked across at Joel when he fell into step beside her. 'How came you to be close at hand when I was attacked?'

'I, too, had been driven from Barkhurst.' His eyes glinted mockingly. 'According to Lady Joan, I was long overdue a whipping for the fun I had poked at her over the years! I ran off before the guards could arrest me.'

'Dear Joel, you did not deserve such treatment!' Alynna said raggedly. 'You have been loyal to Sir Robert ever since I can remember. But how did you find me?'

'Some guards had been sent after me, and I was hiding in the woods,' he answered, again serious. 'I heard your escort approaching and hid in a hollow tree. When I saw the dangerous pace they were forcing upon you, I sensed that something was wrong. I knew then that I must return to Barkhurst and try to warn you of possible danger.'

'At risk to yourself, though. Sir Robert's trust in you was not misplaced!' Alynna was again struck by his loyalty.

Joel shrugged her praise aside, his expression once more serious. 'Sir Robert ordered those mercenaries to leave Barkhurst the day he arrived. He was killed the next day.'

'You think they were responsible for my father's death?' Alynna gasped.

The jester looked away and shuffled his feet. 'Is it not strange that Lady Joan took them back and ordered all Sir Robert's retainers to return to Suffolk before you arrived?'

Alynna shuddered, unwilling to believe that her stepmother had planned Sir Robert's death. She had loved him. She could understand the jealousy that had driven Lady Joan to banish her, for she was not a woman with foresight or quick wits; she would act first and think later. Yet Joel was hinting at something more sinister, and her distress increased. Could she afford to ignore his warning completely?

Cupping her cold hands to her mouth and blowing into them for warmth, Alynna trudged on, her mind a confused jumble of thoughts and emotions. There were so many unanswered questions, and over them all hung the tragedy of her father's death. Yet even through her misery she was still conscious of the presence of the man who had rescued her and was now walking a short distance behind them. If she chanced to look back, his gaze was always upon her. The angular planes of his face were austere, the full lips turned slightly down at the corners as though his teeth were gritted against some inner torment. He did not speak or make any move to approach her, keeping himself aloof, as he did from all the other pilgrims unless someone appeared in need of help, when he would be the first to their side. Why, then, did she feel so disturbed by his nearness—

not threatened, exactly, but something equalling disquieting?

At a crossroads, the pilgrims stopped by a wayside shrine. Kneeling in prayer, Alynna found her mind unable to settle upon the familiar litany. The cold, the discomfort, the gnawing ache in her heart were all like a bad dream. It did not seem possible that her father was dead. It was some weeks since she had seen him, when he had stolen a few days from the celebrations in London to visit her in Suffolk. All too quickly she was passing him the stirrup-cup as he sat his horse, about to set out on his return journey to London. His hand had lingered tenderly upon her cheek when he returned the empty cup to her, his eyes holding a sadness that tore at her heart. Then he had laughed, dispelling her concern.

'Dearest Alynna, it is time a worthy husband was found for you. I am selfish to deny you the chance to love as a woman should be loved.' He had smiled sadly, his voice dropping so that he seemed to speak his thoughts aloud rather than address her. 'Alas, marriage for such as you is not easy to arrange, my dear.'

'But, when I marry, I must leave you!' she had responded in a kind of desperation, thinking his words strange and mysterious.

The graveness had left his still handsome face at her impassioned tones. Now she realised that it was not simply her father's doting that had kept her unwed; her birth would have made a match among the nobility an impossibility.

Distractedly, she glanced about her. The tall pilgrim was kneeling a short distance away, still holding his staff upright, his head bent. Even while praying there was a sense of leashed power in his figure, and she gained the impression of noble pride warring with humility. She doubted that he bent his knee to any man save his king, and to God.

They continued their journey, and Alynna had to drag her attention back to the present. The lights from an inn glowed welcomingly in the dusk a short distance ahead, and as they entered the courtyard, she noticed the unloaded baggage-carts of the noblemen who had ridden past earlier. For a moment she held back as the pilgrims began to file into the inn. The stout friar, who had appeared to be their leader, moved away from his companions to approach her and Joel. Sewn to his brown habit were cockleshells and other amulets from the shrines he had visited at Compostela and the Holy Land, which rattled together as he walked.

'I am Brother Emmanuel. Is it your intention to continue to Canterbury with us?'

'Yes, Brother,' Alynna answered. 'Will you give us your blessing?'

'Gladly, my child.' He raised his hand and made the sign of the cross before them. 'You will need staves for your journey, which can be obtained at the inn. Have you the means to pay for your food?'

Alynna looked helplessly at Joel, who smiled encouragingly at her and replied, 'We shall have enough.'

Brother Emmanuel nodded, apparently satisfied. 'God be with you both.'

Turning from them, the friar entered the inn. The unquestioning way they had been accepted comforted Alynna, certain now that she had made the right decision. Nevertheless, she hesitated to follow Brother Emmanuel. 'I thought we would spend the night at a castle or manor house. Sir Robert always gave hospitality to pilgrims. How shall we eat?'

From beneath his cloak, Joel drew out his fool's stick and waved its bells at her. 'I'll take care of the food by entertaining in the taproom,' he assured her, nodding towards a two-storey building. He handed her his bundle to look after, adding impishly, 'It's not the first time I've had to sing for my supper. You follow the others and get some rest.' Performing a little dance step, he pivoted round and with a bold swagger hurried to the taproom, throwing wide its door. For an instant his wiry figure was silhouetted by the torchlight, then he raised his fool's stick aloft and somersaulted into the room amid a roar of laughter.

Without his company, Alynna felt vulnerable and

alone. Heavy-hearted, she was about to follow the pilgrims who had disappeared from sight, when a firm tread approached and she looked round to see her tall rescuer.

'Your servant has left you. Can I be of help?' He took her arm and led her into the inn, adding, 'If you were robbed and are without money, allow me to buy you food.'

They had entered a darkened corridor, and her step slowed. It was deserted. A single burning flambeau set in the wall showed her three closed doors. Hunger, and something far more disconcerting, clenched her stomach when their arms brushed in the narrow confines. The light touch of the pilgrim's hand seemed to burn through her sleeve, and as she stared up into his shadowy face, her heart raced unaccountably fast. He was a stranger, and after her experience in the woods she was distrustful of men—especially one who had so unsettling an effect upon her senses.

'Your offer is most generous, sir, but I could not accept.' She eased away from him, suddenly nervous. He released her as though sensing her apprehension, and his proud figure stiffened with affront.

'Why not? Because we have not been formally introduced?' He shrugged and bowed to her, 'I am Richard Dreux, at your service. And your name?'

Alynna's throat dried. The Dreux family was one of the most influential in the country, far above her, even before she knew of her bastardy. She had no wish to lie to the man, though there was something about his reserved manner that made her wonder whether he had been entirely honest with her. Ignoring his question as to her name, she countered by turning the conversation back on him. 'From your bearing, sir, I thought you a knight.'

In the torchlight, a glint silvered his eyes and his arched brows rose questioningly. He had not expected to be challenged, and her heart twisted in a way she had never experienced before. His dark looks were devastatingly handsome. Tall, lean and musclar, his broad shoulders seemed to block the corridor. Even his plain garments could not conceal the dignity and bearing few men possessed.

'You flatter me, my lady,' he said crisply.

Suspecting that he mocked her, Alynna looked sideways at Richard Dreux as they moved towards the first of the doors. His proud bearing was never that of a mere squire! Unaccountably, she felt piqued that he remained aloof from her. She bit her lip, and restrained the impulse to question him.

'I am, sir, Mistress Alynna . . .' she began, and was startled when a door to her right opened, sending out a shaft of light as a man strode out so fast that he collided with her.

'By Our Lady, what have we here?' the man exclaimed with a low whistle of appreciation, his hand slipping about her waist. 'My companions said the landlord's daughter was a beauty!'

Recovering from the shock of this unexpected encounter, Alynna stepped back, pushing his hand from her body, her eyes burning with indignation. His back was to the light and she could not make out his features, as she responded hotly, 'I am not the landlord's daughter, sir.'

'Your pardon, dear lady! I was dazzled by the vision of your beauty.' He bent his head to peer at her more closely. With a gasp, he reached out unexpectedly and captured Alynna's arm. 'Have we not met before?'

'That is unlikely, sir.' She jerked her hand to free it from his hold, but his grip tightened and the light fell across his figure. His fair hair was cut above his ears in knightly fashion, and there was an abundance of gold braid and jewels upon his long gown. The boyishly handsome face reflected in the torchlight was that of a stranger.

'I never forget a beautiful face,' he boasted, suspicious. 'Did I see you at Court?'

She stiffened. 'I have never been to Court.'

'Then it must be somewhere else,' the nobleman persisted.

'I do not know you, sir. Allow me to pass.'

'Griswolde!' From behind her, Richard Dreux's deep voice was lethal with warning. 'Let the maiden pass!'

The man started in surprise, and let her go. His eyes widening, he looked past her at the pilgrim. 'By the rood, what are you doing here? There's been no end to the stories at Court as to your whereabouts.'

'The maiden says she does not know you, Griswolde,' Dreux rapped out. 'Leave the matter there.'

Alynna stared at the two men. Clearly they knew each other, but Dreux showed no deference due to a man of higher rank. He stood strong and indomitable, unimpressed by Griswolde's rich attire or arrogant pose.

Dismissively, he turned from the nobleman to face Alynna. 'The pilgrims are in the end room. You had better join them.'

'No!' Griswolde shot out. 'Not before I hear the wench's name. I tell you that I know her.'

'The maid says otherwise.' Dreux's voice hardened.

Griswolde subjected Alynna to an insolent stare. 'Such beauty I would not forget—and those eyes! Perhaps you are related to someone I know?'

Alynna felt trapped. The weaving torchlight played over Dreux's rugged face, as he studied her through partly lowered lashes with an intensity that seemed to pierce her innermost thoughts. A stinging heat warmed her chilled flesh, and her heartbeat quickened. Had her manner towards Griswolde betrayed her? No simple maid would have addressed a nobleman as she had done, but his arrogant tone had angered her. She inwardly cursed her wayward temper. Had not Joel cautioned her to keep her identity a secret?

'I am a simple maid, sir. I would have remembered any meeting with a nobleman as distinguished as yourself.'

Sketching a curtsy, she hastened towards the end door, where the faint sound of intoned prayers filtered through to the corridor. Once the door was closed behind her, she drew back into the shadows of the large room and sat down at some distance from the pilgrims.

She was more disturbed than she cared to admit by the unexpected encounter. Griswolde had been so certain they had met. For whom had he mistaken her?

CHAPTER THREE

'THAT WOMAN is no simple maid!' Sir Geoffrey Griswolde's eyes flashed with sudden anger. 'What is your interest in her, coz? It is not like you to play the knight-errant.'

'She is a pilgrim, and none of your concern!' Richard Dreux warned, seeing the vein throbbing at his cousin's temple.

'Godswounds!' Griswolde raged, his hand resting upon his sword. 'The wench is hiding something. She's a beauty, too!'

For a moment Richard thought that Griswolde was about to let his temper get the better of caution. He regarded his cousin sourly, flexing his fingers over the pilgrim's staff. Often of late he had been forced to intervene when Griswolde had been in the grip of a black, ungovernable rage. It was not the first time he had sought to cross him. He relaxed when Griswolde's hand dropped to his side. His cousin was a womaniser—usually both Court ladies and peasants alike fell prey to his charms—but Mistress Alynna had been unimpressed by his cousin's obvious wealth. He felt a stirring of memory, for he, too, had an uncomfortable feeling that her face was familiar. Why had she been so reluctant to reveal her name? His own curiosity aroused, he was strangely loath to discuss her with Griswolde, and deliberately changed the subject.

'When did you return from the Burgundian Court? I thought negotiations were in hand for your betrothal to the Count de Courcy's daughter.'

'Burgundy!' Griswolde said abstractedly, tapping his lip as he stared back at the door Alynna had gone through. 'I wonder—could it be . . . ?' He caught himself up short, but not before his cousin had seen the crafty gleam in his eyes. 'Yes, they were,' he answered

Richard's question, 'until de Courcy discovered that the estates my late wife brought to our marriage are entailed to my infant son. If you had stayed in France, you could have spoken for me.'

'How so? I was never at the Burgundian Court. I was with the king's army.'

'Always the warrior! Griswolde scoffed. 'You could have won for yourself any French heiress you chose. Every woman at Court was proclaiming you the flower of English chivalry.'

'Then I was well away from there,' Richard replied cynically. 'Your conquests are legion, so I shall leave you to play the gallant lover.'

'It's what I do best!' Griswolde answered with a laugh. 'But then you, my most esteemed cousin, could have any woman in England, with but a snap of those sword-calloused fingers.'

Richard contained a spurt of anger. In recent years it was comments like that from Griswolde which had ended the easy companionship they had once enjoyed. Since his cousin had inherited vast estates from his first wife, why was he never satisfied with the wealth he had? Of late he had become mercenary, seeking every opportunity to enrich himself.

At a burst of laughter from Griswolde's companions, Richard became impatient to rejoin the pilgrims, where he could enforce his wish for solitude. 'I bid you good night, cousin. We leave at first light on the morrow.'

'Do we not travel the road to Canterbury together, coz?'

Richard moved his shoulders to ease the prickling of the hair shirt beneath his plain black doublet, and eyed the trailing jewelled sleeve of his cousin's long gown.

'I travel simply as Richard Dreux.'

'To each man his own kind of piety!' Griswolde patted a bulging money-pouch at his waist. 'For myself, I prefer comfort. These coins will vouchsafe a pardon for my sins. Besides, I go to Canterbury to give thanks for the ransoms won at Agincourt. From Canterbury do you return to Court, coz?'

'No, I go to Thornbank.'

'That remote Manor!' Griswolde snorted in disgust. 'Would you throw away your position at Court to become a hermit?'

Richard stifled his irritation. He had spoken to no one of the events surrounding his mother's death, and had sworn his servants to secrecy to protect his sister's name.

'Have you forgotten that I am in mourning? Meraud is there,' he answered brusquely.

'You were outspoken in your condemnation of the carnage that followed Agincourt,' Griswolde taunted. 'Have you fallen from his Majesty's favour? Is that why you go to Thornbank?'

Richard silenced his cousin's impertinence with an icy glare. 'The battle rivalled the glory won at Crecy. We vanquished our foe, despite their greater numbers.' He swallowed against the distasteful memory of what had followed. 'The slaughter of the prisoners was barbaric and unnecessary.'

At that moment the courtyard door opened and Joel entered. Pushing back his hood, he wiped his sleeve across his sweating brow, his expression grave.

To Richard's astonishment, Griswolde grabbed Joel's arm and dragged him under the torchlight, saying explosively, 'This face I do know! You were in London some weeks back, at a banquet given by Lord Saxby—you were the jester. Now who was your master? It was not Saxby, but . . . Oh, a murrain on this memory of mine! I can never put a name to a face.'

Such a look of horror passed across the servant's face, to be quickly hidden, that Richard again found himself intrigued. How came Mistress Alynna to be travelling with, of all the unlikely companions, a jester? Seeing Joel recover himself quickly, Richard gave way to his own curiosity. 'Are you the jester Sir Geoffrey speaks of? Who was your master?'

'Indeed I was at Lord Saxby's banquet.' Joel answered with only the barest pause. 'Since then, I have been troubled by the evil joint. How can a simple fool amuse his master's guests when he is crippled with rheumatism?

I go to pray for relief from this malady, else I shall starve.'

'You were Sir Robert Freston's fool!' Griswolde declared jubilantly. 'I remember now.'

'Your lordship honours me,' Joel said humbly. 'Sir Robert died recently. After my pilgrimage, I seek a new master.'

Griswolde's brows drew together. He glanced towards the door through which Mistress Alynna had passed, and a stab of unease disturbed Richard at seeing the sly smile on his cousin's face. Had he connected the two as travelling together? Why had the jester been so reluctant to give his master's name? And was Mistress Alynna then in some way linked with Sir Robert Freston? She had skilfully misled him, if that were the case.

'Come, fool, you will entertain my companions,' Griswolde said, cutting through Richard's thoughts. He dipped into his money-pouch. 'Here is a silver coin for your pains.'

The jester seemed about to refuse, but he looked at the silver coin and nodded in resignation. Richard was about to intervene, then checked himself. The fool and his mistress were in need of money, so why did the jester seem so reluctant to go with Griswolde? Was it because his cousin had recognised him? Richard smothered his disquiet. He was being over-protective towards Mistress Alynna because he had saved her when he had been unable to save his sister. He was not responsible for her or her servant.

Griswolde stepped back for the jester to enter the room, his grin insolent as he looked at Richard. 'You have unlikely companions on your pilgrimage, especially the woman! I do not like mysteries. She is a beauty, and I know I have seen her before. I wager, she is not what she seems.'

'Let the matter rest,' Richard warned, stirred to protect her anonymity.

'Have you singled her out for your own amusement, coz?'

The remark was what he expected from Griswolde, yet unexpectedly it slashed at his pride. The mystery surrounding Mistress Alynna had somehow got beneath his guard. He too, did not wish his identity known while on this pilgrimage. 'That may be your way, but it is not mine. I bid you good night, Griswolde.'

'Why, you . . .' Griswolde began, then, encountering Richard's icy glare, thought better of continuing his challenge. 'One day, cousin—' his face mottled with fury '—I'll show you who is the better man.'

The threat was an old one, and Richard dismissed it, his thoughts returning to the dark-haired woman. Just who was she, and what connection could she have with Sir Robert Freston? His hand paused upon the door-latch, and he shackled his thoughts. She was no concern of his, and could not be allowed to become a distraction. Had he not vowed to forsake worldly possessions, and passions, during his pilgrimage? But the woman was beautiful enough to tempt any man, and he had never considered himself a saint.

When he entered the room, he beckoned to the potboy to bring wine and food. Then his glance was drawn, despite his resolution, to Mistress Alynna sitting on the floor in the shadows away from the other pilgrims, her chin resting on her drawn-up knees. As though sensing his gaze upon her, she looked up. The torchlight fell upon her face, and the tears on her cheeks, glistening like stars, roused Richard's latent chivalry.

Alynna quickly turned away on discovering him watching her. Believing herself unobserved, she had given way to her grief. Angrily she brushed the tears away with the edge of her cloak. She did not want pity from anyone, especially him. There was no need for her to look up to know he was coming towards her; every nerve-end prickled with awareness of his closeness. A horn cup was thrust against her hand.

'Drink this!' he commanded gently. 'It will give you strength.'

Knowing it would be churlish to refuse his kindness, she reached up to take it, and inadvertently their hands touched. A sensation like rustling silk spread up her arm, and she barely managed to stifle a surprised gasp at the effect of that brief, potent, contact as Richard Dreux bent over her.

'Your servant is likely to be occupied for some time,' he said, seating himself on the rushes beside her. 'Will you share my meal with me?'

Without waiting for her refusal, he placed the wooden platter filled with cold meats and bread between them. With a knife from his belt he cut a thin slice of spiced capon and held it out to her. She shook her head, the events of the day having robbed her of her appetite.

'There is no place for false pride on a pilgrimage,' he said sharply, misinterpreting her refusal. 'Eat! The jester will need his coins for another day.'

When she made no move, Richard bent one knee, resting his elbow upon it as he thoughtfully rubbed his hand across his beard-shadowed jaw. Beneath the sinuous grace of his movements she sensed the controlled power of his lithe body, and was suddenly tinglingly aware of his masculinity. His skin was golden from riding in all weathers, his eyes lighter and brighter against the contrast of raven-black hair and lashes. His nearness was physically threatening, not with violence, but in a way she could not define, only that it was unsettling to her peace of mind.

'I am not your enemy.' His voice softened unexpectedly. 'I would help you if I can.'

'Why?' she asked, again suspicious of his motives.

The grey eyes flashed dangerously as his gaze burrowed into hers. From the rigid set of his countenance, it was obvious that the knight did not like, or expect, to have his actions questioned. Why could she not learn to curb her tongue? Now he would leave her, and she found she wanted him to stay. She caught the sound of a muffled oath beneath his breath, then his mouth tilted sardonically.

'Because I wish it,' he said significantly, as though that answered all her questions. 'Now will you eat?'

He offered the meat once more in a manner that

brooked no argument. Her stomach knotted at the tantalising aroma of spices, and with a shy smile she accepted it graciously. The stern line of his lips relaxed into a cynical smile as he nodded his satisfaction. They ate for a while in silence. Absently she noted the other pilgrims casting curious looks in their direction, but gave them little attention. Several times Richard cut the meat, presenting it to her in a courtly manner. It was not until she caught his questioning gaze on her, Alynna realised with dismay, that by her natural acceptance of his actions she had revealed more than she intended of herself. He was treating her with the deference due to a woman of rank. No lowly maiden would have accepted food in the manner she had done.

Alarmed, she drew back. Her wrist was caught in firm fingers that snapped over it like an iron fetter, yet did not hurt. Stiffening with defiance, she met his piecing stare. 'Let me go!'

He turned her palm upwards, running his thumb across the smooth umblemished skin and sending a flame of heat through her. 'These hands have toiled upon nothing more arduous than a sewing-needle. How come you to be travelling with Sir Robert Freston's fool?'

The words were like a thunderbolt resounding through her brain. How had he recognised Joel? She despised deceit, yet to tell him the truth would bring shame to her father's name.

At her hesitation, his eyes glinted like glazed steel. 'I know little of Sir Robert Freston,' he said coldly. 'Was Barkhurst his manor? The fool said that his master was dead. Your tears were not for yourself, but another. Were you weeping for Sir Robert Freston? What were you to him?'

Alynna dropped her gaze from his fierce stare. For a long moment she stared at the mud-stained gold braid trimming the hem of her gown, fighting to overcome her rising panic. The pilgrim missed nothing.

Richard hardened himself against Alynna's beauty as he watched her expression grow first wary, then set into

a blank mask. She denied being a noblewoman, and
obviously she was not a servant, therefore she could
have occupied but one role in Sir Robert's household.
And that would account for her being dismissed on his
death.

'Were you Freston's mistress?' he asked gruffly, oddly
disappointed that her innocence was only skin deep. 'Is
that why you could not return to Barkhurst?'

Alynna felt her body burn with humiliation. Aware
that the other pilgrims might overhear, she kept her
voice low, although it throbbed with fury. 'I most
certainly was not! How dare you suggest such a thing!'

'How hotly you defend your honour!' His tone
mellowed with returning warmth. 'Your pardon. I had
no wish to offend.'

'Did you not? Then you were insolent, sir.' Alynna
sprang to her feet. 'Who do you think you are? I thank
you for the food, but that did not give you the right to
insult me!'

In a single graceful movement he stood up, to loom
above her, dark and menacing as a siege tower, the
angular planes of his face taut with affronted pride. Her
heart raced. Again she had spoken out of character for a
humble maid. But then Richard Dreux's self-possessed
manner was unlike anything she had encountered during
her sheltered life. She refused to look away from the
ice-tipped arrows glittering in his eyes.

'My assumption was not an unnatural one in the
circumstances.' His tone remained cool. 'If you have
been insulted, it is because you are not who you claim to
be.'

Although she had given herself away, he apparently
had no idea of her identity, and she forced herself to
relax. There was much about *his* manner that did not fit
the role of humble knight! 'Perhaps I am not what I
seem.' She tilted her head proudly, defying him to pity
her circumstances. 'I suspect you, too, sir, are not the
person you pretend to be?'

Richard passed his hand across his jaw, guarding his
expression from her. Behind him, Alynna saw Joel

approaching. Richard followed her gaze, and bowed to her. 'You have wisdom as well as beauty,' he complimented, but from the deepening grooves about his eyes, Alynna sensed that his thoughts had withdrawn from her, as he added. 'In this band of pilgrims, as in God's eyes, are we not all equal?'

He bowed, and without thinking, Alynna held out her hand to him. Quickly she made to snatch it back, but was too late. Catching her fingers, he raised them to his lips. Again she had betrayed her upbringing! The interest had rekindled in his eyes, and the warmth of his mouth was like a candle flame playing across her skin. Even after he straightened, the impression of his lips still lingered on her hand and he made no move to release it. When he lifted an arched brow, knowingly, Alynna's heart lurched. Now she, too, knew what it felt like to have a gauntlet flung down at one's feet in open challenge.

She stood her ground. Even if she had willed it, she had no ability to drag her eyes from his entrancing stare. When at last he spoke, the normality of his tone startled her, as though she had expected condemnation.

'Good night, Lady Alynna,' he said softly. 'I place you once more in the care of your jester.'

'No, Sir Richard,' Alynna gasped out, horrified that he had guessed her secret. 'I am not . . .' Her voice broke, and she swallowed painfully against the returning memories. Endeavouring to keep the quiver from her voice, she answered his challenge. 'It is not "lady"—but "mistress".'

'God go with you, Alynna,' he answered with a disconcerting smile. 'And, if you please, I am Richard.'

Their gaze held, linked by an unspoken bond to honour each other's wish for secrecy. Then Richard Dreux turned away. Watching him nod curtly to Joel, Alynna felt momentarily suffocated, her heart pounding wildly as though she had escaped a dangerous encounter. It was then that she glimpsed the sadness once more settling upon his handsome face. He waved aside Brother Emmanuel's invitation to join him, and moved to the far side of the room, seeking isolation. When he settled in the darkest shadows she frowned, wondering what burden haunted such a lion of a man.

The mystery surrounding Richard Dreux bedevilled Alynna as their journey continued. In the following days, whenever she pushed her thoughts from her own grief, her mind turned to the tall knight—as she was certain he must be, despite his protestations. The Dreux family was a large one, the most powerful member being the Earl of Trevowan, who was King Henry's friend and counsellor. Perhaps Sir Richard had too often been importuned by petitioners to plead their causes for them. Was that why he remained aloof from their companions?

Her thoughts broke off as a shuffling figure appeared at her side, and she glanced down at Hester, who often sought her company while they walked.

'Always you look so troubled, my dear,' the lame woman said. 'Tomorrow we reach Canterbury. God willing, your prayers will be answered and you will find peace.'

'Will you find peace at Canterbury, Hester?'

'If not peace, I would ask for forgiveness,' Hester said heavily, touching her face.

'In time your scars will be less noticeable,' Alynna comforted her. 'How did it happen? So many women are burnt, and often blinded, when their skirts catch on the flames as they tend the cooking-pot.'

'It was God's punishment for my sins. I was a vain and foolish woman.' Hester looked away, clearly unwilling to talk about herself. She nodded towards Richard Dreux, who walked just ahead. 'You have made a conquest! He watches you often.'

Alynna shook her head, feeling a rush of heat colouring her cheeks. Once they reached Canterbury, she would never see the handsome pilgrim again, and the thought left an hollow sensation in her breast. 'He has spoken no more than a dozen words to me since that first night at the inn.'

'Your beauty must attract many men. Master Dreux is

not the only one!' Hester added with a chuckle. 'There was a man yesterday evening who kept watching you. I saw him again in the village we just passed, though he seemed to take pains that you did not notice him. As a matter of fact, I think he is not far behind our group now on the road.'

A shiver of alarm sped down Alynna's spine. She had thought herself overfanciful in believing she was being observed. Had Lady Joan sent her spies after them? Yet surely Joel would have said if he had noticed anything suspicious. She glanced at the jester, who was chatting to Brother Emmanuel, and her unease grew. Every few moments Joel kept glancing back along the track. Following his stare, Alynna saw several people walking, and on horseback, travelling in the same direction as the pilgrims, but to her relief none of them looked familiar. Something must be happening in the village ahead. None the less, she remained ill at ease.

Through a gap in the hedgerow, she looked down from the hill into the valley. They were approaching a large sprawling village, and the winding road was surprisingly crowded. When they entered the village a short time later, the pilgrims were forced closer together, jostled by the gathering number of people. There was an air of suppressed excitement. What was happening? It was not market day, for there were no livestock blocking the road.

Alynna's ankle was suddenly wrenched as she stumbled into an unseen hole in the road, and she stifled a cry of pain. The soft leather of her riding-boots was worn through, and although the rooftops were whitened with frost, each step upon her bruised and blistered feet was like walking on burning coals. She leaned heavily on her staff and took a steadying breath, attempting to blank out her discomfort.

Hester also stumbled, and Alynna took her arm, concerned that her companion would be pushed to the ground by the impatient people around them. When the apparent excitement running through the crowd increased, Alynna stood on tiptoe to look over the heads of the people. Some distance ahead, the village green stretched out at the foot of the street. The open space was filled with people, and at its edge, several stalls and booths had been set up, but the atmosphere of tense expectancy was not that of a country fair. Then, from out of the church opposite the stalls, a procession emerged surrounding a man standing in a cart. A great shout went up from the green, its tone menacing.

Within moments, the shouts turned to angry jeering. Several burly men in front of Alynna began pushing their way through the crowd. A pie-seller was knocked aside, his wares spilling from the tray he carried on his head. Temporarily diverted, a group of youths pounced on the enraged pieman's scattered pastries and ran off, munching their stolen treats. Alynna temporarily lost sight of the procession, which had merged with the crowd. All she could see were the rotten vegetables hurled in the air towards what appeared to be a prisoner.

'What's happening?' A note of fear tinged Hester's voice.

Alynna scanned the village green. 'A procession led by a priest has just come out of the church,' she explained. 'Behind him is an ox-drawn cart. A man—he looks as though he's bound—is standing in the cart.'

'From the church, you say?' Hester's voice quaked.

'Yes, but I fear it is no ordinary procession,' Alynna stressed. 'There's something sinister about it.'

'Merciful God!' Hester muttered a prayer, her voice rising with alarm. 'Let it not be a punishment—or worse.'

The shouting increased as the procession approached the centre of the village green. Angry mutterings came from the people behind them on the street who were held up by the slow-moving pilgrims, and all at once they surged forward. Alynna lost her hold upon Hester, and was roughly thrust against a low wall. As she clutched it to regain her balance, she saw Richard Dreux start towards her, but Joel was nearer and caught her about her waist, and Richard stepped back.

Returning to Hester's side, Alynna responded to

Richard's gesture with a shy smile. He inclined his head
in friendly acknowledgment, but remained at a distance.
With an effort, she dragged her gaze away and a movement in a doorway caught her attention. Her throat
contracted. A bearded man was staring at her, but
before she could see him clearly, he had darted into an
alley. She swallowed against a lump of fear. Dear God!
Was her mind playing tricks? In that brief glimpse,
he looked like the ferryman who had attacked her at
Barkhurst.

At that moment a low growl filled the air from the
direction of the green, and a plume of smoke rose
skywards from where the procession had halted.

'The fire's been lit!' a harsh voice shouted close by, its
macabre implication ousting all thoughts of the ferryman from Alynna's mind. 'Get a move on, sluggards!
The Lollard will be roasted before we get there.'

Alynna went cold at the mention of the word Lollard.
The followers of the priest Wyclif, who openly spoke
out against the tyranny of the church, were being persecuted throughout the land for heresy. King Henry had
no love for them, especially since they had been behind a
plot to murder him the year before. She shuddered as
the smell of smoke drifted over her. Was there to be a
burning today?

Fights broke out, the crowd becoming violent in their
haste to witness the gruesome spectacle. From the
corner of her eye, Alynna was aware that although
Richard Dreux still did not approach her, he kept close
by. After the sensations his nearness had aroused at the
inn, she had been wary of close contact, but today she
was reassured by his presence. It was only then that she
became aware of the trembling which racked Hester's
hunched figure.

'It's all right, Hester. We need not go near the green.'

'Don't let them get me!' Hester whispered fiercely,
her eyes glazed and starting with fear.

Puzzled by her intense terror, but sympathising with
her friend's desire not to witness a burning at the stake,
Alynna turned to Joel. 'We must get away from here!'

Her words were drowned by a hoarse scream, which climbed rapidly to a bloodcurdling pitch. They both crossed themselves. But Hester was thrown into a frenzy and, wrenching herself free of Alynna's hold, she broke into a limping half-run and threw herself at the foot of Brother Emmanuel.

'Come, my lady,' Joel urged, taking Alynna's arm.

'But Hester . . . I cannot leave her. She is upset.'

'She's better off with the friar. We will not be able to walk across the green for some time,' Joel told her. 'Brother Emmanuel is taking Hester to sit by a well near the market cross. Shall we join them? At least it is out of sight of the stake.'

They stood back as a man leading an ass passed them. He waved a roll of parchment aloft, from which dangled an impressive seal.

'Repent of your sins,' the pardoner cried out. 'See here a relic of St Anselm. Make offerings for his mercy. Repent! Come up and offer in God's name, and I will give you pardon.'

'There is the true scoundrel of this gathering, with his false relics and promises,' Joel muttered angrily, while they waited for the last of the spectators to clear the road. 'Not the wretch who smoulders on the fire.'

Alynna hurried across the village square towards the well, and sat down on a wall. She glanced anxiously at Hester, whose head remained bent as she spoke with the friar. Each time the dying heretic screamed, a violent tremor gripped Hester's body. Knowing that Brother Emmanuel, on this occasion, could comfort her more than herself, Alynna curbed an impulse to intervene and deliberately turned her back on the stake. Moments later, the screams abruptly stopped, and she closed her eyes, appalled. A hand touched her shoulder.

Richard Dreux regarded her with concern. 'Are you all right?'

'I have no heart for such barbarity,' she replied sharply, unable to contain her disgust.

A group of peasant women passing by turned to glare,

the naked contempt in their expressions shocking Alynna.

'Have a care of what you speak!' Richard warned her sternly. 'Consider well any words which appear to criticise the church.'

Her hot retort withered on her lips. He was not condemning, but cautioning, her for her own safety. It was another reminder that she no longer had the protection of her father. She must learn to curb her quick tongue. 'I shall heed your words.'

'Take care that you do. The church teaches meekness and submission in women.' His glance flickered over her indignant figure. 'From the anger in your eyes, I can see that is not your way, so you must be especially careful.' He cupped her chin in his hand, forcing her to look into his serious expression. 'Promise me you will take care.'

His touch, together with the concern evident in his voice, drained the heat from her cheeks. She ran her tongue over lips suddenly dry, wishing her heart would not beat so loudly, for she was certain he could hear it. The grey eyes gazing so piercingly into her own darkened to a smouldering intensity, and with a visible effort he recollected himself and released her.

Joel pushed closer. He had the look of a dog guarding his master. 'I shall look after my mistress,' he bristled, his voice heavy with meaning, 'from any who would harm her.'

'I am sure you will.' Richard eyed the jester haughtily. 'Your mistress looks pale. Should you not draw her a cup of water from the well?' At that, he turned on his heel and marched off.

She was puzzled by his sudden change of mood, for there had been more to the exchange between the two men than had appeared on the surface. Richard had spoken in a tone, chillingly arrogant, putting Joel firmly in his place as the servant and himself as the master. It had been done without spite or rancour, but with the naturalness of one used to command.

Belatedly, realising that Hester and Brother Emmanuel had also moved off to rejoin the other pilgrims, Alynna stood up, stifling a gasp at the pain and stiffness in her feet. Joel handed her a cup of icy water and she drank it thankfully, its coolness refreshing her, before they hurried to catch up. When they skirted the village green, she averted her eyes firmly from the stake.

The persecution of the Lollards was growing, encouraged by the piety of the king. She reflected that although Henry V had returned from Agincourt a hero, the ruthless manner in which he dealt with the Lollards did not seem that of a compassionate man, but more the act of a religious fanatic. Her throat tightened with misgivings, since it was to this man that she must plead her cause for her future.

Troubled, she began to think what steps she must take to gain audience with the king. It still was hard to believe she would be a royal ward. And how would Joel and herself live until then? The problems seemed never ending. What she needed was a champion, but who?

Distractedly, her glance roamed over the column of figures. The road from the village was crowded with people returning to their homes. Hester was a short distance ahead, talking to another pilgrim. At least outwardly, she seemed to have recovered from her terror. Behind her, Alynna could hear Joel's taunting voice entertaining the travellers. What would she do without him? He was astute enough not to waste an opportunity to earn money. The people he had looked on with contempt an hour earlier were now throwing coins at him as he capered and poked fun at their companions.

Her thoughts turned again to the problem of her future, and she sought the tall figure of Richard Dreux walking some way in front. His kinsman, the Earl of Trevowan, would be an ideal choice to speak of her case to the king, but immediately she thrust the thought aside. Already she was indebted to this knight and it would appear ungracious to ask more of him.

Wearily Alynna trudged up the hill on the far side of the valley. As they began their descent, the road narrowed along a river, and the icy water beckoned temptingly. It would be good to bathe her aching feet in its coolness, but there was no place to climb safely down. The bank was steep and treacherous, while below it, the river was channelled into a fast-flowing mill-race.

Over the drone of voices she became conscious of the distant rumbling of a water-mill just visible through the trees. As she approached, she became fascinated by the swirling water forcing the heavy wheel into constant motion. She paused by a tree, her taut nerves soothed by the sight and sound of churning water, until her attention was drawn to a small boy laughing shrilly as he ran in and out of the crowd.

'Look at me!' he shouted, his chubby face glowing with devilment as he walked along the edge of the bank.

Alynna's heart missed a beat. The ground was slippery with frost—all too easily the boy could fall. A white-faced woman, obviously the boy's mother, screamed. Her hands outstretched, she tried to force her way back through the press of people, but her cries were ignored. The revellers, intoxicated by the sight of the burning, jeered at her efforts. A youth waving a wine-skin urged the boy on, and the lad's body began to wobble. Impulsively, unthinking of the danger to herself, she threw down her staff and rushed forward, hauling the boy back as he teetered on the edge.

'Leave me be!' he screamed, unaware of his danger, and wriggling free, he ran towards his mother.

At that moment, a smell of wild garlic and rotting fish assailed Alynna's nostrils. Before she could turn, suddenly nervous, something rammed into her back. As she toppled sideways, her foot caught in a frozen tussock. She snatched at the air, her heart thumping wildly as she desperately tried to regain her balance.

She screamed. There was no longer solid ground beneath her feet—she was falling. Pain shot through her ribs as her body caught the edge of the bank and she slid over its side. Frantically she clutched for a handhold. When a thick tree-root jabbed into her side, she grabbed it with both hands. The gnarled wood bit into her flesh, but she held tight, her weight ripping part of the root from the thin soil. Mercifully, it held, and she hung suspended over the gushing water, her arms almost wrenched from their sockets as she sought a supporting ledge.

'Help!' she shouted, striving to master her terror.

Her blood chilled at the sight of the turbulent mill-race directly beneath. Weighted down in her heavy gown and cloak, she would not survive plunging into those icy depths. Within moments she could be sucked by the current into the blades of the water-mill and drowned. Above her on the road, she saw a blur of watchful faces. Some called out encouragement, others waited in morbid curiosity to see if she would fall. A coarse bearded face loomed into vision, then disappeared into the throng. It was Hugh—the ferryman—she was certain. There had been the smell of wild garlic and rotting fish just before she fell! Had he not stunk like that? Was it he who had pushed her?

'Alynna! Hold fast!'

Richard Dreux's urgent command cast everything else from her mind. Gritting her teeth against the pain in her straining arms, she gazed up at him. Careless of his own safety, he was climbing down the bank to rescue her.

The mill-wheel ground on perilously close. Already the tree-root sagged in an alarming fashion, and she stretched her legs, desperately seeking a foothold, but there was only empty space all around her.

Then, with an ominous tearing noise, a shower of earth fell on to her face. The root juddered. It was being dragged free of its anchoring rock.

CHAPTER FOUR

ALYNNA SCREAMED again. Stinging beads of sweat broke out between her shoulder-blades, and she tasted blood as she bit into her lip to still the terror gripping her. Her body was pitched several feet down, fire shooting through her arms and hands as the tree retained its tenacious hold.

'To your right, Alynna!' Richard Dreux shouted. 'A ledge!'

'Stay calm, mistress!' Joel added his encouragement from high above.

Trembling, she obeyed, extending a foot, and to her relief it touched solid rock. Above her a small crevice provided a handhold. Summoning her failing strength, she heaved herself towards the ledge, but her foot slipped on the frosty surface and she fell back, gasping. With an alarming crack, the tree sagged further.

'Forget the ledge,' Richard ordered. 'Give me your hand!'

Alynna saw the strong capable fingers several inches above her face. Dear God, she would never reach them! He was too far away. If she let go of the tree, and failed to grasp his hand, she would plummet to her death.

'Do as I say, Alynna!' Richard commanded.

The confidence in his voice gave her the encouragement she needed. Offering up a hasty prayer, she tensed. Then, like a spring uncoiling, she launched herself into the air, her hand stretching upwards. It was caught and held. At the same time, her foot found a niche in the jutting rock.

'Don't look down!' Richard warned. 'Go carefully. I've got you.'

Mastering her terror, Alynna stared into his lean beard-darkened face. The determined set of his mouth and the encouraging gleam in his grey eyes banished her fears. His grip was firm upon her hand; he would not let her fall. Guided by him, she carefully placed each foot as they began their slow climb upwards. When they came level with the top of the bank, Richard ordered the crowd back. With a final long stride, he stood above her on the road, his hands steadying her as she scrambled the last few feet to safety. She leaned against her rescuer, breathing heavily, and her heart raced. To her dismay, she could no longer control the trembling in her body.

'You little fool,' he said gruffly.

Then his arm tightened about her waist and he clasped her against him. Closing her eyes, Alynna leaned against his chest. Through the thinness of her cloak, the warmth of his body was like a flame against her chilled flesh. She knew she should pull away, but the touch of his strong arms about her, after the terror of her fall, intoxicated her disjointed senses. Her hand, trapped between them, felt the quickening beat of his heart and a deeper fire stirred within her. Unconsciously she nestled closer.

Richard sucked in his breath and tensed, his hands moving to her shoulders. Then he eased back, anger now edging his voice. 'You could have been killed!'

She jerked back, hurt by his tone. He looked fierce and aloof as he glared at the people gaping at them, and ordered sharply, 'Get about your own business!'

Alynna flinched at the scorn in his voice. Even Joel and Hester, who stood at her side, their faces drawn and anxious, moved several paces back.

'The child was in danger,' she began, cursing the quiver in her voice as she fought to overcome her fright. 'Besides, I was . . .' She stopped, defensive and defiant. Why should she explain herself to him, when he had been so censorious of her actions? In her confusion, she had been about to say she was pushed, but that was absurd! Surely it had been an accident caused by the press of people on the narrow track. Yet she had seen Hugh . . . and that smell of rotting fish just before she fell! The memory nagged at her. After her ordeal in the wood, she would never forget the reek of her attacker.

'You were what?' Richard's hand tightened over hers.

Alynna winched, pain shooting through her fingers. He looked down at her hands, his expression softening when he saw the lacerated, bleeding flesh.

Brother Emmanuel stood before them, his face serious. 'Your injuries should be tended to, mistress, but our band must continue on our way.'

'I shall stay with Mistress Alynna and her servant,' Richard said, his glance settling upon Hester. 'Will you tend Mistress Alynna's injuries?'

At Hester's nod of assent, Brother Emmanuel added, 'Our pace is slow. You will catch up with us before nightfall, when we rest at Cissford Abbey.' He smiled at Alynna. 'It was a brave but dangerous risk you took in saving the boy. That lout who fell against you should be punished for his drunkenness. God be with you, my child.'

Brother Emmanuel left them, and Richard's gaze flickered over Alynna. He still held her hand, his thumb gently probing the torn skin. When she looked up and saw the admiration in his eyes, her breath caught in her throat.

'I did not realise you had saved a child's life.' His tone was subdued, betraying nothing of his emotions. 'Alas, your gown is ruined. It is a poor reward for your bravery.'

Self-consciously she shook out the muddied folds of her skirts, noting with embarrassment a long rip in both her surcoat and kirtle which reached from the hem to her knee, indecently revealing her leg when she moved. She blushed, humiliated that he should see her like this. She had nothing else to wear, nor the means to buy new. Looking down at her broken nails, the skin grazed and bloodied, she reflected that they bore little resemblance to a lady's hands. Indeed she doubted whether her fast-swelling fingers could even hold a needle to patch her gown.

She swallowed hard. Her hands would heal, and the garments could be mended. 'Once again I owe you my life, sir. I fear I have become a burden to you.'

He smiled, grimly. 'I do seem to find myself rescuing you from the most unlikely scrapes!'

'I only wish I could repay you in some way.'

Their gaze held, and beneath his stare, Alynna's blush deepened. The bond of understanding she had first felt at the inn became fused more powerfully between them. And something more—much more, indefinable, but unnervingly sensual. Silver lights sparkled from behind his long, dark lashes, the boldness of his appraisal causing a glow to spread over her body. Drawn by a force outside her willpower, she swayed closer to him.

'Alynna!'

The sound of her name was a tortured groan, almost a plea. She saw his eyes darken and knew he desired her. Although he did not move, she was aware of the charged emotion sparking like lightning between them. She moved restlessly. The unexpected pain darting through her feet brought a gasp of shock from her at its viciousness, and the mystical spell was broken. Richard's glance swept over her figure, his brows drawing down. Then, without warning, he lifted the edge of her ripped gown.

'By Our Lady!' he rapped out, staring down, 'how long have you been walking barefoot?'

At the anger in his voice, Alynna glanced down with dismay. Her riding-boots were in shreds, their worn leather ripped away by her fall had been unnoticed by her until now, and her hose were torn past mending, exposing her feet, naked and bleeding.

'Oh, I look like a beggar waif!' All that was female in her cried out in frustration.

'You were almost killed in saving that child's life, and all you can think of is your ruined clothing!' He stared at her incredulously.

She was sore and aching in every limb, and must look frightful enough to scare the crows—no wonder he looked at her with horror! The impulse to burst into tears almost overwhelmed her, and biting her lip, she fought down the angry tears welling in her eyes.

'If I had drowned in the mill-race,' she responded obstinately. 'I would be past caring how I looked.'

His brows went up, merriment replacing the anger in his eyes. 'Forgive my laughter, but your logic is astounding! You are a very courageous woman.'

'No, I am not.' His compliment destroyed her composure as his mockery never could. Tears rolled down her cheeks, and no power on earth seemed capable of stopping them.

He uttered a muffled oath. 'You are exhausted, fair lady, and near to collapse.'

Before she could guess his intent, his arms were beneath her knees and about her waist, and she was lifted to his chest as effortlessly as though she were a small child. The boldness of his action dried her tears, but for several moments she was unable to retaliate. At the touch of his breath caressing her hot cheek, her pulse raced alarmingly. Captured so intimately against him, her whole body was stingingly conscious of the play of muscles in his arms. The intensity of her awareness shocked and frightened her, so that she gasped out, desperately, 'Put me down!'

'You are in no fit state to walk!' He glowered at her threateningly, as if expecting her to disagree. 'Hester will attend you once we can bathe your feet in the river.'

'Ay,' Hester readily agreed. 'You must not walk, Alynna. Would you make yourself crippled for the rest of the journey?'

Joel stood before them, barring the way, his expression antagonistic at Richard Dreux's audacity.

'Stand aside, man,' Richard demanded impatiently. 'I mean your mistress no harm.'

Alynna looked beseechingly at the jester, silently pleading with him to make Richard put her down, but after a long stare at him, Joel ignored her plight and stepped aside. Whistling a jaunty tune, which drowned Alynna's protest, the jester picked up the discarded pilgrim's staves, and Richard strode forward, leaving her to seethe with impotent rage. The harder she tried to suppress the emotions he stirred in her, the more devastating they became at the next encounter. The path was too slippery for her to risk struggling against him and bringing them both down, but at least she was spared the embarrassment of being gaped at. The road was now deserted; even the pilgrims had disappeared from sight. She stared rebelliously up at Richard, who grinned unrepentantly.

'What is to become of you, fair Alynna? You have the courage of a enraged tigress, and are just as unpredictable!'

'I shall manage very well,' she returned primly, her moment of self-pity vanishing as she became increasingly disturbed by the pressure of his body against hers.

'I believe you will, even against all odds.'

Admiration, and a higher accolade—respect—reluctantly entered his eyes. His grin broadened, his white, even teeth shining like pearls against his black beard. A lock of hair fell forward over his brow making him appear less formidable, while the masculine smell of his skin had a riotous effect upon her senses. She found herself wondering how it would feel to run her hand over the bearded roughness of his face and the raven-black hair curling over his collar. Then, annoyed at her fancies, she clenched her knuckles, the pain curbing her wanton impulse. A provocative smile tilted his lips, and to her further chagrin she realised he had seen her movement, and worse, read her thoughts. Exasperated, she stiffened, refusing to look at him, and was vexed when she felt, rather than heard, the deep laughter rumbling in his chest.

A low branch hung over the track, and when he bent his head to pass under it, his mouth brushed against her temple. Was she just imagining that the touch of his lips lingered too long for the contact to be accidental? She had no experience of flirtation, while he, she instinctively knew, was accomplished in the art of love. Worse, the knave was making the most of his appointed role of knight-errant!

Her quelling glare was lost upon him; if anything it

brightened the amused glint in his eyes, and she felt that
the bond she had earlier sensed again intensified. Hardly
checking his pace, Richard carried her past the mill and
along the track until the river bank became a gentle
slope. Only then did they move down to the river's edge
and he placed her on a boulder.

'Thank you,' she said stiffly, sweeping back her hair
which had fallen about her face, but she did not look at
him, lest her composure again deserted her. 'If you
would turn your back, I can remove my hose,' she added
tersely, aware that he continued to watch her. When he
made no move, she scanned the road above them, and
was disconcerted to see that Hester and Joel were still
some distance away, the lame woman unable to keep up
with Richard's tireless stride. A stone slithering into the
water told her that Richard had at last turned away, and
she removed the remnants of her boots, hastily stripping
off her garters and discarding her torn hose. Once her
legs were again covered by her skirts, he propped his
foot beside her hip on the boulder and bent forward, his
finger lifting a stray tendril of hair that clung to the side
of her mouth.

'I could help you if you would let me,' he persisted,
still holding the curl between his fingers.

At the unexpected gentleness of his words, together
with the impact of his compelling stare, so disarmingly
close, Alynna's fragile barrier against him crumbled.
'You have done so much already.' She hoped he would
not discern the tremor of anticipation in her voice. 'I
could not ask more of you.'

'I do not make such offers lightly.'

Silver sparks flared through his grey eyes. His hands
moved to her shoulders, his eyes heavy-lidded as they
stared fixedly at her mouth. Her breath hung suspended
in her throat. Imperceptibly their bodies moved closer,
and their lips wavered, a finger's breadth apart. Then
she was crushed in his arms, his beard lightly grazing her
skin before his mouth claimed hers with a fervour that
caught her unawares. Her initial reaction was to push
him away, but as though sensing her fear at the passion

of his kiss, the touch of his lips gentled. The supple warmth of his mouth moving expertly over hers became deliciously sweet, stilling her resistance. Her murmured protest was smothered by the insistence of his lips, their pressure demanding until, dizzily, her lips parted and their breaths mingled.

Caught up in a turmoil of exquisite emotions she had not imagined possible, a moan of pleasure rose in her throat. Even the tickling sensation of his beard enhanced the mastery of his kiss. The promise of the delights imparted by the message of his lips kindled a craving deep within her, and she clung to him, lightheaded, her blood afire.

A fall of earth from the direction of the river bank shattered the intimacy of the moment. Alynna started guiltily, the wantonness of her response leaving her shaken.

'You should not have done that!' She drew back, appalled at what he must be thinking of her.

'I will not apologise for so pleasurable an act.'

Her heart raced at the desire smouldering in his eyes. He had taken advantage of her innocence, and her anger rose at the light manner in which he had seized upon the opportunity to kiss her. 'I trusted you! If that were not enough, we are on a holy pilgrimage.'

He straightened, releasing her, his black brows slanting ominously and fine lines of contempt spreading from the corners of his eyes. He curbed the self-anger tearing through him. How had this woman pierced his armour? He had forsworn worldly passion during his pilgrimage, but constantly he found himself fascinated by her courage and beauty. She had looked so youthful and beguiling, with the sunlight enriching the sheen of her hair, that her beauty had moved in a way no woman had before. What madness had possessed him so to forget his vows and give in to the temptation of kissing her? He eyed her warily, studying the proud lines of her oval face, and was annoyed at the intensity of his need to make love to her. She constantly surprised him by her actions. He would have sworn that she was a virgin and without guile, but he had sensed a deeply passionate nature rising in response to his ardour. A blush stained her high cheekbones as she watched Joel and Hester climbing down the river bank, but apart from that, her thoughts were carefully shielded from him. His ingrained suspicion returned. Was her innocence a pretence?

'Your plight is desperate, is it not?' he asked roughly.

'Not desperate enough to forget my honour,' she responded, her sapphire eyes flashing with challenge. 'I am ashamed that I did not stop you sooner.'

At the coldness of her tone, his eyes narrowed. Then he checked himself, amusement overriding his anger. Many women in her position would have offered themselves to win his protection. 'I meant no insult,' he drawled, disconcerted by the levelness of her stare. Few men eyed him with such defiance. 'Will you allow me, then, to help you?'

'I cannot deny that I need a champion.' There was obstinacy and pride in the set of her chin, and a sad smile touched her lips. 'But my plight is such that only the king can help me.'

Disappointment stabbed through him. During his years at Court he had been offered every bribe imaginable by petitioners eager to win his favour. So that was her game! She had played it well, and almost fooled him.

'You aim high,' he said harshly. 'Do you wish me to speak with my kinsman, the Earl of Trevowan? He has some favour with his Majesty.'

'Oh no!' Alynna looked taken aback. 'Why should the Earl interest himself in my case? I doubt that he even knew my father.'

The instant she had spoken, all colour drained from her face. His curiosity was aroused at her independent nature, and he again wondered what she was hiding. Did she truly not know who he was? Or was this a ploy to gain his interest? He had to be sure.

'Who was your father?' he demanded.

She glanced, as though seeking guidance, towards her servant, who was helping Hester to climb down the shallow river bank. When she refused to answer, he gripped her shoulders, forcing her to gaze up at him. Her eyes were sad, their brilliant depths muted, and he was struck afresh at their unusual colour. Only once had he seen such eyes, and that had been many years ago.

'I could help you. But I can do nothing unless you tell me what happened to leave you penniless. You were not robbed, were you?'

She shook her head. 'It is painful for me to speak of it. My father was Sir Robert Freston.' Her voice cracked. 'Please . . . no more. Not now.'

Richard rubbed his hand over his jaw, recalling all he knew of Freston. A country knight, not often at court. Yet, when he had appeared in the late king's court, he had been shown favour by his Majesty. Uneasily, Richard remembered that Griswolde had mistaken Alynna for someone. Was it possible that his cousin had met Sir Robert's wife? He could not remember a wife accompanying Freston at Court. A dozen questions sprang to his mind, but he refrained from asking them and appeared to dismiss the matter. If Freston was her father, it was likely she had guessed his own identity. At Canterbury he would have the truth from her, and until then he could learn much by watching and waiting.

He stepped back as Hester hobbled forward. Taking some coins from the pouch on his belt, he tossed them to Joel. 'Your mistress needs shoes. Go to the village and buy some.'

'I cannot take your money,' Alynna declared hotly.

'What you cannot do is to walk barefoot from here to Canterbury,' Richard snapped, irritated that she continued to defy him. He saw pride warring against reason in her face. Her vivid blue eyes lifted, sparkling with helpless fury. Their gaze merged in silent combat, and he felt the excitement akin to the moment when he couched his lance and prepared to enter the tourney lists.

Meeting the force of his commanding stare, Alynna shifted uncomfortably. Richard was right: it was she who was being unreasonable. Was it because she was drawn to this man in a way that no other had affected her?

When Joel did not immediately respond to Richard's orders, she looked askance at him, wondering what was wrong. He was watching her, his brow wrinkled as though he were deeply troubled.

'Would you go to the village for me, Joel?' she said, guessing he had resented Richard giving him orders. Her own father had never treated him as a servant, and neither did she intend to. 'I fear I do need shoes.'

'Ay, for you I will go.' He looked pointedly across at Richard Dreux, adding stiffly, 'Hester's presence will protect my lady's honour while I am gone.'

'What the devil do you mean by that?' Richard blazed.

Joel paled as he met his glare, but he continued to stand his ground, his short wiry figure braced ready to defend Alynna by force, if he had to. His loyalty touched her, but she feared his conduct was sadly out of order. Joel was wrong to disobey Richard—he had meant no offence. If his tone had been abrupt, it was because he was used to unquestioning obedience, she suspected. The knowledge pitted her stomach, for she did not want to believe his rank could be higher than that of a knight.

'I take no orders except from my mistress.' Joel cut across her thoughts. 'I was honoured by the friendship of her father. In his stead, I would protect her with my life.'

'You are a good servant, Joel,' Richard surprised Alynna by saying, his stare no longer antagonistic. It was obvious that, in any contest, he would emerge the victor, yet he seemed to be deliberately holding back, respecting the jester's courage. 'I, too, would like to help your mistress,' he continued smoothly. 'We will not do that by quarrelling. If we are to reach the abbey before dark, we must leave within an hour.'

Joel lowered his gaze, inclining his head in a gesture of respect. 'I had better make haste, then.'

He took off up the bank, and Alynna breathed more easily now that the two men had come to some kind of a truce. Her future was uncertain enough, without dissension among her few friends. She caught herself up quickly. It was wrong to regard Richard Dreux as a friend; he was a . . . She sighed. What was he, or indeed ever could be, to her?

A shadow passed across the sun as Richard bowed to her. The shuttered, gaunt expression had returned to his face, and she felt his thoughts were already far from her as he said absently, 'I shall leave you in Hester's hands.'

Too weary to think clearly, she abandoned the attempt to understand why he had chosen to help her. When he wandered further along the river bank, she tore a strip of material from her ragged kirtle to bathe her feet.

'Allow me to do that. Your hands are too sore,' Hester insisted, kneeling at her feet and taking the cloth.

Hester made no comment on the fine quality of the silk, although Alynna saw her frown as she soaked it in the water. She had never once probed her to speak of her life, and for that she was grateful. Now, in view of what had happened in the village, she wondered if Hester also had her secrets.

The cold water stung Alynna's skin, then gradually, beneath her friend's gentle touch, the pain and discomfort eased. That task done, Hester refused to let her sew her ripped kirtle and gown, and feeling at a loss, Alynna looked along the bank to where Richard sat on a tree trunk, with one knee drawn up against his chest.

Again she was struck by his almost regal aloofness as he stared at the water rushing over a group of boulders. He was too far away for her to see his expression, but she sensed a great sadness in him. She fought against the desire to go to him and offer him comfort, until the effort to restrain her impulse caused a painful ache within her breast. Unable to drag her eyes from his figure, she could not banish the memory of his kiss. He was all she had dreamed a chivalrous knight to be, but what use were such dreams to her now? Since she had been born out of wedlock, what knight would marry her? If Joel had spoken the truth, and there was no reason why he should lie, her mother had been a noblewoman. As a ward of the king, her dowry would be quite substantial, but would that make a difference? She clenched her hands, the pain of her torn flesh bringing a return to sanity. She was foolish to build her dreams upon a single kiss. Was it not likely that he would more readily make her his mistress than his wife!

The thought was sobering. With her wits once more clear and rational, she could not understand why she still harboured a sense of unease that had nothing to do with her emotions concerning Richard Dreux, and she sat very still. Then the hair at the base of her neck prickled and she glanced over her shoulder, convinced that she was being watched. Joel must have returned. The river bank and road were deserted. She shrugged. The fall had shaken her more than she realised. Why should anyone be spying on them?

There was a shout from the direction of the road, and Joel came into sight. He skidded down the bank, holding a pair of bright red shoes, and with an exaggerated bow presented them to her, together with a pair of green knee hose.

'The finest the shoemaker could offer!' He wielded his purchase aloft like a war-prize. 'They were made for the steward's wife at the Manor, but she has not paid for the last pair he made for her. That will teach her to neglect her debts!'

The expression on his craggy face was so comical, that she laughed—for the first time since she had learned of her father's death.

'It is good to hear you laughing again, mistress,' Joel beamed at her, and after a brief hesitation nodded towards Richard. 'We reach Canterbury tomorrow, so why not speak to him of your plight? I am not sure I trust his intentions, but he could help you to gain an audience at Court.'

'He has already offered, but I already owe him so much. I only wish there was some way I could repay him.' She pulled on the hose and pushed her feet into the shoes, which although too large were surprisingly comfortable.

'Take care what you offer,' Hester warned. 'A man such as he is used to taking what he chooses.'

Alynna lowered her eyes, as Hester's words echoed her own suspicions. At Richard's approach, she cautioned Hester and Joel to silence, and leaning heavily on the staff Joel returned to her, she stood up. Richard held out his arm, and when she hesitated to take it, his expression became stern.

'Joel will look after Hester.' His tone had returned to cold informality. 'Permit me to assist you.'

Resting her hand on the soft wool of his sleeve, she was conscious of the powerful strength in the lean muscled forearm as he adjusted his long stride to her slower pace. Although his manner was courteous, she felt that somehow he had distanced himself from her, and his coolness was puzzling. Had she unwittingly offended him in some way? She stumbled on the rutted track, and his hand was quick to seek her waist to steady her, the firm touch playing havoc with her senses. When she tried to thank him, she was appalled to find herself as tongue-tied as a village idiot. They walked for some distance in silence, a tangible tension building between them, until her taut nerves could stand it no longer.

'I have angered you,' she blurted out, as they turned off the road on to a cart track leading to the abbey, which had just become visible. 'Was it my refusal to speak of my past, or . . . ?' Her voice broke off with embarrassment. 'Do you despise me as a wanton? I must have appeared brazen and shamefully immodest at the river.'

Richard's crack of laughter shattered her composure. 'You looked beautiful and provocative . . . and—very much as though you wanted me to kiss you. I thought you enjoyed the experience.' He raised a mocking brow.

'Yes, curse you, I did enjoy it,' she retaliated before she could consider her words. Then catching herself, she added warningly, 'But honour is more important than pleasure.'

'A noble sentiment, sweet Alynna.' He caught her hand and raised it to his lips. His eyes became serious. 'So now you regret what happened?'

He looked at her strangely. Did he feel himself compromised? His expression was infuriatingly guarded. Her instinct was to tell him the truth—that she had wished that magical moment could last for ever, but it was unthinkable for a maid to speak of such things. Unwilling to lie to him, she protested, 'I wish to forget the incident, sir. A true knight would do the same.'

'Now you would question my chivalry!' He laughed softly, but there was a glint of steel in his eyes.

She launched her last attack, knowing it would be impossible to win any battle, verbal or otherwise, against him. 'I do not understand the rules of this game you play. I speak honestly, and mean no offence.'

She tried to pull her hand free, but found it held tighter. His lips twisted into the taunting smile that had become so familiar. 'Little firebrand! How like Meraud you are!'

A sharp pain gouged her heart at the affection mingled with sadness in his voice. 'Meraud?' she queried tentatively. 'Your wife?'

'My sister,' he replied, the haunted look she had noticed at their first meeting returning to his eyes.

She was about to ask more of his family, but was warned by the severe line of his mouth that he would not be questioned. The sound of a bell carried to them from the nearby abbey, and as it faded, a twig snapped in the wood alongside the track. Again Alynna's neck prickled; this time she was convinced they were being watched, and she clasped Richard's arm in mounting alarm. 'Someone is following us!'

He scanned the wood, frowning, before addressing Joel and Hester. 'Did you see anyone following us?'

Joel looked blank. 'There are only two peasant women carrying faggots.'

'What makes you think we are being followed, Alynna?' Richard looked at her thoughtfully.

'I heard a noise. It was just a feeling I had,' she said, feeling foolish at allowing her glimpse of the ferryman at the mill to make her nervous. 'Probably I was mistaken.'

'It has been a long and eventful day.' Richard

squeezed her hand. 'You probably heard a fox in the wood.'

'That must be it,' she reluctantly conceded, withdrawing her hand. His touch had confused her further. Too disturbed to say more, she fell silent, relieved that the tall buildings of the abbey were directly ahead.

A blind beggar squatting by the enclosing wall cried out for alms as they approached. Richard tossed him a coin, and rang the admittance bell on the gate. After a short wait, a panel slid back from behind an iron grille in one of the two huge studded oak doors, and a face appeared.

'We are pilgrims who became separated from Brother Emmanuel,' Richard explained.

The panel was snapped shut, and a small door set within the large one opened. Gesturing for Alynna to go first, Richard pulled the hood of his cloak further over his face as he walked past the monk. Why did he hide his face when meeting new people, she wondered. What was he hiding?

Once inside the abbey, the porter directed them to the two guest houses—one for the men, the other for the women. Richard bade her farewell, and as she entered the women's quarters there was an emptiness within her at being parted from him so abruptly. From then on, the routine life of the religious house carried her along in its wake. Food was brought and they were later led to the chapel for Vespers, where the women remained separated from the men by a wooden screen. The service ended. Alynna returned to the cell she shared with Hester, and sank tiredly on to the straw pallet. She had never felt so exhausted, and to add to the discomfort of her sore feet, her body was bruised and stiffening after her fall. Closing her eyes, she lay listening to Hester's chatter.

'Have you decided what you are to do once the pilgrimage is over, Alynna?'

'I should go to London.' Alynna turned on to her side and propped her head on her elbow. 'But I have not yet decided. First I must find a way of supporting myself through the winter. I will not be a charge upon Joel.'

'Has Richard Dreux anything to do with your indecision?' Hester said with a languishing sigh. 'I have seen
the way he looks at you when he thinks he is unobserved.
And you at him. Do you love him?'

Startled by her bluntness, Alynna sat up. 'Of course
not! I hardly know him.'

Hester chuckled. 'Love strikes where it will, and
without warning! He kept himself very aloof from the
pilgrims until you joined our band. He is more relaxed
these days, but those not blessed with his favour are still
in awe of him. He is a mystery, that one—but a handsome devil!'

The odd fluttering that affected Alynna's heart
whenever Richard was mentioned returned. Could she
be falling in love? The knowledge shook her. How could
fate be so cruel?' He had shown her kindness, but that
did not mean he loved her. Yet he had offered her help,
and she knew he desired her. But desire was not love.
Was the physical attraction she felt for him just the
blossoming of her womanhood? The memory of his lips,
warm and demanding upon her mouth, turned her blood
to molten liquid, her body throbbing with an indefinable
yearning. A shiver of pleasure possessed her. Closing
her eyes, she mentally scolded herself. That had been a
moment's madness; it did not mean that she loved
Richard Dreux!

Hester laughed delightedly. 'Your eyes betray you,
Alynna.'

'Is it so obvious that I find him attractive?' she sighed.
'He is far above me in rank. Whether I loved him or not,
nothing could come of it.'

'Well, not marriage, but . . . you need a man's protection. I do not like to think of a woman, young and
innocent as yourself, thrown into such a life, but . . .'

'No. I will be no man's leman,' Alynna cut in. 'My
children will not be . . .' She paused, the pain of her own
bastardy lancing through her. She drew a shaky breath
and went on more steadily, 'I would not shame my
family.'

'If you see that as shame, then you regard yourself as his equal.' Hester eyed her keenly. 'I was once maid to the lady of the manor, and I know a noblewoman when I see one. So does Master Dreux. Are you sure thoughts of marriage are hopeless?'

'Oh, Hester—I know so little about him! I do not even know if he is already married. And I am . . .' Alynna lay down on her back, covering her eyes with her forearm. With difficulty at first, she began to speak, but once started, she was unable to stop, and her story since she had arrived at Barkhurst tumbled out. Hester said nothing until she had finished.

'Oh, my lady! I have never heard of such injustice.'

'*Not* "my lady",' Alynna cautioned, 'Promise me you will keep my secret?'

'I'll not betray you,' Hester promised. 'But is there no hope that Lady Joan will relent?'

Alynna shook her head. 'My stepmother made her hatred clear. I must make a new life for myself.'

'Put your faith in God, my lady.' Hester squeezed her hand. 'His ways are not always easy to understand. If he has brought you and Richard Dreux together, then it is with reason.'

More than anything Alynna wanted to believe that, but when eventually she began to drift into sleep, she tossed and turned, her mind harassed by doubts.

The next morning, when the pilgrims assembled in the abbey courtyard, Alynna was still edgy from her night's discoveries and could not meet Richard's gaze as he came to stand at her side behind the pilgrims. The band had begun to walk to the gate when the abbot stepped from the building opposite, moving towards his travelling litter. They stood aside for him to pass, and he paused to give them his blessing, but his hand froze in mid-air as he was about to make the sign of the cross. He was staring at Richard. With a start he recovered himself, and to Alynna's astonishment, he bowed respectfully to him.

Her heart sank. Abbots did not show such deference

to humble knights, so Richard must be a great nobleman. It was a harrowing thought, confirming her fears, and her heart wrenched. Was it possible that she was falling in love with a man whose rank was far above her own?

Joel touched Alynna's arm. 'Mistress, the others are leaving.'

Heavy-hearted, she followed, and at the gate she paused. She glanced back at Richard's handsome, grave face. When he knelt to kiss the abbot's ring, there was nothing subservient in his manner. At her side, Joel drew in a sharp breath and took her arm roughly, dragging her forward past the beggars gathered outside the gate.

'Do not look round, mistress,' the jester whispered harshly in her ear. 'That beggar with the bandage about his head—I am sure it is Wat, who was with the ferryman when you were attacked at Barkhurst.'

CHAPTER FIVE

'WHAT ARE we to do?' Alynna demanded. 'I am sure I saw the ferryman at the mill. Has Lady Joan sent them to spy on us?'

Joel, his face grey with worry, glanced over his shoulder at the group of beggars, while urging her forward. 'Lady Joan does have much to fear from you, and there is no point in taking unnecessary risks.' When they were some distance ahead of the other pilgrims he pressed a new leather belt with a sheathed dagger into her hand, saying, 'This is the knife you took from the ferryman. I bought the belt in the village yesterday. Wear it always. Sir Robert taught you how to defend yourself with a such weapon—you may have to use it in earnest.'

Alynna stared incredulously at him. 'Do you think Lady Joan wishes me dead? No, I do not believe her so evil.'

He took her staff while she fastened the dagger belt over her hips. When he handed it back to her, his voice was ominous. 'Lady Joan acted rashly when she cast you out, without thought of the consequences. If those two scoundrels are following us, they are up to no good. Sir Richard should be told.'

'No, Joel!' She looked back at their companions strung out along the track. Richard Dreux emerged from the abbey, striding past the slowly trudging pilgrims. At the strength and vigour in his graceful, untiring pace, she crushed a wave of emotion, saying firmly, 'I will not be a further charge upon him.'

'He has not seemed to mind until now.' Joel regarded her, openly curious.

'Which is why I will not trouble him with my problems.'

'Mistress, now more than ever we need his help!' His

tone was urgent. 'Yesterday you were content in each other's company, so have you since quarrelled?'

Alynna evaded the jester's gaze. She did not want to be reminded of the transformation that had come over her when Richard had held her in his arms.

'So he has captured your affections,' he observed. 'I would not see you hurt, my lady, but the Dreux family are powerful and high in the king's favour. That he is not immune to your charms, could be to your advantage.'

'It is not so simple.' She looked beseechingly at him, her voice firm and without self-pity as she explained, 'You still regard me as the Lady Alynna, but until I learn who my real mother was, I am no one—without rank or position. I see now that at Higham I was deliberately sheltered from any unexpected visitor from Court. But why? When my father spoke of suitors, he referred to them as being worthy of me, yet his most frequent lecture to me was with regard to the structure of rank and the rules governing it. Cross them at your peril, he would say, for disaster will surely follow. A knight cannot marry a peasant, no more than a duke or earl a lowly knight's daughter. I feel I have lost my identity, Joel. For the moment I exist in a void as Mistress Freston—a temporarily pilgrim—soon to become a vagabond.'

She pulled herself up short with a wry smile, realising that she was in danger of becoming maudlin. 'As for Richard Dreux . . .' she added, reminding herself as much as the jester. 'He is no mere knight, of that I am certain.'

Joel shrugged. 'All the better. He can speak for you at Court.'

She shook her head. 'How could I repay him? I could not bear his pity, nor would I live upon his charity.'

'But, mistress . . .'

'Enough, Joel. My mind is made up. Let me be alone with my thoughts for a while.' She kept her step even, although her torn feet began to feel on fire. 'Go to Hester, she needs you more than I. She is exhausted.'

'You will miss her when you have to part.'

'I have grown very fond of her.'

'The poor creature needs a friend.' Joel brightened. 'So Hester shall stay with us. We will manage somehow.'

'You mean *you* will! Oh, Joel, do you really think we could all stay together?' Her spirits lifted at the thought.

'How can you present your petition to the king without a lady's maid in attendance?' He grinned impishly. 'Besides, your reputation must remain untarnished if your future is to be truly secure. Hester will be your chaperon and companion.'

Impulsively, Alynna kissed his wrinkled cheek. 'Dear Joel, you have been a good friend these past days. I shall not forget.'

A blush stained the fool's face, and for the first time Alynna could remember, he was at a loss for words.

'Go and ask Hester if she will stay with us,' she urged. 'She knows how I depend on you, and will need convincing that she will not be a burden to us.'

When Joel fell behind to speak with Hester, Alynna ignored the pain in her sore feet, relying on her sturdy staff to take some of her weight. In the distance, dark grey against a wintry-white sky, the towers of Canterbury Cathedral rose skywards above the city walls. Soon their journey would be at an end. She touched the dagger at her waist. Once in the city, she could lose herself in the crowds and would be safe from the menace of Lady Joan's spies. At the sound of a firm tread at her side, she tensed.

'Your feet seem to have healed remarkably well,' Richard remarked. 'I wanted to speak with you before we reached Canterbury.'

'What about, my lord?'

His brows slanted down with suspicion. 'Why so formal? Yesterday I was Richard. And I thought we had agreed that I was a humble knight?'

Alynna stilled the clamouring of her heart, aware that the other pilgrims were some way behind. She was too vulnerable to the spell he so effortlessly seemed to weave over her, and her only defence against her wayward emotions lay in attack. 'Yesterday I said much that

would have been better left unsaid.' She stared at him
accusingly. 'You are no mere knight, my lord. I saw the
respectful way the abbot treated you.'

'That signifies nothing.' Richard's tone roughened
with annoyance, and his eyes flashed dangerously beneath black brows. 'The abbot was grateful. At Court,
I was able to bring the king's attention to a matter
concerning his family.'

'You move in exclusive circles, my lord,' she said
caustically. 'You know something of my story, and it
must be clear to you that our stations are far apart.'

They were approaching a wide stream with several
large flat stones sunk into its bed. She lifted her skirts
above her ankles, preparing to step on to the first stone,
but Richard took her arm, preventing her movement,
his voice gruff with exasperation, 'Have I not said I
would help you?'

'I owe you too much already,' she countered.

He controlled the anger stabbing through him at her
obstinacy. Never had he met such an independent-
minded woman! Or anyone so determined not to allow
him to help. Strangely, that knowledge rankled. 'There
is a way in which you can repay me,' he conceded. 'But
now I would know what you are fleeing from?'

Her only indication that he had chanced upon the
truth was the quickening of her shallow breathing, but
he detected the trembling she was taking pains to conceal. Stubborn minx! A fierce need to protect her welled
up in him. She had been so soft and yielding yesterday;
now her slanted brows lifted with cool hauteur in a way
that was both courageous and infuriating.

'Trust me, Alynna.'

Wary as a cornered vixen, her eyes searched his. Then
thick, dark lashes veiled their sapphire depths and her
mouth set in a determined line. She was so proud—so
defiant, just like Meraud used to be. The reminder of the
change in his sister, and the reason why he had under-
taken this pilgrimage, returned to haunt him. He bit
back his command for Alynna to answer him, and
repeated smoothly, 'You should let me help you.'

Alynna sighed. To refuse his help was madness. Joel
was right. What choice had she but to accept his offer?
The decision made, she eyed him steadily. She would tell
him the truth—everything—and if he turned from her in
disgust at her lowly birth, so be it. Far better now than
later, when each meeting made it harder to accept that
once the pilgrimage was over, she might never see him
again.

'I was not mistaken yesterday. I am being followed.'

His fingers tightened over her arm, but he made no
comment. They walked on, their slower pace adding
gravity to her words. 'When you rescued me from those
men near Barkhurst, we had not been robbed, as Joel
led you to believe.'

He listened, without interruption, throughout her
story. From time to time she glanced across at him,
trying to judge his expression. It remained inscrutable
until she spoke of her treatment at Barkhurst. Then his
eyes grew thunderous.

'Such injustice cannot go unpunished!' he flared.

'I will not have my father's name discredited,' she
returned.

'God's wounds!' Richard exploded, outrage darkening his face. 'What I would not give to get my hands on
those villains! One is dressed as a beggar, you say?'

The fierceness of his anger clutched at her heart. Was
it aimed at Hugh the ferryman or because she had misled
him from the start?

'I bear the stain of bastardy,' she said hollowly, unable
to judge his thoughts and fearing the worst. 'I shall
understand if you wish to withdraw your offer of help.'

He stood so still, like one of the giant pagan stones she
had seen on a desolate moor on her way to London; only
his eyes looked alive, and the glint in their stormy depths
filled her with dread. Something of her alarm must have
shown in her face, for her hand was taken in a warm, firm
grasp and lightly squeezed, although his expression
remained forbidding. He had proved himself a worthy
friend, but that look—glacial and dangerous—warned
her that he would make a terrifying enemy. 'You are still

Sir Robert Freston's daughter, and apparently the king's ward. I recall that Freston was held in some regard by the late king.' He rubbed his hand across his beard, his eyes troubled. 'Are you sure you have never met Sir Geoffrey Griswolde before?'

Alynna's pride smarted at the suspicion roughening his voice. 'No, never!'

'And you have no idea who your true mother is?' he persisted ruthlessly.

'I have told you all I know. Except . . .' She frowned, remembering. 'At the inn, Sir Geoffrey was so certain he knew me. Could he have met my mother? I must seek him out at Canterbury.'

They were almost at the city walls, and the road in front was crowded with wagons and people. Richard glanced over his shoulder to where the other pilgrims were now very close.

'Beware, Alynna. Sir Geoffrey is not to be trusted. *I* shall confront my cousin.' He pushed back a lock of black hair that fell forward over his brow, the terse movement and darkening glower showing that there was little love lost between him and his noble kinsman. 'We can speak no more of the matter now. The city gate is ahead,' he added at her questioning glance. 'I shall spend three days in prayer here. After that . . .'

He paused, pensively rubbing his jaw. 'Then we shall discuss your future,' he said casually, though the slight tilting of his mouth hinted at something more, and her heart fluttered in anticipation. 'It may not be possible to approach the king immediately. I shall, however . . .'

He broke off at hearing a discreet cough near by. Discovering Brother Emmanuel behind them, they drew apart. Before giving his attention to the friar, Richard leaned closer to Alynna, adding in an undertone, 'I shall not always be on hand to protect you in Canterbury. Take care, my dear. Stay close to Joel.'

She moved to the side of the road to wait for Joel and Hester to join her. Hester was limping heavily, but her face was flushed with pleasure as she excitedly agreed to stay with them after the pilgrimage. Alynna was

unaware that she had failed to answer several of
Hester's questions as they trudged on, the conversation
with Richard having left her emotions in turmoil.

Relieved that he had not condemned her for her
bastardy, her initial delight that he would be her
champion was tinged with apprehension. And what of
her own attraction to Sir Richard? Would she be able to
find the strength to resist temptation? For resist she
must, or betray all the teachings of her father.

The clamour around her indicated, to her surprise,
that they had already entered the city. Somehow she had
expected there to be a calm reverence filling such a holy
place, but instead, the noise was deafening. The booming voices of pardoners competed with the cries of
pedlars selling medals and ampullae of holy water.
Strolling players performed on raised platforms, while
friars preaching on street corners vied to win the attention of the crowd against performing bears, acrobats and
the constant whine of beggars.

In the streets, rickety handcarts and ox-wagons were
jostled by the litters of noblewomen. Above the rooftops, the long grey cathedral dominated the city, but as
Alynna stared about her, her excitement died. Too often
her gaze fell upon the sick and crippled, even soldiers,
their wounds or stumpy limbs still bandaged and un-
healed from Agincourt. After the open road, it was
uncomfortable to be pressed in by so many.

She looked round for Richard, and was dismayed to
see him some distance behind, still talking with Brother
Emmanuel. Even Joel and Hester had become separated from her by the crowd. She began to push her way
back towards Richard and, alerted by the creeping
sensation raising the hair on her neck, her hand sought
the dagger at her waist. Was she still being watched? Her
glance darted over the crowd. Most of the men had their
hoods pulled low over their faces against the cold, and
many were bearded. If Wat or Hugh were following
her, they would be indistinguishable among so many
similarly dressed. A blast from an outrider's horn made
the crowd ahead flatten themselves in doorways and

against the timber-framed houses. A party of nobles were pushing their horses through the throng. Alynna drew back, clutching her staff tight to her body as the riders began to pass.

Opposite, through an archway, she saw a gypsy girl, her skirt whirling high to her knees as she danced to the music of a piper, while another man collected the coins thrown to them. Two of the nobles, obviously intrigued by the sound of music, reined in, leaving their companions to ride on. She was surprised to recognise the scarlet-cloaked figure of Sir Geoffrey Griswolde before he and his companion turned their horses under the arch to watch the dancer. The knight roared his approval as the gypsy's skirt twirled higher, revealing her olive thighs. With the arrival of the two knights, the dancer's mood changed. Raising her arms above her head, she swayed her hips in time to the sensuous rhythm as she provocatively circled her noble admirers. When the dance came to an end, Sir Geoffrey tossed her some coins and, leaping from his horse, captured her in his arms and kissed her. With a throaty laugh, the gypsy pulled away but, even from where Alynna stood, every movement of the young woman's body was a blatant invitation for him to follow. Tossing the reins of his mount to a groom, Sir Geoffrey pursued her, placing his arms about her waist as they entered the inn.

At that moment a man stumbled against Alynna, and she stiffened when he placed his hand on her hip to steady himself. Knocking his hand aside, she turned her back on him.

'You look lost, my pretty,' a gruff voice spoke in her ear. 'If it's company you're looking for, join me in a mug of ale.'

She spun round. After the easy way Griswolde had won the gypsy's services, she was outraged that she had been so lewdly accosted. She glared haughtily at the ugly, squat creature who, in his worn velvet gown trimmed with squirrel, looked like an impoverished merchant. 'How dare you address me so!' she fumed. 'Leave me alone, or I shall . . '

'You will do what, beggar?'

A cruel light appeared in his squinting eyes, and Alynna felt her first prick of alarm. A crowd was beginning to form round them, and a voice muttered darkly, 'Respectable women do not roam the streets unattended. Too many vagabonds are a charge on this city.'

Drawing her tired body up proudly, she refused to show her growing fear as she rounded on the merchant. 'I shall call the watch.'

He grinned at the crowd straining to listen, his voice low. 'Who will take your word against mine?' He leered at her. 'I can be generous when paying for a woman's company.'

'You vile creature!' she raged, shaking her staff at him. 'I am a pilgrim. Get off with you before I use this!'

The merchant laughed derisively, turning to the crowd for support. 'We see too many so-called pilgrims here—whores who would lure Godfearing citizens into temptation, and sham-cripples, who by trickery beg alms from true penitents and pilgrims. They will not be tolerated.'

A frightening roar of abuse rose around her. They sided with the merchant, not her. Even in Suffolk she had heard of people believed to be vagrants being set upon by villagers. This was the fate to which Lady Joan had condemned her, and she had been saved only by Richard's and Joel's protection. Concealing her fear, she repeated haughtily, 'I am a pilgrim. It is this man who lies!'

'Why should we believe you?' shouted a woman in a bright blue cloak beneath which she wore an abundance of paste-jewels sewn to her crimson gown.

'Ay!' Others joined in, sounding like baying hounds about to close in for the kill.

Alynna drew her knife, brandishing it at the merchant, who made a lunge at her. 'Poverty is not a crime.'

'Beggar—or more likely thief—that's what you are!'

the gaudily dressed woman screeched. 'Our shop was robbed last week by a beggar-pilgrim such as you. She spoke like gentry, despite her ragged cloak. Next thing we knew, she had stolen two silver goblets and run out of the shop before we could stop her.'

Alynna stood her ground, proud and dignified, the knife her only defence as the crowd pressed closer. Suddenly she saw Joel. 'There is my servant,' she declared. 'He will tell you I am no begger!'

Several faces turned towards Joel as he thrust his way to the front of the gathering, his wrinkled face contorted with fury. 'What is happening here? Are you safe, my lady?' At her nod, he spun round, his large owl-like eyes fixed scornfully on the crowd. 'For shame! Is this how you treat pilgrims in your town—by ridicule?'

The merchant backed off, scowling. 'No decent woman walks unattended.'

Joel started forward, bristling for a fight.

'No, Joel!' Alynna commanded, determined to avoid a further scene. 'Let the matter rest, my friend,' she added urgently. 'I came to no harm.'

She moved forward, eager to put the unpleasant experience behind her. At least Richard Dreux had not witnessed her humiliation! He had rescued her from so many incidents that he must think her weak and foolish. The thought left her angry with herself. His opinion of her should not matter, but it did. More than she cared to admit.

Their progress was slow through the press of people in the narrow street, but finally they entered the cathedral grounds. Here Alynna hesitated, feeling small and insignificant as she stared up at the immense three-towered building. She had come to the end of her journey. Would she find the answers she sought here? Her glance alighted on the pilgrims making their way into the cathedral, and unerringly she picked out Richard, who, accompanied by Hester, was walking towards them. Her heart ached at seeing his solemn, world-weary expression. If only she could help to ease whatever burden troubled him, as he had eased her grief! When he halted at her side his austere countenance relaxed, but he still appeared distracted.

'Brother Emmanuel and the others are lodging at a hospice in the city,' he pronounced. 'You will be better to stay within the cathedral precincts.'

At the sound of approaching riders, Richard pulled his hood further over his face and hunched his shoulders to conceal his height as Sir Geoffrey and his companion rode past.

'Will you lodge with your cousin at the prior's house?' Alynna asked, puzzled that he did not wish to be recognised by his kinsman.

'No.'

She frowned at the suspicious note of his tone. He knew her story, but she still knew nothing of him. Her heart wrenched as she recalled the tender moments between them and the air of command he assumed so naturally. In his company, her spirit and senses could one moment soar to heights of unbelievable pleasure, the next be cast down into a pit of inconsolable misery. She saw that Hester was watching them both closely, a secretive smile playing on her lips. Was the lame woman right—had she unwittingly lost her heart to Richard Dreux?

To mask her feelings she looked up at the sky. It was dull and overcast, its bleakness as depressing as her thoughts. The casual, almost possessive, way Richard took her arm, coupled with the contact of his shoulder and the muscular hardness of his body against hers as they walked, unnerved her. Thankfully, he seemed too preoccupied to notice the effect his slightest touch had upon her, as he nodded for Joel and Hester to follow. While they walked he bent closer, his breath, warm in the cold air, stroking her cheek, his voice a low confidential whisper.

'Our ways must part for a time. Promise me, you will not leave Canterbury before I can speak with you about your future. Meet me in the cloisters tomorrow afternoon an hour before Vespers.'

Unaccountably his words threw her into confusion. It

was what she wanted—to stay at this man's side. His manner was brisk with no hint of affection or any other emotion. How could she remain in his company, feeling as she did? Flustered, she pulled away from him, but his fingers tightened over her arm.

'Why do you look at me with such fear? Have I done aught to make you think me your enemy?'

How wrong he was! If she feared anyone, it was herself, because of the powerful emotions he roused in her. With difficulty she forced out, 'I do not fear you, my lord. Nor do I regard you as my enemy.'

'It is a beginning.'

The unexpected warmth of his smile disarmed her, and she lowered her eyes from his challenging gaze. His hand slid along her arm to take her shoulder, easing her body round to face him. The touch of his fingers was cool as his other hand lifted her face to meet his stare. When her gaze remained lowered, he stroked the softness of her neck, drawing her nearer.

'Alynna,' he ordered huskily. 'Look at me!'

Her lids seemed weighted with lead as she raised them and encountered his spell-binding gaze. His stare bored deep into hers, the irises of his eyes darkly ringed, the grey depths smouldering with emotion. She held her breath, becoming dizzy with expectancy as she waited for him to speak.

He swallowed with apparent difficulty. Then, as though only just recalling their surroundings, he smiled wryly. 'This is not the place nor the time for us to speak,' he declared, softly. 'Will you meet me tomorrow?'

Caught in the spell woven by his sensuous touch and gaze, Alynna was powerless to resist. She nodded agreement, not trusting her voice to sound normal.

'Until tomorrow.' His voice was uncharactistically rough and hesitant. He lifted her hand to his mouth.

Brief though the warm pressure of his lips was, it sent a shock through her. Gradually the wild tempo of her heartbeat steadied as she watched him stride away, but the insidious yearning spreading through her body could no longer be denied. Layer by layer the pretence was stripped from her, until only the truth remained. She loved Richard Dreux!

Yet the knowledge did not fill her with elation. Instead, fiery talons of despair raked at her breast. Nothing could overcome the stain of her bastardy. And Richard's background was swathed in mystery, no less so than her own. Why could she not extinguish the notion that love and happiness were an impossible dream? Would she be doomed, like her father, to give her heart to someone who would be forever unattainable?

CHAPTER SIX

ALYNNA TURNED to Joel and Hester. Her mind was too full of thoughts of Richard for her to feel ready to enter the cathedral just yet. 'Shall we find lodgings first?'

By the time they had entered the Almonry Yard and been shown by an official to their quarters, Alynna felt calmer. Joel had found himself a room and was waiting for them as they left the hospice and made their way to the cathedral.

'I would first pray at the Chapel of Our Lady Undercroft,' Alynna suggested. She needed time to settle her thoughts and to come to terms with the uncertainty of her future.

Hester looked uneasy. 'Forgive me, Alynna, if I do not join you. I would prefer to go straight to the shrine. I shall see you back at our rooms.'

'Of course,' Alynna agreed. Hester's needs were different from hers. With Joel at her side, she entered the small chapel. She had hoped for quiet and solitude, but even here it was packed with pilgrims.

At first her prayers were jumbled. It was impossible to clear her mind of the image of Richard Dreux and to pray for her father's soul. Gradually the beauty of the paintings decorating the roof and walls of the chapel brought her the peace she craved, and after an hour of prayer, she rose stiffly, her knees aching from the cold, and left the crypt to pray at the scene of Becket's martyrdom. From there she joined the pilgrims who had paused at the Altar of the Sword Point, on which lay the shattered end of the knight's sword which had cut straight through Becket's skull and struck and broke on the stone floor. A monk was reciting the story of Becket's death when the four knights, too eager to do Henry II's bidding, had murdered the Archbishop of Canterbury.

Alynna listened to the familiar tale, but when the monk described the saint's brains spilling from his skull, her blood chilled, and she gestured for Joel to move on to the saint's shrine itself. Here the chanting of the monks became drowned by the voices of the pilgrims crying out for the saint's intervention. The smell of incense was dulled by the acrid musk of unwashed bodies and the stench from running sores and sickness. She was shocked at the afflictions of many of the pilgrims. The blind were led or groped their way slowly forward, the cripples either carried by relatives or crawled on their hands and knees up the smooth hollow worn steps towards the shrine.

In front of her, a woman screamed out and collapsed on the steps, her arms and legs thrashing as her body seemed possessed by demons so that it took two men to hold her down until the spasms passed. Shaken, Alynna leaned against a marble pillar.

Instantly Joel was at her elbow. 'Are you all right, my lady? You look pale.'

'There is so much suffering. How unimportant my troubles seem, compared to those of others.' She was standing beside the tomb of the Black Prince, and stared down at the bronze effigy of England's warrior prince. He had been her father's hero, although he had died the year before Sir Robert was born. She closed her eyes, her grief at her father's death returning fourfold. Although it had never left her, during the last days in Richard's company it had lessened to little more than a dull ache.

'Sir Robert came often to pay homage to the Black Prince's tomb as well to pray at the shrine,' she added, her voice tightening with sadness. 'He told me so many stories of the Prince's valour and chivalry. I believe he tried to model his life on that of his hero. It is too cruel that Sir Robert was struck down while hunting.'

'Ay, Sir Robert rode like the devil!' Joel spoke with pride as they moved slowly on. 'He feared no man in the lists and was a handsome, gallant knight, a favourite with the Court ladies, even the queen. In his younger

days there were few to rival him. His death was a tragedy
. . . And timely for a certain party.' A hard note crept
into his voice. 'There is one who has richly benefited
from it.'

At her questioning look, Joel clamped his mouth shut.
Was he implying that Lady Joan was involved in her
father's death? Her stepmother had loved Sir Robert.
Loved him—but she had been scorned by him? A
disquieting thought nagged at her. If he had been killed
by mercenaries, why had Lady Joan allowed them to
return to Barkhurst? She quashed the notion at once
—its implication too terrible to be borne, seeing that
they had taken her there.

They filed into the Trinity Chapel, and in this dark
part of the cathedral the golden shrine gleamed in the
light of hundreds of candles. She glanced round, hoping
for a sight of Richard. Despite his hood pulled down
over his face, there was no mistaking the proud lines of
his long body kneeling in prayer at the far side of the
chapel. He resembled a carved effigy, so still was his
figure. He seemed unaware of the discomfort of the cold
stone floor—but then he would have undergone a
knight's vigil, kneeling at prayer throughout the long
hours of the night.

There was no sign of Hester, and she guessed she had
already left the shrine. For some time she was too
conscious of Richard's rapt devotions to concentrate on
her own, but when the mass of pilgrims hid his figure
from her, she cleansed her mind of earthly thoughts and
stared at the glittering shrine. Wherever she looked,
precious stones, carved cameos and onyx encrusted the
structure. With growing awe and reverence she became
unaware of the passage of time, or of the loud pleas of
the pilgrims.

The shimmering brilliance of the shrine dimmed before her eyes, and it was as though her father's presence
was with her, comforting and reassuring. She could hear
him encouraging, urging her to fight for her rights, so
that he had not died in vain. Yet as to the strange
circumstances of his death, she could find no answer.

Fewer pilgrims came to the shrine as night fell and the cathedral became darker. Alynna stood up. Joel, stiff with rheumatism from his hours of vigil at her side, rubbed his swollen joints. Before leaving, she looked back at Richard. His proud head was still bent in prayer, oblivious of everything around him. At some time, unnoticed by him, his hood had slipped back, partially revealing his features. Since she had first seen him, his beard had thickened, its blackness harshening the lean contours of his face. Where the soft light of the candles fell across his features it revealed deep lines scored into his brow. Were they caused by sorrow or remorse, she wondered. Seeing him vulnerable to human suffering, her heart went out to him.

How complex was this man's character. He had the valour of a lion, but beneath the gruff soldier's exterior, there was a deep sensitivity. And whoever he was, he was no underling! When he had spoken of helping her, it was with unquestioned assurance that he would succeed. Did that not make him a man far above her in station? The question haunted her.

'Come, Joel,' she said tiredly. 'Let us return to our lodging.' Aware of the painful way the jester shuffled along, Alynna linked arms with him to give him support. They stopped at the pilgrim's well, from which it was said Becket drank daily, and each purchased a lead ampulla, filling it with the holy water before leaving the cathedral.

Later, when Alynna returned to the room she shared with Hester and several other women, she found her friend quieter than usual. They both retired early, but she was too restless to settle. Too many questions remained unanswered. What had she expected from this pilgrimage? The journey had given her the time she needed to accept her father's death, though nothing could dull the pain of her loss.

She tried to shake off a sensation of approaching danger. She was over-tired. Tomorrow she would learn the truth of Richard's identity, and until then there was no point in speculation. Her ears pricked at a muffled sound audible above a woman's snores. She sat up, straining her eyes in the darkness. It was just possible to see Hester lying curled up on the next pallet bed. The sound came again. Concerned, Alynna put out her hand to touch her friend's shoulder.

'You are weeping,' she whispered. 'What is wrong, Hester?'

The sobs stopped on a watery hiccough. 'It is nothing.' Hester croaked. 'Go to sleep.'

'But you are upset,' Alynna persisted in a low voice. 'Will you not tell me what is amiss?'

Hester kept her face averted, her voice taut. 'I cannot speak of it now. Not with others present. I met someone I knew before . . . before I was scarred. They said some horrible things . . . I should be used to it by now.'

'Oh, Hester.' Alynna swung her feet to the ground and, unmindful of the cold floor, knelt at her friend's side. 'You must not let people upset you. It is not what is on the outside, but what lies within that counts. I have never met a more caring person than you.'

'That is because you always look for the good in people,' Hester groaned. 'I do not deserve your kindness. I have been wicked and sinful.'

Alynna reached out for Hester's hands and squeezed them. 'I do not believe that.'

'But it is true.' Hester whispered. 'I value your friendship, but I am not worthy of it. I cannot travel with you. I shall bring you harm.'

'I will listen to no more of this nonsense!' Alynna declared softly. 'You are overwrought.'

As she began to straighten, her hand was taken by Hester, whose tone was low and resigned. 'Are the others all asleep? I do not want anyone else to hear this. You have been kind, and deserve to know the truth.' There was a pause, then she went on, sounding as though she had suddenly aged thirty years. 'These scars . . . they are not from an ordinary fire. They come from the stake. My father and brother were burned that day . . . for heresy. I was condemned with them—only I . . .' Her voice cracked.

'There is no need to tell me, Hester. Not if it wounds you to speak of it.' Alynna hid her initial shock, and stroked the cold limp hand. She could guess what must have happened, and her heart wrenched as she imagined the horrors endured by her friend. 'It makes no difference.'

'Oh, but it does!' Hester tearfully exclaimed. 'We were Lollards. Or my brother and father were. I never fully understood all their preachings. Father was strict, and I had little choice but to follow their ways.'

'I can understand that,' Alynna soothed her. 'But that does not make you wicked or sinful. Just misguided.'

'In my father's eyes I sinned,' Hester groaned, her hand trembling. 'He died reviling me. I was so frightened. I did not know for what I was about to die. When the fire was lit, I screamed out, begging for mercy. I recanted. But the wood was dry and the breeze stiff. The flames caught at my gown and hair before they could douse it.'

Hester snatched her hand free, and in the pale moonlight from the window Alynna saw her touch her face. 'Mercy! Was this mercy?' Hester sobbed. 'The world can see me for what I was. If you befriended me, you will be reviled too.'

Alynna raised her hand to Hester's scarred cheek and gently wiped away a tear. 'You recanted, Hester. You are free. That is all behind you now, and we shall start a new life together.'

Hester's tears splashed hotly upon Alynna's hand and she put her arms round her friend, but realising the last thing Hester wanted from her was pity, she argued, 'We have to stay together, Hester. I need you. You must forget the past.'

'The past will not forget me,' Hester sniffed. 'I have visited shrines throughout England to pray for forgiveness. Some people will never let me forget. You do not need me, Alynna. You have Joel, and I doubt that handsome knight will leave you unprotected.'

'So you would desert me!' Alynna countered, in her need to make Hester see reason. 'You told me you had no family, so how do you propose to support yourself? By begging? You know I cannot travel about the country unchaperoned. My reputation would be ruined! I do need a female companion or maid.' She gave a soft, derisive laugh. 'Unfortunately, I have no means of paying for her services.'

Hester hung her head. 'You know I would not willingly desert you. But I act for your own good.'

'Then we shall talk no more of the matter.' Alynna was resolute. 'We stay together.'

The next morning Alynna returned to the cathedral. Knowing that any sight of Richard would distract her, she avoided the usual places of pilgrimage and visited the quieter St Gabriel's Chapel. Throughout the day she was aware of Joel watching over her and of Hester occasionally leaving the chapel to return later. As the hours passed, her prayers became ritualistic: she had no sense today of her father's presence. Yet from time to time she shivered, seeming to hear a distant voice calling out 'Beware!'

Twice she glanced over her shoulder, feeling herself observed, but each time all heads around her were bowed. Except for Joel who, too, appeared on guard and watchful.

Eventually he touched her shoulder. 'If you are not to keep Sir Richard waiting, we must go now, my lady.'

Upon leaving the chapel, Alynna looked round to see if they were being followed. Only a hooded monk, his head bowed in meditation, was some distance behind them. She shrugged, growing impatient at her nervousness.

After the musty, incense-laden atmosphere, Alynna inhaled deeply as they walked out into the cloisters, where the air was fresh after a morning's rainfall. They were joined by Hester, as they strolled beneath the vaulted arches, looking for Sir Richard. She glanced at a group of brightly dressed nobles sauntering in the central courtyard, and recognising Sir Geoffrey, she drew back into the shadows. It was unfortunate that he was here. She was sure Richard would not want their conversation interrupted by his cousin.

Without warning, a sudden cloudburst drenched the people outside in the open, and Joel ushered Alynna and Hester behind a large stone archway as the cloisters quickly filled with wet, complaining pilgrims. Alynna stood on her toes trying to make out Richard's tall figure among the crowd, but he was nowhere in sight. Disappointed, she dropped down onto her heels. Someone stepped on her foot, and she was suddenly rudely elbowed aside. Then everything seemed to happen at once. A fat woman, her hair dripping from the rain, pushed past Alynna, grabbed Hester, and began shouting.

'Here she is—the Lollard!'

'What's a heretic doing here?'

A dozen angry voices shrieked abuse as Hester was dragged from Alynna's side.

'To the prior with her!'

'Blasphemer!'

'Satan's apostle!'

Joel sprang forward to protect Hester as her assailant began to strike at her with her fists. At the same instant Alynna caught the smell of decaying fish, a sixth sense warning her of danger. Reaching instinctively for the dagger at her belt, she spun round, placing her back against the stone arch, expecting to see the ferryman. Round-eyed, she stared in disbelief at the figure of a bearded monk aiming a dagger at her heart.

'Holy Mother, help me!' she screamed, her blood freezing as she recognised Hugh the ferryman beneath the shadow of the monk's hood. Her cry was drowned by the noise of the jeering throng surrounding Joel and Hester. Managing to parry the blow, she brought up her own blade to attack. Why did no one notice her plight? Frightened, she glanced over her shoulder. The stone pillar partly obscured her from the crowd, who were intent on watching the fat woman's attack on Hester.

'Damned bitch!' the ferryman snarled, lunging at her a second time. 'Anyone else would have died at the mill!'

His rank breath hit her full in the face, almost choking her. She dodged aside, and lashing upwards, her blade nicked the flesh of his neck. Hugh's face twisted murderously. Alynna's throat was too dry to scream a second time as she concentrated all her energy on staying alive. Surely someone must realise what was happening! But the crowd had moved further away, presumably as Hester tried to escape their abuse.

'Hell-brat!' Hugh growled as his free hand touching his wounded neck came away covered in blood. 'There's no one to save you. My woman has seen that the crowd are distracted by the fate of your Lollard friend.'

Alynna ducked his upward jab, gasping, 'Who sent you? Was it my stepmother?'

His lips curled back evilly, revealing his broken black teeth. Ignoring her question, he slashed his knife across her body, but somehow she managed to side-step in time and her own blade jarred against his parry. He caught her wrist. Knowing she had only moments before he plunged the dagger into her, she kicked out, scraping her foot down his shin—a trick taught her by her father's captain of the guard. Hugh emitted an animal grunt and limped sideways, while at the same time she flung all her weight against him before he could fully recover. Thrown off balance, he toppled over the step between the cloister's arches.

Alynna staggered away. A quick assessing glance along the cloisters showed her that Hester was still being hounded by the crowd and had retreated to the furthest corner. Joel was at Hester's side, his face white with fury as he argued that she was innocent. After days of being hemmed in by people, Alynna found herself suddenly isolated. It was like riding the night mare. The crowd had pushed past her, unaware of her desperate fight for her life. Jeering and hostile, they were concerned only with what was happening to Joel and Hester. Hugh had planned it well! He had meant to strike swiftly and kill her, while his woman roused the crowd against Hester, then to disappear into the throng.

A bellow from Hugh as he swayed to his feet filled

Alynna with alarm. Arms outstretched, he lurched over the cloister step. Panic gripped her. Where was Sir Richard? In vain she scanned the shadowed arches as she backed away from the ferryman. Hester needed her, but with her own life in danger, how could she stop to help her friend?

Behind her, Joel's persuasive tongue seemed to be calming the incensed crowd. Then her thoughts of Hester scattered as Hugh came at her again. Lifting her cumbersome skirts above her ankles, she fled back along the cloisters in the direction in which she guessed Sir Geoffrey had taken cover from the rain. In Richard's absence, he was her only hope.

Above the violent hammering of her heart, she heard Hugh's lumbering step close behind. The corner of the cloisters was menacingly dark, but voices carried to her from its shadows. Too frightened to slow her pace, she rounded the corner at a run.

'For the love of God, help!' Her gasping plea floundered on a groan of agony, pain shooting through her foot as she tripped over an uneven flagstone. Plunging forward, she put out a hand to save herself. It slammed against a man's hard body, and his arms slid round her waist to prevent her fall.

'Such ardour, sweet Alynna,' Richard chuckled against her ear. 'I had no idea you were so eager for my company!'

'Thank God it is you!' she cried breathlessly. 'Hugh . . . the ferryman from Barkhurst . . . He tried to kill me.'

Realising that by now Hugh should have been upon them, Alynna glanced round fearfully. He was nowhere in sight. He must have seen Richard and run off through one of the many openings out of the cloisters. Shaken and trembling, she swayed, and laid her head on Richard's chest.

'Go and search along there,' he snapped out to someone behind. 'The man is heavy-set and bearded.'

'He was disguised as a monk, and armed with a dagger.' Alynna's voice was muffled against Richard's

doublet as she clung to him, her body quivering with
reaction at yet another near brush with death. She was
safe. But not so Hester.

'Hester is in danger too,' she gasped. 'That com-
motion across the way—she is accused of being a
Lollard.'

'Bring the lame scarred woman to me,' Richard
ground out over her head to his companions.

As he drew her aside, there was a clatter of booted
feet from several men breaking into a run in response to
his command. The authoritative tone he had used, and
the way it had unquestioningly been obeyed, disconcerted Alynna, and then her fears for Hester pushed all
else from her mind.

'I must see that Hester is safe.'

'Are you sure you are unharmed?' he asked with
concern.

'Yes. I was just frightened and shaken,' she answered
honestly. 'But Hester is in danger! Please take me to
her.'

Side by side they hurried to the far side of the cloisters.
Richard carved a way through the crowd in his own
indomitable fashion, and any who turned to snarl their
displeasure were immediately silenced by his stern
countenance and moved aside without protest. In the
centre of the circle of faces, Joel with his arm about
Hester's shoulders was leading her away. The fat woman
who had caused all the trouble had vanished.

'I must go to Hester,' Alynna said, worried.

'One moment.' It was a command, not a request. 'She
is safe with Joel. I would speak with you.'

Startled by Richard's change of mood, she felt a
flicker of unease. He was different, somehow. When she
met his piercing stare, her heart jolted. There was no
mistaking his noble lineage in the way he held his head
and the strong contours of his angular jaw. Gazing into
his lean, beard-shadowed face, yearning tugged at the
core of her being. She could feel a void opening between
them. All sign of the humble knight had left his proud
countenance, and something of her trepidation must

have shown in her face. He smiled warmly, his eyes glowing with an iridescent light.

'You are safe now, Alynna,' he assured her, misinterpreting her anguish. 'Now that my pilgrimage is over, I can openly give you my protection. No one will dare to harm you.'

Instead of comforting her, his words filled her with alarm. He spoke so naturally of the power he wielded, and the chasm widened. Irrationally, she felt betrayed and stepped further away from him. His nearess was too disturbing, destroying her ability to reason clearly.

'Sweetest Alynna.' His hand tight over her arm preventing her from putting further distance between them. 'The ferryman will be caught. There is nothing to fear.'

'Is there not, my lord?' she contended, trying to break free. 'Please let me go.'

Two passing monks looked across at them as her voice rose. It was obvious that Richard Dreux had no intention of releasing her, and unwilling to provoke a scene, she fell silent.

'Do you fear someone will see us?' he chided, as he manoeuvred her into a secluded alcove. 'I shall let no one harm you.'

When his hand moved up her back to slide into the thickness of her hair, she moved restlessly, dangerously close to losing her self-control. The touch of his fingers, cool and persuasive on her neck as he gently eased her head back, caused a ripple of pleasure to race through her.

'Look at me, Alynna,' he demanded. 'Trust me. I shall speak to the king.'

The confidence of his tone confirmed her growing dread. Just who was he?

'A tender scene!' Sir Geoffrey mocked from behind them. 'Do I intrude, my lord?'

Richard Dreux stiffened, and removed his hand from her neck. 'I shall talk with you later, Griswolde.'

Alynna drew back, troubled by his dismissive tone. Sir Geoffrey was a nobleman of some standing, yet Richard had addressed him as an underling.

'Why, it is the wench from the inn . . . the pilgrim!' Sir Geoffrey observed slyly. 'I knew there was something special about her. Who is she?'

'Not now, Griswolde,' Richard snapped. 'I said— later!'

Sir Geoffrey backed away, his pouting lips showing his resentment at the manner of his dismissal. Bowing to Richard, he continued perversely, 'Special, is she, coz? She must be. Why else should the noble Earl of Trevowan so trouble himself?'

Alynna felt faint with shock. It was much worse than she had imagined! As an earl, Richard was far, far out of reach of such as herself. And that if that were not barrier enough, his estates were some of the largest in England. No wonder he had said with such assurance that he would speak to the king. He was his Majesty's friend and counsellor. She conquered a wave of dizziness. How could she have been so blind? The way he had fought —his self-assurance—was something he had been born to, not acquired. She, fool that she was, had lost her heart to one of England's most powerful nobles—the acclaimed flower of chivalry and hero of Agincourt.

She stared up at him as Sir Geoffrey left. He answered her look for look, his full lips compressed, his grey eyes sharpening to flint hardness as he defied her to pass judgement upon him. Belatedly aware of the homage due to him, she somehow managed a stiff curtsy.

Exasperated, Trevowan muttered an oath beneath his breath and raised her up. Good God! The last thing he wanted was her to fawn at his feet.

'I am honoured that you have given me so much of your time, my lord,' Alynna said frostily.

'Nothing has changed between us.' His anger flared at her stubbornness. Anyone else in England would be grateful for his intervention, whereas this woman had the temerity to resent it!

'You mock my ignorance.' Fury blazed from her sapphire eyes. 'I guessed that you were no humble knight, but this . . .' She turned away, her voice splintered with pain. 'Why did you let me go on believing in you? I trusted you.'

'You saw what you wanted to, Alynna.' Just what had she expected from him? He supposed he should be glad that she had not used her wiles to win his favour. Instead, the knowledge touched a raw nerve. Again she had found a chink in his armour. 'I have said I will help you. I mean it.'

'And for your interest, Lord Trevowan, what payment will you require? I have nothing.'

Seeing the suspicion in her eyes, he decided to teach her a lesson. No one dared to question his actions as she did. He touched a dark curl laying upon her breast. 'You have a great deal to offer, my dear.'

At the slight pressure of his fingers through the fine wool of her gown, Alynna paled, and encountering the dangerous glitter in his eyes, she drew back.

Trevowan was swifter. Pulling her against him, he lowered his head, devouring her lips in a hard punishing kiss. Her lips burned beneath the roughness of his beard as she struggled to twist her head away, knowing that her defences against him were too insubstantial to deny him for long. His embrace was relentless. Already her blood was on fire, her limbs turning to molten supplication. Still she resisted, but instead of freeing herself, her movements, disastrously, moulded their bodies closer together. A shudder passed through his powerful frame, the touch of his beard sensuously stroked her chin and his lips gentled, moving expertly over hers in an exquisite, all-consuming caress.

She swayed dizzily, her hands pushing against his chest as she tried to resist the treacherous surge of desire his kisses roused in her. She should hate him for this! Was he so used to taking what he wanted with impunity that he cared nothing for propriety, or the wishes of others? Why, then, did her soul cry out for him to make her his completely? She closed her eyes, the insistence of his mouth sending her senses spiralling until she clung to him, dazed and breathless.

'No!' She finally summoned the will-power to free her mouth and force out, unsteadily, 'You would bring shame to me, my lord.'

He raised a brow, his eyes changing to the colour of woodsmoke before his lashes hid their expression from her. 'Many would not see it so. The arrangement could prove most satisfactory—and to your advantage.'

Disillusioned, Alynna stared mistily at him. How could she have so misjudged him? Drawing an uneven breath, she poured out her scorn. 'I will die a pauper before I dishonour my father's name!'

He folded his arms across his chest, his expression forbidding. 'You offer me a glimpse of paradise, then think to retreat behind maidenly virtue.' A wicked gleam sprang into his eyes. 'Or is it a ploy to win me to your cause? The enticement of Eve is as old as time . . . You would not be the first to use it.'

'I use no lure,' she said coldly. 'I shall always defend my honour. I will be no man's whore. And for all your noble titles, the Earl of Trevowan is but a man.'

His crack of laughter bewildered her. There was no anger in his appraising stare. Had he somehow been testing her? Her pride smarted that he had thought it necessary. 'I bid you good day, Lord Trevowan. Unlike you, I do not find the situation amusing.' Summoning what little dignity he had left her, she spun on her heel to leave him.

'I have not dismissed you!'

The imperious tone raised her hackles. Turning slowly, her eyes burned with suppressed anger as she regarded the equally incensed earl. For a long moment they glared at each other, then, unexpectedly, with the change of mood Alynna found so disconcerting, he smiled.

'I did not arrange this meeting for us to quarrel. Or to seduce you. You are a beautiful and very desirable woman, and provocative enough to tempt a saint.'

She blushed, torn between indignation and a secret thrill at his admission. 'From your conduct, Lord Trevowan, you are more devil than saint.'

He looked taken aback. Then a shield dropped over his eyes, his expression again grim and uncompromising.

This time, she wondered, swallowing painfully, had she goaded him too far?

'That is the spirited answer I have come to expect from you. Your honesty is barbed, Alynna. But it is honesty for all that! You are impetuous, often speaking when silence would serve you better. Do you not fear the consequences?'

'I act as my conscience demands.'

'Yes, you are a woman of rare qualities and high principles,' he said sombrely. 'It shows in the way you rescued the child and protect Hester. By befriending her, you have given her confidence and self-respect. She was withdrawn and nervous before you joined the pilgrims.' He paused, and she sensed that what he was about to say did not come easily. 'There is someone, very dear to me, who needs the guidance of a friend. Will you become that companion?'

Stunned by his words, she took a moment to recover her senses. 'My lord, I—I do not know what to say. I am indebted to you. I would help in any way I can.'

'I would not have you do this out of indebtedness,' he said gruffly, as though he had expected her to accept without reservation. 'It must be done because you want to. You will have to travel to Thornbank Manor in Cornwall, and for a time it will mean living in comparative seclusion.'

Alynna searched his expression, trying to gauge the true depth of his feelings. It was in his power to order her to obey, but he had given her free choice. Was that not a mark of the respect in which he held her?

'To whom am I to be companion.'

A wariness came into his eyes, and a catch was obvious in his voice. 'Lady Meraud—my sister.'

'What need has Lady Meraud of me, my lord?' she asked, astonished. The nagging pain of uncertainty gnawed deeper. Was this a ruse by Lord Trevowan to get her to Cornwall to serve his pleasure?

She subjected him to a searching stare, and his eyes challenged her to defy him. If it was not that, then what reason lay behind his strange request?

His brows drew down impatiently at her hesitation. 'I can see that my suggestion is unacceptable.' He turned to go.

'Wait, Richard!'

In her consternation, she forgot the respect due to his rank. 'M-my lord, f-forgive me,' she stammered, appalled that she had allowed her uncertainty to anger him. 'I am honoured that you think me worthy of such a position. But you know my story—my birth makes me an unfit companion for a noblewoman.'

'Would I have asked you, if I thought that?' he said tautly. 'And how can a king's ward be the lowly bastard you say you are? Enough of such objections! Meraud needs you. When you see her, you will understand.'

'My lord, I cannot abandon Joel and Hester.' Her heart jumped. Was it truly so? Dared she hope that her birth was not as humble as Lady Joan had scornfully told her?

'Naturally they will accompany you.' A taunting sparkle lit his eyes. 'Besides, you will need a chaperon, if we are to travel together. You are the king's ward—your reputation must be guarded.'

So his intentions were not dishonourable! Why, then, all the mystery about Lady Meraud? 'How can I accept your offer, my lord, when you have not told me all there is to know?'

She held his glare levelly, uncertain whether her obstinacy would anger him. The troubled light returned to his eyes, but he gave no sign that he was annoyed.

'I should have known that those sharp wits of yours would sense something amiss. Meraud has become a recluse.' The words were dragged from him. 'She is sick with melancholy. Unless someone can help her soon, I fear she will lose her sanity.'

Taking Alynna's shoulders, he turned her to face him. Tense lines furrowed his brow, setting her heart yearning to bring him peace. Yesterday she would have done so with spontaneous compassion. Now, knowing his true identity, she felt as awkward as with a stranger. Instead she stood very still, conscious of his need to talk.

CHAPTER SEVEN

'I HAVE spoken to no one of this,' Trevowan went on gruffly, leading Alynna to a stone bench in a quiet corner and drawing her down to sit beside him. 'On my return from France, I remained at Court throughout the pageantry and feasting, intending to travel to Trevowan Castle at the end of the month.'

Alynna nodded; her father had told her that although the king's counsellor, the Earl of Trevowan, had been outspoken on the carnage of Agincourt and there had been talk of a rift between them, the king had honoured his favourite by riding side by side with him through the City, and a troubadour had composed a song commemorating Trevowan's deeds in the joust and leadership in battle.

'My mother and sister journeyed there from Thornbank to prepare for my arrival,' he continued. 'On their way through Cornwall, their baggage train was attacked by outlaws.'

The bitterness in his voice ridiculed the acclaim he had won at Agincourt. His fingers pressed Alynna's as he spoke, and she felt the torment raging inside him. She did not move, despite her discomfort, realising that by lowering his guard and confiding in her he was according her a singular compliment. His eyes darkened stormily, the bronzed skin stretched tautly over his high cheekbones. Suddenly she had an anguished feeling she knew what he was about to say.

'My mother was killed that day. And Meraud—Meraud was brutally raped.'

Horror went through her, and instinctively she covered his hand with hers, saying softly, 'To say I am sorry sounds so inadequate. I can understand how you feel, but you blame yourself unjustly, my lord.'

'Unjustly!' he ground out savagely. 'Had I not been

with the king, it would not have happened. I should have been with them when they needed me.'

'Your first duty was to his Majesty,' Alynna suggested, although inwardly she realised how little it would lessen his guilt and pain. 'Your mother, more than anyone, would understand that. Like any woman she would be proud of the son, who had not only won the king's friendship, but was loved by the people and honoured for his prowess in battle. How could you have known what would happen?'

His eyes flashed contemptuously and he pulled his hand from hers. 'I would willingly have renounced my rank and glory to have saved them.'

At hearing the pain in his voice, Alynna's heart ached to find the right words to bring him comfort. 'That is what makes you worthy of your position, my lord.'

'Hollow words!' he flung back, again distrustful, his face a stony mask. 'I have had my fill of them at Court.'

His scathing tone flicked at her pride, even though she understood the hurt behind his harsh words. 'I have no need to feed the vanity of the great Earl of Trevowan,' she retaliated. 'I spoke truthfully—as one pilgrim to another. If I was misled as to your true rank, my lord, it was because of the consideration you showed towards the common people.'

The fierce light died in his eyes, and for some moments he stared above her head, fighting some kind of inner battle. 'The truth is often painful. This pilgrimage has taught me much. I have many faults, Alynna.' The ridicule was back in his voice. 'Do not endow me with virtues I do not possess.'

Was that a warning? She studied his face. There were no visible sign of dissipation; even the sensual fullness of his mouth was thinned by remorse. All his life he had been indulged. She recollected he had inherited his earldom on his father's death when he was twelve, but for some years before that he had been the Prince of Wales' companion, and as such, his education and training to bear arms had been as unremitting as that of the warrior kings. Now for the first time something outside his control had struck at his own, and he had been powerless to act. That was what gnawed at him. It was not sympathy he needed, but sound reasoning.

'There was an old wise-woman in the kitchens at my father's castle. She used to say that the pattern of our destiny is shaped before our birth.' Alynna saw his eyes brighten with interest. 'However much we try to mould it to our will, the inevitable will always await us. Perhaps it was so: there are many cruel lessons we must each learn in life, my lord. It is not always easy to accept God's will.'

'As you have discovered for yourself. You have a wisdom that is peculiarly your own.' He reclaimed her hand, his lips curving upwards. 'I have had more than my fill of sycophants to console me. Because you do not fear to speak out, I ask you to be Meraud's companion. She was once like you: indefatigable, bubbling with energy and gaiety. Now she hides away, speaking to no one —not even to me.'

Looking down at their hands he raised hers to his lips. 'You are wise as well as temptingly beautiful, Alynna. If anyone can help Meraud, it is you. For that reason I shall sacrifice my own needs and desires.' His smouldering gaze set her pulses tumbling. 'And it is sacrifice indeed, my sweet Alynna. I offer you my protection. On my return to Court, I shall speak with the king on your behalf.'

He dropped her hand and the tenderness of moments earlier was replaced by the guarded look she had come to dread, his tone again formal. 'That will not be for some weeks. In the meantime, it would be as well to solve the mystery of your birth. The matter must be dealt with by stealth and diplomacy. For that purpose, if you are agreeable, I would send Joel to find out what he can. His wits are sharp, and in his guise as a jester he can travel freely from castle to manor. Most important—we can count on his discretion.'

'You have thought of everything, my lord.'

'Then it is agreed that you will become my sister's companion, Lady Alynna?'

'It is agreed, Lord Trevowan.'

'I had planned to stay for another day at prayer, but it is best we leave tomorrow. My men are already lodged in the town.' He looked her up and down assessingly. 'You will need garments. Some will be sent to you, for you must be dressed as befits my honoured guest.'

With a sinking heart she realised he was telling her that if she accepted his protection, she would be treated as his sister's companion and thereby safe from his attentions. Sound reason told her that after the wanton way she had reacted to his kiss, she should be grateful that the incident would not be repeated. Why then did her heart twist with disappointment?

The sound of running footsteps deflected their thoughts. A soldier wearing a black tunic with the gold lion device of Lord Trevowan bowed stiffly to the earl, and pronounced breathlessly, 'The man disguised as a monk has been captured, my lord.'

'Keep him under guard. I shall question him later.' Dismissing the man-at-arms, he stood up and bowed to her. 'I have much to attend to. Until tomorrow, Lady Alynna.'

Suddenly bereft, she felt like a wind-torn leaf wrenched from its branch by the autumn gales. Buffeted and storm-tossed, where would she settle, she wondered. At Higham Mote she knew every servant and villager by name. Over the years she had visited the sick, consoled the bereaved and listened to their problems, for they were like a family to her. It was humiliating to be dependent on strangers. The easy companionship shared with Richard, the pilgrim, during the past days was over—Richard Dreux, the Earl of Trevowan, was a stranger to her.

Her pride rebelled at allowing another to take control of her life, yet in her heart she knew Lord Trevowan was right. Not only did she need a champion, but she was responsible for Joel and Hester. False pride must not prevent them from having the security offered by the earl. And was she not indebted to Trevowan for saving her life? She must honour that obligation, no matter what the cost.

Back in her room, Alynna was relieved to discover that Hester, although looking pale, was apparently recovered from her experience in the cloisters. She had expected to find her shaken and crying, but she was exclaiming with delight as she laid on the bed the contents of a large oak coffer.

'What are you doing?' Alynna enquired. 'You should be resting after what you have been through. Are you sure you are all right?'

Hester nodded. 'I am now—praise be to Joel and Lord Trevowan's men for arriving in time! It has happened to me before, and always it brings back the horrors of the torture chamber and how I was dragged through the streets to be burnt.' She shuddered, but there was a new confidence about her Alynna had not seen before, and her eyes glowed with fervour. 'From now on it will be different. Under Lord Trevowan's protection, we shall both be safe.'

'How did you know Lord Trevowan had given me his protection? I have only just accepted his offer.' Alynna glanced suspiciously at the surcoats and kirtles spread across the bed. 'Where have all these come from?'

'Lord Trevowan had them delivered a short time ago,' Hester babbled in her excitement. 'He is the king's favourite, and he will make sure your inheritance is returned to you. Your future will be safe and secure, never fear.'

'I do not doubt he will achieve all that for me.' She averted her face so that Hester would not see the tears pricking her eyes.

'So . . . that is the way of it!' Hester responded sadly. 'He has stolen your heart. I am sorry, my lady. He can never be for you—not in marriage, anyway.'

Alynna attempted a brave smile. 'Lord Trevowan wants me to become companion to his sister.'

'From the way he looks at you, he has more than that in mind. You take care, my lady,' Hester warned as she picked up a blue silk kirtle from the bed. 'Come and try on these beautiful clothes. His lordship left instructions that if you needed anything else, you had but to ask.'

Lord Trevowan had known that she would agree to his proposal, and it rankled that he had taken her acceptance for granted. However, realising she was being unrealistic, Alynna acknowledged that he had acted with foresight and expedition, for time was short. He left for Cornwall on the morrow. Besides, as she fingered the rich brocade of a ruby red gown, she was flattered he had been so thoughtful of her needs.

'Where could Lord Trevowan have purchased all these?' she said, draping a fur-lined cloak about her shoulders.

'I dare say he arranged for an army of seamstresses to sew all night. That would be his way,' Hester answered with a grin. 'And look!' She held up a velvet-covered box containing needles and thread. 'I shall set to work at once altering the gowns to fit you, my lady.'

Alynna was about to protest at Hester's servility, but seeing the determined light in her friend's eyes, she realised that Hester accepted that their roles had changed. She, too, had her pride. She was content to be Alynna's maid—a position that gave her a dignified place in society without becoming a burden upon her friend.

Alynna sat on a stool, her eyes closed as Hester brushed the tangles from her knee-length hair. The brush paused in midstroke, and she stiffened as Hester peered closer at the side of her head.

'Do you fear to serve a woman who carries the devil's mark?' she asked as she pulled a lock of hair over her ear, hiding the tiny hole at the top of its lobe.

With an impatient tut, Hester continued with her brushing, making the dark tresses crackle. 'Devil's mark indeed! 'Tis no more than a birthmark. I dare say others of your family have the same.'

Alynna was about to say that it was not so, when a knock on the door prevented her. At her command, a page entered wearing the earl's black and gold livery. Behind him came two burly servants carrying a huge wooden wine-vat which had been cut in half. They put it down in the centre of the room, whereupon a dozen women armed with pitchers of steaming water hurried forward to fill the tub.

'Lord Trevowan regrets that the facilities are primitive,' the page announced. 'His lordship thought you would wish to refresh yourself after your long journey.'

Alynna looked at the tub with pleasure. Richard really had thought of everything! 'Tell his lordship I appreciate his kindness,' she called out after the departing page, who was being shooed from the room by Hester.

It took several journeys by the maid-servants to fill the tub, but at last Alynna was able to immerse herself in the hot water. Sighing with contentment, she leaned back against the rim. The tiredness drained from her limbs, and as she lay in the water, her thoughts returned to Lord Trevowan. That he could order the luxury of this bath, and also with obvious ease produce a magnificent wardrobe for her, made her ever more aware of the differences between them.

A sleepless night filled with apprehension left her tense and edgy the next morning when Joel came to escort her to the earl.

'My lady,' Joel beamed, his gaze sweeping appreciatively over her silver-edged blue velvet gown. Placing his hand over his heart, he bowed with courtly extravagance. 'Your beauty will win many a heart this day. Just wait until you see the size of his lordship's escort!'

The jester's praise banished the nervous fluttering in her stomach. 'Has his lordship spoken of his plans?'

'I leave immediately, my lady, to visit the monastery endowed by Sir Robert. Do you remember Father Dominic? He was Sir Robert's chaplain in the early days of his marriage, and is prior there now. He may know something of your birth.'

'I had not expected you to leave so soon,' Alynna said in dismay. 'I shall miss you, my friend.'

Joel shuffled with embarrassment. 'I am just an ageing fool, my lady. You will not be lacking company in Cornwall.'

'Do not belittle your worth.' Overcome with emotion, Alynna kissed both his cheeks. 'God go with you, dear Joel.'

Outside in the courtyard, Lord Trevowan checked an angry rejoinder as he glared at his cousin. Griswolde showed no remorse at the inhumanity of his action.

'The ferryman died because of your interference.' Trevowan forced himself to speak levelly. 'You had no right to question him.'

'I told you I thought I knew that girl he tried to kill.' Griswolde's eyes flashed maliciously. 'You show undue interest in the pilgrim wench, coz.'

'That is my concern, not yours!' Trevowan warned, wondering what his cousin was hiding. He was used to Griswolde's devious ways—what was his cousin planning? But now he was more concerned with what had happened the night before. 'We are talking of my prisoner. I take your action amiss.'

Griswolde's eyes darkened with fury. 'The man deserved to be flogged!'

'But not to death. It is not the first time you have allowed your temper to rule your head.'

'The ferryman would have hanged anyway. He was the leader of those mercenaries—or so he claimed.'

Trevowan looked meaningfully at his cousin's hand poised on his sword. 'Take care, Griswolde,' he said with lethal coldness. 'Draw that blade against me, and you know the consequences . . . I have warned you before—curb your devil's temper, or you will live to rue it.'

The sword snapped back into its scabbard. 'One day, coz,' Griswolde snarled, his face flushing with mounting rage, 'you will push me too far. You are not my guardian.'

'I am head of our house. You will obey me, or make your own way in the world.'

Griswolde opened his mouth to retort, then the light in his eyes changed as he caught sight of someone approaching. Alynna entered the courtyard, where

Lord Trevowan's entourage was already assembled.

She looked for the earl's tall figure, and saw him standing with his back to her talking to Sir Geoffrey. The knight in scarlet cloak and yellow doublet and hose, looked garish against the earl's sombre black. Sir Geoffrey raised an eyebrow in open admiration and bowed low. Richard turned to face her, and she felt her heart stop, then leap into a wild, erratic rhythm. He was clean-shaven, looking less stern and younger than the eight and twenty years she knew him to be. For the first time, the lean high cheekbones and strong determined jaw were revealed to her. How could she ever have believed he was other than a man used to command even the mightiest?

Dismissing Sir Geoffrey, Lord Trevowan came towards her, his eyes sparkling with pleasure and admiration as his gaze travelled the length of her figure, while she noted every detail of his elegant appearance. A large ruby adorned his flat turban hat, which was tipped at a rakish angle, one end of the flowing velvet draped casually across his shoulders. Beneath his long cloak he wore a gold-bordered black doublet sewn with emeralds and pearls. A jewelled sword-belt emphasised the slimness of his hips, and his tight black hose displayed the muscular curve of his thighs and calves. Alynna's throat tightened with yearning. In her eyes he was the most handsome knight in all Christendom. He was all, and so much more than, she had dreamed a lover to be.

With an impatient gesture he stripped off his jewelled gauntlets, and taking her hand, kissed it in greeting. 'Can this regal beauty be my little pilgrim? I trust my sister appreciates the sacrifice I have made on her behalf! It is not her companion I would have you become, sweet Alynna, but my own.'

Shocked by his bluntness, and aware that Sir Geoffrey was watching their every move in the same perplexed manner he had observed them at the inn, Alynna drew back. Lord Trevowan laughed softly, misunderstanding her fears.

'Do not fear, Lady Alynna.' He did not relinquish her

hand. 'Our bargain is made. I shall not go back on my word.'

Waving aside a page who had brought a wooden mounting-block for her to stand on, he gripped her waist and lifted her into the saddle of a white palfrey, adding for her ears alone, 'No woman has tempted me as you do, Alynna. My sister will not always have need of you. Then you would do well to remember that I am but a man.

The ardour in his voice set her whole body aglow, but innuendo aside, his words were a chilling reminder of the plight which had placed her under his protection.

'My lord,' she spoke quietly, unwilling anyone should overhear, 'what did you learn from the ferryman? Why did he try to kill me?'

Trevowan swung into the saddle of his huge black destrier, and wheeled it round to stand at her palfrey's side before answering, the low pitch of his voice edged with steel. 'Griswolde, in his zeal to please me, had the ferryman questioned while I was closeted with my officers yesterday. The man died before I could talk to him. According to Griswolde he was no ferryman, but the leader of a mercenary band. He swore he had acted out of vengeance against Sir Robert, who had dismissed his troop without payment.'

'He lied! My father never used mercenaries.'

The flint hardness in Trevowan's eyes softened at her anguish. He seemed about to speak, then his lips compressed before he added coolly, 'We shall discover the truth, I promise.'

With a curt nod in salute to Alynna, he rode to the head of his mounted men-at-arms. An iron band tightened about her heart. After the closeness they had shared during the pilgrimage, she must learn to adjust to her new role. The days of friendship must be forgotten; she was now his dependant.

She waved farewell to Joel, who was helping Hester to mount behind one of the many liveried servants, and gathering up her reins, prepared to ride forward. Her passage was blocked by Sir Geoffrey, and when she tried to guide her mare round him, he grabbed the palfrey's tasselled bridle.

'So our mysterious pilgrim is to travel to Cornwall under his lordship's protection!'

Alynna tensed. Because of the carelessness of this man, she would never know if anyone had sent the mercenary after her. That information would have been vital, for despite so much evidence to the contrary, she did not want to believe it was Lady Joan.

'From your censure, Lady Alynna, I presume my cousin has told you that your attacker died before he could talk.' Sir Geoffrey's light blue eyes clouded. 'I wished but to serve you. And I failed lamentably,' he added regretfully.

'You did your duty as you saw fit, Sir Geoffrey,' she conceded. He was Lord Trevowan's cousin, and she would not treat him discourteously.

Sweeping his long peaked hat from his head, he bowed to her, taking care that the pheasant feathers adorning its rim did not trail in the puddles of the courtyard. 'That miserable wretch deserved to die for trying to harm you! Your beauty will be the shining light that draws me to his lordship's remote lands.'

Unused to such blatant flirtation, Alynna blushed. Her anger at Sir Geoffrey's interference began to dispel. He seemed so eager to please, and despite her disapproval of his forwardness, she felt a smile tugging at her mouth. In contrast to Trevowan's sardonic looks, Sir Geoffrey reminded her of the golden-haired painting of the angel Gabriel on the chapel wall at Highham Mote.

'I would not have you ride so far on my account, sir. You must have weightier matters which keep you at Court.'

'Weightier indeed, but far less intriguing. There is not a woman there to hold a candle to your beauty, fair Alynna. Do you now own that we have met before?'

Alynna's smile faded. 'We met at the inn. Nowhere else.' She tried to jerk her mare's head free of his hold, her voice icy when he maintained his grip. 'I shall listen to no more of your nonsense. Release my palfrey's bridle!'

'You are cruel, Lady Alynna.' He smiled slyly as he released the reins. 'Until we meet again in Cornwall, then. I never could resist a beautiful woman—or a mystery.'

She forgot the disturbing few moments with Sir Geoffrey as the troop of Trevowan's riders clattered through the narrow streets of Canterbury, accompanied by the fanfare of the outriders' horns clearing the way. It was a new and exciting experience for Alynna to be a part of such a magnificent cavalcade, for her father's entourage had been small by comparison. People scattered from the path of the riders, but as Trevowan's black standard with its golden lion rampant was recognised, a great cheering went up, proclaiming the earl's popularity. A lump of pride formed in her throat, then, fast upon the wake of her excitement, came the bitterness of despair. She stared forlornly at the long line of retainers and baggage-carts. The display of wealth and splendour humbled her. Richard was master of all this; hundreds of vassals acknowledged him as their liege lord. And how insignificant was her own lowly station.

She stifled a sigh. Loving him as she did, she wondered whether she could live so close to him and still keep secret what lay in her heart. From this moment she must forget the tender exchanges that had passed between them. They had been borne out of a bond forged between two humble pilgrims. Pomp and ceremony had replaced the simplicity of those days, and those two people no longer existed.

There was also Lady Meraud to consider. Lord Trevowan trusted her to help his sister, and she was determined not to fail him. From the affection in his voice, it was obvious that they had once been close, but if Lady Meraud refused to speak to the brother she loved, how would she react to a stranger?

In the bleak tower room at Thornbank Manor, Alynna stepped closer to the carved stone fireplace. The heat from the burning logs was barely adequate, and she shivered and pulled her fur-lined mantle closer about her. Every other room she had seen was warm and luxurious, the walls hung with rich tapestries or painted silk hangings. Here in the tower, Lady Meraud had ordered every sign of luxury to be removed, and the chamber was as cheerless as a hermit's cell. For the dozenth time in as many minutes Alynna glanced anxiously at the black-clad figure engrossed in her spinning. The ceaseless drone of the wheel and creak of the treadle were the only response she received to her remarks or questions.

During the four days she had attended upon Lady Meraud, her companion had not spoken a single word. Hour after hour Meraud continued with her spinning, and when the wheel did fall silent, she sat motionless on her stool staring at the bare whitewashed walls, existing in a closed world of her own, allowing nothing and no one to reach her.

Frustrated by her failure to communicate, Alynna picked up a lute, seeking to lighten the dreary atmosphere by playing a tune. As her nimble fingers plucked out the notes, she studied Meraud, refusing to give in to her own despair at having failed to penetrate the young woman's consciousness. There could be no more than a year's difference in their ages, herself at seventeen being the elder. From the first she had felt warmly towards her, but the problem was how to break down the barriers Meraud had erected against others.

The elfin face was as white as the gauze veil she wore and almost as transparent, the pale blue veins visible beneath the skin. On a silver platter at her side, the spiced duckling in its succulent sauce was left untouched, and she had eaten only a mouthful of the crisp white bread. But what troubled Alynna most was the dullness of her coal-black eyes. There must be some way to penetrate her stupor. She refused to acknowledge defeat, for Lord Trevowan had not brought her all this way for nothing.

During the ten-day journey from Canterbury, every

moment of that time she had been on her guard lest she unwittingly betray her love for Richard. At times, it seemed that the bond between they was as strong as ever: he sought her company for no apparent reason, and acted as though nothing had changed. But his moods were unpredictable. Often when the affinity had seemed at its strongest, he would leave her abruptly, his manner becoming remote and restrained. Then she had striven to harden her heart against him, for how else would she expect a great noble to treat the illegitimate daughter of a lowly knight?

At the sound of the door opening, she was jerked from her bitter reverie. Lord Trevowan entered. When Meraud did not even turn at his greeting, Alynna despaired, knowing how his sister's lack of response would pain him. He squared his proud shoulders, his expression grave as he came towards herself. She put down the lute and spread her skirts to curtsy, but impatiently he took her elbow, preventing her from paying homage to him.

His voice was taut. 'Has there been no change?'

'No, my lord. I fear I have disappointed you.'

He shook his head, his fingers tightening about her arm. 'It will take patience and understanding. I know you will not fail me—given time.'

'But Meraud does not even notice that I am there,' Alynna persisted worriedly. 'Why did you bring me to Thornbank? I am a stranger to her. I talk, but she never answers.'

'Her maid tells me she is sleeping more peacefully at night, and she is certainly more calm during the day since your arrival,' Trevowan observed quietly. 'At least she now tolerates my presence in her chamber. Before my pilgrimage, she used to flee sobbing at any sight of me. Perhaps your words are getting through to her more than you realise.'

A muscle pulsed along his jaw, revealing the tight rein he was keeping upon his emotions. Meraud's silence was eating away at him. Several times since their arrival he had visited his sister, and it plucked at Alynna's heart to see the way she ignored his presence, yet not once had he lost his temper, although each time the planes of his angular cheeks became more hollow and his eyes more haunted.

'Does he hate me for failing her?' he murmured, less to Alynna than to himself.

Alynna ached to take him in her arms and bring him solace, but that was a gesture forever denied her. Instead, she reasoned softly, 'You are too harsh in your judgment, my lord. I believe Lady Meraud feels tarnished by her experience. She probably feels unworthy of your affection.'

'That is absurd!' Richard looked at her incredulously.

'Is it, my lord? I think that is why your sister has withdrawn into herself.'

'Have I not shown her every consideration?' The pain was evident in his voice. 'Surely she must know I place no blame on her.'

Alynna regarded his frowning black brows for several moments, hesitating to speak her mind lest her words wound him more deeply. 'Could it not be, my lord, that your very kindness makes it harder for Meraud? If you were angry with her, or even punished her, it would be like a penance and she would feel herself cleansed.'

'I have no intention of beating her!' he growled. 'She is scarcely more than a child.'

'No, my lord, she is very much a woman,' Alynna persisted, dropping her voice so that Meraud could not hear.

His grey eyes flashed, his low tone condemning. 'I had not thought you so insensitive.' He turned to address Meraud. 'Come, sister dear, it is time you forgot the past. In ten days it will be Christmas, and there is much to be done. You are mistress here, and the servants need your supervision.' As he spoke, he placed his arm about her shoulders.

Meraud flinched, her eyes large as trencher plates, staring at him with horror. 'Do not touch me!'

All colour drained from his face, the pinched whiteness of his nostrils warning Alynna of the control he was exercising upon his temper. She hurried to his side.

'Meraud does not know what she is saying, my lord,' she said, drawing him away from his sister. Out of the corner of her eye she saw Meraud relax. 'She is overwrought. Cooping herself up in this room does not help. Once the weather brightens, we must encourage her to ride again.'

'You are right, of course.' His anger gone, he looked at her quizzically, holding her gaze for a long heart-stopping moment. For an instant he seemed about to make a taunting rejoinder, but then his long black lashes veiled his eyes and the moment passed. 'Try and get Meraud to speak of the attack,' he said gruffly. 'It is an evil which must be exorcised.'

'Is that not dangerous, my lord? Who knows how she will react.'

'I trust you. You will know how to deal with her, Alynna. Meraud cannot go on as she is. Her betrothed, Sir John Holcombe, arrives in two days. The wedding was to take place on her birthday in January, and it must go ahead as planned.'

'Does Sir John know what happened?'

'It is not something that could be kept from him,' Trevowan declared. 'Meraud could have won for herself a duke. Instead, she fell in love with Sir John. For weeks he has ridden with my men to hunt down her attackers, but they have vanished without trace. Sir John loves Meraud, and still wants to marry her.'

'Lady Meraud is doubly blessed to have two men who care for her deeply! Once she realises no one blames her for what happened, I believe she will pick up the pieces of her life. There was a girl—the daughter of my father's reeve—who was beaten and raped by a drunken soldier of the sheriff. For a time she hid herself away, terrified of all men. Our miller, a gentle, understanding man, asked my father for permission to court her. It took some months for him to win the girl's confidence, but now they are happily married with four children.'

Trevowan looked across at Meraud, his expression again haggard. 'I pray that will be so for Meraud also.

Until then, I leave her in your care. Get her to talk. It is our only hope of saving her sanity.'

Alynna stared at the door closing behind him, and wondered how she could succeed where he had so far failed. She did not look directly at Meraud, who had resumed her spinning, and kept her voice light. At first she spoke of everyday things, and although Meraud gave no sign that she heard her words, she persevered until the light began to fail. Lighting a candle to brighten the room, her voice crackled hoarsely as she began to talk of her arrival at Barkhust. Did she imagine it, or was there a flicker of response in Meraud's black eyes as she spoke of her own father's death and the way she had been cast out?

Meraud had stopped spinning and was staring unseeing at the wall. There was a scratching at the door, and a maid appeared, accompanied by Trevowan's physician. Alynna excused herself and left the room, tired from the long hours in the cramped confines of the tiny space. The next day in Meraud's company, she spoke once more of her life, not knowing whether her words were heard or not. When a distant rumble of thunder drowned the incessant drone of the spinning-wheel, she paused briefly, finding it difficult to speak of the attack by the ferryman in the forest, especially as Meraud had not been fortunate enough to be saved from a similar incident. She forced herself to go on, while all the time the storm rumbling overhead grew in violence. Although Meraud became restless as it reverberated through the tower, she began to glance in Alynna's direction. Was she at last beginning to get through her reserve?

At that point the room was illuminated by a blue flash of lightning, followed by a crack of thunder, which set Alynna's scalp tingling beneath her butterfly headdress. She was forced to wait for the deafening boom to fade before describing the attack. Glossing over the more horrifying details, she spared Meraud nothing of her own feelings of terror, and shame at what she had been subjected to. The spinning-wheel came to an abrupt halt.

This time, there was no mistaking the curious light in Meraud's eyes.

'Is that why my brother brought you here?' Meraud's voice was strained. 'Because he blames himself for what happened to me—and wanted to save another?'

Anger pricked Alynna at the way she made Lord Trevowan's pilgrimage and sacrifice sound so trivial. 'Yes, Lord Trevowan does blame himself,' she returned hotly. 'And your attitude does nothing to ease his guilt.'

Meraud, her darkly circled eyes huge in a ghostly white face, leapt from the window seat. For several moments she paced the chamber saying nothing, her agitation obvious from the way she wrung her hands. 'I am defiled! Unclean! How can any man look at me and not feel revulsion?'

'Not all men are so unfeeling. Lord Trevowan loves you, and is concerned for your welfare. And what of Sir John Holcombe? He still wants to marry you. You should count your blessings, Lady Meraud.'

'Like all those who surround my brother, you say what he wants you to.' A flash of lightning lit up the room, revealing her violent trembling, and her voice rose shrilly. 'We are strangers. Why should you care for me?'

'Because you are a woman.' Aware of Meraud's suspicion, Alynna checked her rising temper. 'You could not help what happened. Men use their greater strength to take what they want, without caring that they debase us. Lord Trevowan is not like that. Nor, so I believe, is your betrothed. Would you have him see you like this?'

'How can I face Sir John?' Now her silence had broken, Meraud grew more distraught, her words tumbling out in rushes and her movements jerky as she paced the room. 'Besides, he wins for himself a fortune by taking me for his bride—whether I am defiled or not!'

'You judge Sir John too harshly. I was told that yours was a love-match. Surely it is a measure of his love that he will stand by you.'

'I am not worthy of any man's love!' Meraud halted in mid-stride and swung round, eyes wild and the agony in

Discover a world of romance and intrigue in days gone by with 4 Masquerade historical romances FREE.

Every Masquerade historical romance brings the past alive with characters more real and fascinating than you'll find in any history book.

Now these wonderful love stories are combined with more real historical detail than ever before with 256 pages of splendour, excitement and romance. You'll find the heroes and heroines of these spellbinding stories are unmistakeably real men and women with desires and yearnings you will recognise. Find out why thousands of historical romance lovers rely on Masquerade to bring them the very best novels by the leading authors of historical romance.

And, as a special introduction we will send you 4 exciting Masquerade romances together with a digital quartz clock FREE when you complete and return this card.

As a regular reader of Masquerade historical romances you could enjoy a whole range of special benefits — a free monthly newsletter packed with recipes, competitions, exclusive book offers and a monthly guide to the stars, plus extra bargain offers and big cash savings.

When you return this card we will reserve a Reader Service subscription for you. Every 2 months you will receive four brand new Masquerade romances, delivered to your door postage and packing free. There is no obligation or commitment — you can cancel or suspend your subscription at any time.

It's so easy, send no money now — you don't even need a stamp. Just fill in and detach this card and send it off today.

Plus this stylish quartz clock — FREE

FREE BOOKS CERTIFICATE

Dear Susan,

Your special introductory offer of 4 free books is too good to miss. I understand they are mine to keep when the clock. Please also reserve a Reader Service subscription for me. If I decide to subscribe, I shall receive four brand new Masquerade romances every other month for just £6.00, post and packing free. If I decide not to subscribe, I shall write to you within 10 days. The free books are mine to keep in any case.

I understand that I may cancel or suspend my subscription at any time by writing to you. I am over 18 years of age.

4A8M

Signature _____

Name _____
(BLOCK CAPITALS PLEASE)

Address _____

_____

_____

Postcode _____

... please write to: Independent Book Services P.TY. Postbag X3010,

To Susan Welland
Reader Service
FREEPOST
P.O. Box 236
CROYDON
Surrey CR9 9EL

SEND NO MONEY NOW

her voice tearing at Alynna's heart. 'I have brought shame to my family. It would have been better had I died that day.'

Alynna understood exactly how this proud woman felt. Would she not have felt the same if the ferryman had succeeded in ravishing her? The memory made her shudder, spurring her to greater effort to win Lady Meraud's trust. 'You must not think that. Sir John will love and cherish you, and in his arms you will come to forget the horrors of that day.'

The wild gleam in Meraud's eyes warned Alynna that she was precariously close to losing her reason. Where kindness had failed, the harsh truth might yet succeed.

'Do not let yourself be eaten up with self-pity!' she urged above the noise of the storm, and reached out to take her hand, but Meraud backed away. Undaunted, she went on, 'Lord Trevowan told me of your courage. Where is it now? Will you let those coarse brutes crush and destroy all that was so fine in you? Yours is an old and noble family. In your veins flows the blood of Saxon warloads. Fight, Lady Meraud! Fight for what you want. If you love Sir John, you must . . .'

'No. Do not speak to me of love!' Meraud shrieked, covering her ears with her hands. 'That is what makes it so hard to bear.'

A cannonade of thunder directly overhead drowned her words, and as the lightning and thunder simultaneously raged, Meraud hugged her arms tightly to her frail figure. No longer able to hear her words, Alynna watched with growing alarm as Meraud paced wildly up and down. When she began repeatedly to wipe her hands on her gown, as though trying to cleanse them of an unseen filth, Alynna hurried to her side, placing an arm about her trembling shoulders.

'Calm yourself. You will make yourself ill!'

'Leave me alone!' Meraud broke away, and ran to the door.

Alynna sped after her, fearful that in her distraught state she would come to harm. At the door, her fear mounted. Meraud was not making for her apartments,

but was running up the tower steps towards the roof.
Two pages were crouched in the corridor, engrossed in a
game of dice, and Alynna shouted to them, 'Fetch his
lordship to the battlements at once! Lady Meraud may
be in danger. Hurry!'

Without waiting to see if they obeyed, she raced up
the steps. A gust of wind from a door opening above
caught at her veil and blew out the wall torch. Plunged
into semi-darkness, the arrow-slits allowing little of the
gloomy daylight to penetrate the tower, she was forced
to check her pace. Gasping for breath, she rounded the
last bend in the tower steps. Ahead, the narrow arched
door creaked on its hinges, blown back and forth in the
strong wind. Her alarm increased. No one in their right
mind would hazard the battlements in this weather. A
barrage of icy rain struck her face, plastering her veil to
her cheeks as she ran out on to the parapet. Where was
Meraud? Panic churned her stomach. Dear God, she
must not fail Trevowan now! Meraud was hysterical
—her life could be in danger.

Frantically Alynna peered into the gloom, scanning
the crenellated walls that ran at roof level beside several
outbuildings before adjoining the gatehouse at the far
end. Meraud was nowhere in sight. For a moment she
clung to the wall, shivering in her soaking garments, the
force of the buffeting wind making her heart beat so fast
that she had to fight for breath. Then, lowering her head
against the wind, she edged her way round the narrow
ledge outside the tower to its far side. A bolt of lightning,
like a golden whip uncoiling across the blackened sky,
illuminated the sandstone buildings, and her blood
froze. A few feet away, poised on the edge of the
parapet, was Meraud.

CHAPTER EIGHT

THE RAIN-DRENCHED, windswept figure of Meraud teetered precariously as she stared into the moat far below. Alynna stumbled forward, terrified that she was too late.

'No, Lady Meraud!' she shouted above the wind. 'For the love of God, that is not the way!'

In her haste to reach Meraud's side and stop her, Alynna slipped on a mossy patch of the narrow parapet, barely managing to recover her balance in time to avoid slipping over the edge. She realised she could have broken her neck if she had fallen.

'Go away!' Meraud wailed.

Rising shakily to her feet, and with every movement hampered by the wind as her own sodden skirts flapped about her legs, Alynna struggled on until she stood below her.

'To take your life is a sin!' she shouted. 'It is also the coward's way. How could you shame Lord Trevowan thus?'

'I have shamed him already.' The thin voice carried back to Alynna on the wind.

'No. He loves you. He was proud of your valiant spirit. You have everything to live for!'

Meraud slowly shook her head from side to side. 'It would be better if I died.'

'Would you condemn your brother to a life of torment? How could you be so selfish?' Alynna reasoned, brutally trying to pierce Meraud's lethargy and make her see reason.

Meraud stood like a statue, the wind snatching her veil from her head, so that it floated over the battlements and down into the murky moat. Horrified, Alynna watched the frail figure sway. Then Meraud's mouth opened in a soundless scream of terror, and her arms clutching at the stone crenellation saved her from being swept from the ledge. Rigid with fear, she clung to the wall.

'Help me!' The cry was muffled as Meraud pressed her face against the wet stone. 'I do not want to die!'

'You shall not die!' Alynna stretched up her arm, the icy wind setting her teeth chattering. If she did not act quickly, Meraud would be too numb to save herself and could plummet to her death. 'Stay calm,' she commanded. 'Take my hand.'

Still Meraud seemed incapable of movement. Alynna scanned the wall, but there was no room for her to climb up beside her. Why did Lord Trevowan not come? She glanced back along the parapet, hoping rescue was at hand. It remained deserted.

'Do you want Lord Trevowan to see you like this?' she asked in desperation. 'Be quick, and we can return to your room before he learns what has happened.'

Meraud turned her head, looking at her for the first time. 'I cannot move.' A flash of lightning showed the terror glittering in her eyes. 'I dare not! Help me!'

'You will not fall. Keep hold of the wall and bend towards me. I shall catch you if you lose your footing,' Alynna encouraged her. 'You *can* do it!'

Meraud hesitated, then tentatively extended her shaking hand towards Alynna, who gripped it firmly. 'Good! Now, slowly, step down,' she urged. She braced herself as Meraud slid from the top of the wall into her outstretched arms. For a long moment they clung to each other, the sound of running footsteps ignored, as they alternately sobbed and laughed with relief.

'What the devil has been going on here?' Trevowan bellowed from behind them.

Alynna kept her arm protectively about Meraud, shielding her against her brother's anger. 'We are both safe, my lord,' she said calmly, wondering how much he had seen. 'There is no danger.'

After dismissing his curious men, who went reluctantly with many backward glances, Lord Trevowan advanced. The lightning lit up his gaunt face. Silver fire sparked from his narrowed eyes, and his bloodless lips were a mere slit. He was furious, but there was also something else, far more dangerous than anger, that he was struggling to keep bridled.

'God's bones!' he swore fiercely. 'You both could have been killed. Get to your rooms.'

Meraud, her soaked gown moulded to her body, making her look like an exhausted child, freed herself from Alynna's hold and moved unsteadily towards her brother. 'Lady Alynna is not to blame. I owe her my life.'

At Meraud's defiance, some of the tension left Trevowan's face. She reached out her hand to touch him, her trembling figure near to collapse.

'Forgive me, Dickon, I am so ashamed.'

The rain plastered Trevowan's hair to his brow, his throat working convulsively as he scooped Meraud into his arms. 'Thank God you are safe,' he said gruffly. 'Both of you.'

He looked over his sister's head at Alynna, who, without waiting for his words of thanks, was walking back through the lashing rain to the tower. He swallowed against the tightness in his throat, unable to avert his gaze from the voluptuous curves and long-legged slenderness provocatively revealed by the wet clinging gown. Alynna had saved Meraud's life today, thereby proving that he had been right to bring her here.

By the time Alynna disappeared from sight, he knew it was not just Meraud's needs that had driven him to keep Alynna at his side. He wanted her as he had wanted no other woman. She captivated, provoked, tantalised and drove him to near distraction. And by his own hand he had placed her out of reach. He would not break the code of chivalry and take her as his mistress—not while she was under his protection.

Entering Meraud's room, he set her down and called for her maid. Relieved that she was safe and showing signs of recovering from her weeks of lethargy, he smiled and tenderly rubbed her cheek with his knuckles. 'Later we must talk,' he said, moving to the door. 'But now I shall send the physician to you and you must rest.'

'Dickon!' Meraud's voice broke on a sob.

He turned, again anxious for her welfare, but instead of hysteria, Meraud staggered across the room and flung her arms about him. 'I have been such a fool! I thought I wanted to die. But as I stood on the wall and stared into the moat, I knew I had to live.' The words were dragged ashamedly from her. 'Lady Alynna made me realise that I was hurting the ones I loved most by my actions.'

'Then there will be no more of this nonsense? You will marry Sir John?'

She hesitated, her head bent, her eyelids lowered. 'Yes,' she answered softly. Then slowly she looked up and tossed back her black braids of hair, her voice stronger and determined. 'Yes, I will marry Sir John. And I shall be a good wife, worthy of the love and the honour he has shown me.'

Trevowan kissed her chilled brow, at last feeling a measure of peace. His pilgrimage had not been in vain —this was more like the Meraud of old! Although it would clearly be some time before she fully recovered her strength and vitality, the change already apparent was remarkable.

'I am pleased to hear it. The marriage shall take place as arranged.'

Meraud kissed his cheek, and despite her sodden, bedraggled appearance, she smiled. 'Thank you for bringing Lady Alynna here. I am sure we shall be friends. She saved my life today, and I shall miss her when she leaves.'

He stopped in his tracks, a catch in his throat making his voice harsh. 'There is no reason for her to go.'

'I pray not.' Meraud looked at him searchingly, before adding, 'Alynna is unhappy. We must make her want to stay.'

On his way to his own rooms he digested his sister's words. Alynna unhappy! Did she not know he would speak with the king? He frowned. There had been a change in her since they had arrived at Thornbank. While according him every courtesy, he could have sworn she had been avoiding him. His stride lengthened

with indignation. He had done nothing to offend her.
Had he not curbed his own desires and taken pains to
protect her reputation? What more did the wench expect
from him?'

His mood darkened as his squire attended him and he
changed his clothes. Unbidden, an image of Alynna, her
saturated garments clinging with tantalising allure to her
full breasts and hips, returned to plague him. He shook
his head, but the vision was ingrained on his mind. What
was it about her that made him want her with such
intensity? She was not averse to his kisses, and there
had been the sweet promise of a passionate nature in her
brief response—a demon tempted him. With iron will-
power, he smothered the impulse to go to her.

Alynna sneezed violently as she sat huddled by the
crackling log fire.

'My lady, truly you have caught a fever from your
soaking yesterday.' Hester paused in brushing Alynna's
hair. 'To bed with you. It is well you excused yourself from the meal this evening, for all his lordship is
celebrating Lady Meraud's path to recovery.'

Hester continued in the same vein for several minutes
while she finished brushing. When she would have
braided her hair, Alynna waved her aside. Her head
ached, and she preferred it loose at such times.

'You get to bed,' Hester fussed as she crossed the
room to the door. 'You will catch your death if you wear
nothing but a dressing-robe. I shall fetch a posset from
the kitchen.'

Absently, Alynna pulled the edges of her green velvet
robe across her breasts, for in the privacy of Thornbank
she had returned to her usual custom of sleeping naked.
Her fingers stroked the thick band of miniver edging the
wide trailing sleeves as she stared into the fire. Holding
her throbbing head in her hands, she listened to the
distant sound of pipes and tabors coming from the Great
Hall. The atmosphere at the manor had lightened
already since yesterday's near tragedy. Early that morning she had visited Lady Meraud, who, despite being

confined to her bed by the physician, was friendly, her black eyes sparkling for the first time since Alynna had known her. Richard, too, looked less careworn.

'I have not thanked you for saving Meraud's life,' he had said when she joined him for the first meal of the day in the Great Hall. 'I do that most sincerely. You put your own life at risk to help her. How can I repay you?'

'I want no reward, my lord,' she answered haughtily. 'It in some measure repays my indebtness to you.'

He had looked at her strangely, as though expecting her to demand more. When she noticed that his goblet was empty and the page who had been attending him was being given instructions by the chamberlain, she picked up the flagon to refill the cup. Trevowan gripped her wrist, staying her hand.

'You are not a servant, but a guest—an honoured guest—in my house. There will be no more talk of indebtedness. You have been dealt a cruel injustice. As the king's counsellor, it is my duty to see that his Majesty's laws are upheld and his subjects protected.' His dark brows drew together and his voice deepened to a respectful timbre which set her pulses racing. 'I ride out to hunt directly. Will you join me?'

After being cooped up in the manor for so many days, she enjoyed the freedom of the hunt, but although courteous to her, Lord Trevowan had again somehow distanced himself from her. Now that she had fulfilled her obligations to him, she would have to leave Thornbank soon. The thought of leaving Richard left her disconsolate, and the pleasure of the hunt lost its excitement. To her dismay, she had begun to shiver in the wintry sunshine long before they returned to the manor. By mid-afternoon she had taken to her room, her fever worsening after the effects of her soaking the day before. By evening, her throat ached and a weariness had entered her bones.

She stood up, a little too quickly, and the room revolved round her. When she called out to Hester, there was no reply. Her maid had not returned from the kitchen. A spasm of coughing attacked her and she sank

on to the stool by the fire, feeling wretched and dejected.
Never in her life had she felt so cut off and alone. She
glanced round the antechamber, which was far more
magnificent than any room at Higham Mote. The fire
and candlelight played over the rich colours of the silk
hangings, and a sweet fragrance of dried herbs rose from
the freshly-strewn rushes, but all pleasure in the splendour of her surroundings was dimmed by the aching loss
within her. More than ever she missed the carefree
laughter and wise guidance of her father. She brushed a
tear from her lashes. She would always miss him, but she
refused to mourn the loss of material possessions. Deep
in thought, she did not even look up when the door
opened, thinking Hester had returned.

'Alynna! What ails you?' Trevowan's voice brought
her head up with a start. 'Why did you send to say you
would not dine in the Hall? Are you ill?'

'My lord, your pardon. I fear I have taken a chill.' She
managed to stand up to greet him, and self-consciously
held the edges of her robe together and curtsied.

He took her hand, and with gentle firmness led her to
the stool by the fire. 'Please sit. You look feverish and
should be resting,' he said stiffly. 'After your bravery
yesterday, I would not have you taking a lung-fever.'

He was studying her with an intensity which set her
heart racing. Standing a few paces from her, his body
was tense while he absently twisted a large gold ring
bearing his crest on his little finger. His tall, broad-
shouldered figure dominated the room, the overwhelm-
ing power of his masculinity threatening her as never
before. A black lock had fallen rakishly over his brow,
and she locked her fingers together, curbing the impulse
to brush the curl aside and run her fingers over his
clean-shaven cheek. Aware of the inpropriety of being
alone with a man—and in such circumstances—she
glanced nervously towards the door. What had delayed
Hester?

Trevowan neither moved nor spoke as he continued to
stare at her. The boldness of his gaze as it lingered over
the curves of her body was as blatant as a caress. She

should feel shocked and repelled by his appraisal; instead, her love betrayed her, and her body tingled with anticipation. She still wished Hester was there, giving her protection. There was a predatory stillness about Trevowan's lithe figure as he continued to watch her. When he made no move to leave, Alynna stood up, feeling less vulnerable when he ceased to tower over her. The room seemed to crackle with an indefinable tension, heightening her awareness of him, until her breathing became shallow. Half-fearing, half-yearning that he would take her in his arms, she had to do something to break the spell.

Trevowan spoke first. 'You are aware, of course, that we are in mourning for our mother—as you are for your father. Christmas will be celebrated quietly here, but on the morrow, as I feel Meraud's recovery is well forward, I leave for Trevowan Castle. There is much I must attend to there first, and I would leave easier knowing you will watch over my sister.' He moved closer, filling her mind and vision, his change of mood disconcerting her. 'I shall return to Thornbank before the first day of Christmas.'

'I shall do all in my power to speed Lady Meraud's recovery,' she said throatily, attempting to conquer the sensual, nerve-throbbing spell his nearness aroused. 'I bid you Godspeed, Lord Trevowan, for the morrow.'

A smoky light sparkled in his eyes, and the corner of his mouth lifted with amusement. 'You are well to be on your guard, fair Alynna. Those eyes of yours will be your downfall. But is that all you would say to me on the eve of our parting?'

The glimmer of mockery in his eyes belied the lightness of his tone. He was punishing her, but for what? His barbed taunting confused her. She was exhilarated by the hidden promise behind his words, but was poignantly conscious of the danger he presented.

'My lord,' she began, then hesitated. She could hardly order him from a room in his own manor. The effort it cost her to appear calm brought on a coughing fit.

'Where is Hester?' Richard looked askance towards the inner door leading to the bedchamber.

Alynna mastered her coughing enough to reply, 'She has gone to the kitchen to prepare a posset.'

'I did not realise you were alone,' he said hoarsely. Turning away, he filled a goblet from the wine flagon on the chest and held it steady as he pressed it to her lips. The cool liquid soothed her throat, and as she raised her hand to push the goblet away, their fingers touched. It was like a spark kindling a fire between them.

She took a step back, only to be brought up short by her shoulders touching the wall. Breathlessly she met the force of his silvery gaze. Aware that someone could burst in on them at any moment, and of the state of her undress, she nervously toyed with a tress of her hair that had fallen across her breast. As though bewitched, his gaze followed her movements, then his hand brushed hers away to coil the chestnut ringlet over his fingers. Through the velvet of her robe, his touch was like a brand. A soft gasp rose to her throat, her blood igniting, a shimmering heat spreading through her body. She knew she should move away, but her limbs refused to obey her, a power greater than her own will keeping her captive.

Hardly daring to breathe, she held his desire-darkened stare. His hands moved to her shoulders, and for a moment she thought he would put her from him. After the barest hesitation, when she sensed he was fighting an inner battle, Richard's arms closed round her. His mouth descended, treasuring the taste of her lips, then drew back as he looked at her, gauging her reaction before he reclaimed them. There was no restraint in the fierce demand of his lips hungrily savouring hers. Her senses whirling, she clung to him. She forgot that they might be discovered, forgot all but the rapture of this stolen and forbidden moment.

'Sweet Alynna, there is no woman to match your fire or beauty,' he groaned against her ear. 'You are my damnation!'

With the agony of one vanquished, he crushed her against him, the force of his ardour leaving her

breathless. When her lips parted in response, it was
no seasoned warrior who laid siege to her defences, but a
tender and practised lover. Her body was a torch,
burning with the need to find surcease from the exquisite
torture building within her.

When his lips continued to caress her own, their
breaths mingled, nectar sweet, and when his mouth
wandered in a blazing trail to her ears and throat, she
answered him kiss for kiss, tasting the tangy freshness of
his skin. Cradling her over his arm, with tantalising
slowness his mouth travelled lower as he parted her
robe, and the teasing, sensual flame of his tongue as he
buried his head against her breast drew an ecstatic sigh
from her throat. She felt no shame, only a sense of
inevitability. Was this man not her one and only love?
She was possessed by a fever, driven by a wildness which
transcended reason. If she was destined to spend the rest
of her life without love—let there be this night to
remember.

Her fingers followed the line of his jaw, its smooth
touch so different from the bearded roughness of their
last embrace, and entwining her fingers through his thick
hair, she bound him closer. Then the sharp stinging
building in her throat could no longer be ignored, and
she turned her head aside, gripped by a coughing spasm.
Trevowan drew back from her, his hand lingering
momentarily on her waist, until her coughing ceased.
He tensed, and when she looked up at him, his hand
dropped to his side, his expression carefully guarded. He
had proved how much he wanted her, but the tightly
drawn line of his lips showed how determined he was to
fight against his desire.

'My pardon, Lady Alynna,' he said hoarsely. 'That
was unforgivable of me. You are here as my sister's
companion, and supposedly under my protection.'

She bit her lip and pulled her robe across her breasts.
His mood had changed, his expression hidden from her
by the shadows of the dimly lit room. 'The blame was not
all yours, my lord,' she said, covering her hurt at his
apparent coolness. 'It was a moment's indiscretion. I

would hate to think that, because of it, we had become enemies.'

'No . . . we are not enemies, Alynna.' He folded his arms, looking at her quizzically. 'What would you have us be?'

'My lord, I . . .' She broke off, too embarrassed to speak.

'Lost for words, Alynna? That is not like you.' There was an icy edge to his voice he had never used to her before. 'Where is that honesty you pride yourself upon?'

'What more can I say—in honour, Lord Trevowan?' she parried.

'Ah, honour!' he murmured so softly that she barely caught his words. 'It is the cross we must bear—when temptation would prevail.'

'Lord Trevowan!' Hester's astonished gasp came from the doorway. 'With respect, my lord, you should not be in my lady's chamber . . . and she alone.'

He moved back into the light, and the glare he fixed upon Hester caused the maid to grow pale and stammer, 'N-not that anything untoward w-would have happened, I am sure, m-my lord. B-but my lady's reputation . . .'

'Indeed, Hester,' he stated. 'Lady Alynna's reputation is my greatest concern.'

When his attention returned to Alynna, his voice and manner were once more those of the remote and unattainable Earl of Trevowan. 'I have received a message. Father Dominic has gone to Lindisfarne Holy Island, and Joel is following him there. There is also a woman who could know the truth of your birth, but he has not yet discovered her whereabouts. After Meraud's wedding, I shall return to Court and bring your case to the king's attention. I have sent word for Joel to join me there. For your safety, you will remain here.'

Recovering her composure, Alynna curtsied. How easily Trevowan had changed from lover to the role of master, and her heart ached at the formality now between them. She schooled her voice to match his cool politeness. 'Your lordship honours me by his consideration.'

Lord Trevowan bowed stiffly, and with a last searing look, he marched from the room. Alynna sank down before the blazing fire, hugging her arms about her body to ease the pain grinding through her. She felt trapped —skilfully manoeuvred against her own will or judgement—as though she were the lure about to be seized by a trained falcon. Meraud needed her here. There was no way she could leave Thornbank, or escape its master, until after Meraud's wedding.

Tonight Trevowan had proved there could be nothing between them. He had given into temptation—but where a lesser man would have succumbed totally to his need, he had withdrawn before honour was irretrievably lost. Her reputation and virtue remained intact, but she had never before regarded it as such a useless and burdensome commodity. Her nails bit into her arms as she was torn by the dictates of her conscience. She could never be more than Trevowan's mistress. One day he would marry, and though she might have his heart, it would be his wife who would always have first claim upon him. It would be his wife who would bear his legitimate sons. It was that knowledge which cut deepest of all. The priests emphasised that the sins of the fathers were passed on to their children. Unable as yet to come to terms with her own bastardy, even for Trevowan, she could not recklessly condemn, to a similar fate, the children she longed to give him.

She took the posset Hester held out to her, and drank it down. In silent misery she endured her maid's reprimand, warning her of the danger of entertaining a man—even Lord Trevowan—in her bedchamber. Where his lips had touched, her body still glowed with remembered pleasure. And that memory would be all that she would have in the future.

When at last she climbed into the huge canopied bed and the bed-hangings were closed around her, she turned her face into the pillow, smothering her sobs. Courage took many forms, she reflected bitterly. It would be a harder battle to find the strength to walk out of Lord Trevowan's life for ever than to surrender to his will. But it was a battle she was determined to win.

Christmas this year, she thought darkly, with all the enforced intimacy between the household and the Lord of Trevowan in particular, would likely be one of torment, not of joy.

CHAPTER NINE

THE NEXT morning, Alynna awoke late and was disappointed to have missed Lord Trevowan and his men riding away from Thornbank. Her long sleep had combated most of the debilitating effects of her chill, and she rang the handbell at the side of the bed to summon Hester, urging her to dress her quickly, so that she could attend upon Lady Meraud.

'Lady Meraud is in the solar,' Hester said brightly as she adjusted the veil over Alynna's crescent-shaped headdress. 'It is the talk of the manor how changed her ladyship is—almost like her old self.'

When Alynna knocked on the solar door and curtsied to Trevowan's sister, to her surprise and delight, Meraud immediately jumped to her feet, her face brightening. She came forward to link her arm through Alynna's, saying worriedly, 'I feared you had taken to your bed with a lung-fever after your drenching on the battlements, and I am not ill at all! Forgive me for acting as I did. It is my fault that you became ill. I hoped we could be friends.'

Alynna smiled. Just seeing some colour in Meraud's cheeks and a liveliness in her black eyes made her forget her own troubles. 'I would like that.'

'And you will be one of my attendants at my wedding,' Meraud promised.

Touched by the warmth and sincerity in her voice, Alynna responded in kind. 'I am glad you are to marry Sir John. Lord Trevowan said you were a fighter, and he was right. I can see I have fulfilled my obligations to his lordship, but I had planned to leave once my purpose here was at an end.'

'Oh, indeed you will not!' Meraud exclaimed. 'Where, pray, would you go? Dickon warned me you could be stubborn to a fault. I will not hear of you leaving.'

'My task here is done. I will not live upon any man's bounty.'

'Did my brother say you were stubborn?' Meraud rose to her feet, her eyes flashing with exasperation. 'Pig-headed, rather! Of course you have a place here. There are the Christmas festivities to attend to.' Her eyes saddened. 'As we are in mourning for our mother, they will naturally be quiet this year. But there is also my wedding to plan.' She paced the room, the violence of her agitation causing the white veil draped over her steeple headdress to stream out like ripples in a pond behind her. 'Much needs to be done, and everyone will be judging me. I need a friend I can rely upon. My mother, the countess, was so capable when it came to arranging such matters. I—I fear I will fail Dickon. If you leave, I shall have to summon my great-aunt, Lady Agnes—and my brother will not thank me for subjecting him to her company!' She sank wearily into a chair, a shadow passing across her face. She was making a great effort to overcome her melancholy, but Alynna glimpsed it lurking just below the surface. 'Lady Agnes will descend upon us like a raging tempest!' Meraud sighed. 'Within a day, she will have the house-servants sullen and unbiddable; every last detail will be planned, changed and then changed again. My aunt is a scold who finds fault with everyone and everything. Dear Alynna, I thought we were friends. Would you condemn Dickon and me to that?'

Suspecting that Meraud was exaggerating, but moved by the impassioned speech, Alynna shook her head, laughing, her merriment ending in a cough. 'I would not condemn you to such a fate,' she said, recovering her voice. 'Is your wedding to be in January?'

'Yes.' Meraud brightened. 'Sir John will arrive in a few days—and you will like him very much. Not too much, I hope—I could not bear to share him!' Her eyes sparkled with a greater radiance as she rattled on. 'But you will see why I love him so!'

'I can see why he loves you,' Alynna said warmly. 'I am pleased you are to marry as planned.'

Some of the sadness returned to Meraud's eyes. 'You made me see that it is the right thing to do. Sir John is kind and understanding. He will be gentle, not like . . .' She turned alarmingly pale.

'Do not think of the past, Meraud. You have the future to look forward to. You will be happy with Sir John.'

Meraud nodded. 'Besides—once my future is settled, my brother will have no excuses to delay his own betrothal. Our lady mother was distraught that before Dickon left for France he had not finalised the arrangements for a match with Lady Celia. And still he has made no declaration . . .'

Alynna almost cried out. Drawing a quick breath, she succumbed to another coughing fit. Meraud poured her a goblet of wine and handed it to her, saying, 'I prattle on like a fool, and you truly are ill.'

'No,' Alynna insisted, covering her heartache at the news that Lord Trevowan was about to be betrothed. 'But no more talk of the past. I would rather hear your laughter. What is Lady Celia like?' she could not stop herself asking. 'Is Lord Trevowan to marry her?'

Meraud glanced across at her through lowered lashes and, for a moment, Alynna thought she had guessed the truth. 'Dickon has not withheld himself from marriage for so long to fly into it now.' Meraud's eyes widened speculatively as she continued to regard Alynna. 'He has not committed himself, for all Lady Celia is the ideal match. And her father, the duke, is eager for my brother to return to Court and resume negotiations. But I do not relish Lady Celia as a sister-in-law. She never hunts, and is a rather vain, frivolous creature. But I suppose Richard, like all men, is dazzled by beauty, not by sharp wits. And Lady Celia is very beautiful.'

Each word was like a hammer-blow straight at Alynna's heart, but she took a hold upon herself. She had no idea Richard was so close to marrying. Did he love the beautiful Lady Celia?

She forced herself to appear serene while inwardly her head pounded and her heart seemed cleaved in two. While Meraud was talking of the arrangements to be made for the Christmas feasting, the transformation and animation in her was startling after her melancholy of a few days earlier. But then Lord Trevowan said she was spirited and strong willed. Once Meraud had come to terms and accepted what had happened to her, she would strive to overcome the pain. In so many ways their characters were alike and, despite her own unhappiness, Alynna could not help but be drawn to the vivacious creature blossoming before her. She had never been close to her staid and prim sisters, and already she felt that she had known Meraud for years.

'There is much to be done before the guests arrive,' Meraud babbled on. 'At least it will keep us busy, and I shall not miss Dickon so much.'

The mention of Richard's name set Alynna's mind aflame with the memories of his kisses and touch. Her cheeks grew hot and she looked away confused, glad that a further fit of coughing covered the awkward moment.

'I have tired you with my chatter, and you look feverish.' Meraud was contrite. 'I have matters to discuss with my brother's chamberlain as to the form of the celebrations, so I will leave you to rest.'

Once Meraud left, the room was unbearably quiet. Alynna stared into the flames of the fire miserably, her whole being twisting with shock from Meraud's news.

If Alynna's heart was inwardly breaking, she refused to allow anyone to see it. The days leading up to Christmas were hectic, and although Lord Trevowan was never far from her thoughts, the growing friendship between herself and Meraud eased some of the pain and loneliness. Meraud sometimes suffered moments of withdrawal, shutting out her companions, but those were getting less and less frequent.

Today Meraud was irrepressible. It was impossible for her to settle, and by midday she had changed her gown

no less than four times as she fretted upon the arrival of
Sir John Holcombe.

'Alynna, do you think there is enough holly and laurel
decorating the walls?' Meraud halted in the centre of the
Great Hall. 'Is there ample mistletoe in the kissing bush,
or should it be hung with more ribbons?'

The servant at the top of the long ladder held by three
men paused in his struggle to suspend the kissing bush
from the centre of the roof beam. Seeing the strained
expressions on the faces of the men holding the ladder,
Alynna returned hastily, 'The mistletoe and ribbons are
perfect.'

'Very well, it shall remain as it is.' Meraud's anxious
glance swept round the room. 'But what of the silver
plate? Did the . . .'

'I pray you, Meraud, stop worrying!' Alynna threw
her arms wide to indicate the evergreen garlands, the
sprigs carefully arranged in groups. 'Already Thornbank
has caught the joys of Christmas, and we have checked
everything . . . twice. The hall looks lovely—the cooks
and scullions are busy in the kitchens—even the Yule
log has been cut and awaits Lord Trevowan's arrival to
be brought in and lit. Now, no more fussing, or you will
be too tired for the dancing this evening.'

Meraud looked crestfallen. 'There can be no
dancing—not for us. We are in mourning.'

'Perhaps Lord Trevowan will permit a stately measure? Christmas is a time for rejoicing—my father was
the first to proclaim that.' Alynna bit her lip against an
onrush of grief. 'He would not see it as a tribute if I
curtailed all pleasure. He lived life hard and encouraged
others to do the same. This Christmas, he will be with me
in spirit if not in body.'

A look of compassion and understanding flashed be-
tween them, making further words unnecessary. Then
Meraud exclaimed, 'Is that the herald's trumpet? Has
Sir John arrived, or Richard?'

A page ran into the hall and spoke to the chamberlain,
and with dignified grace, as befitted his high position in
the household, the chamberlain proclaimed in a loud

voice, 'Sir John Holcombe's party has arrived, my
lady.'

Meraud momentarily froze, her dark eyes widening,
and Alynna guessed that she feared Sir John would have
changed in his manner towards her. Then she squared
her shoulders and, recollecting her duties, gave orders to
the servants. 'Bring mulled wine to warm our guests. We
shall greet Sir John in the privy parlour.'

Alynna followed Meraud out of the hall along a
narrow corridor to the new wing completed the previous
year. Of all the magnificent rooms at Thornbank, the
privy parlour was her favourite. More intimate for entertaining guests than the great draughty Hall, and larger
than the otherwise cramped solar, it was a room any
woman would envy.

A welcoming glow greeted them from the blazing fire,
which reflected off the black and red tiles on the floor.
The shutters were still open, and Meraud seated herself
in the curve of the oriel window where the wintry
sunlight streamed through the stained glass of the
central panel decorated with Lord Trevowan's coat of
arms.

At the sound of voices, she glanced anxiously at
Alynna. Then her gaze flew to the door as Sir John was
announced, and a slim, handsome man of medium
height entered. He had eyes for no one but Meraud.
Crossing the chamber, he knelt at her feet, his gaze
adoring as he raised her hand to her lips.

Meraud flinched at his touch, but relaxed and smiled
waveringly as Sir John said devotedly, 'God's greetings, Meraud. I rejoice and daily give thanks for your
recovery.'

The unconcealed love in his eyes brought a catch to
Alynna's throat. Murmuring an excuse, she moved to a
secluded alcove on the far side of the room to give the
lovers privacy, and she could not hear what Meraud
replied. Self-consciously she watched several others
guests file into the room to cluster round their hostess.
The initial greetings over, Meraud led Sir John towards
her.

'Sir John,' she said, smiling and now at ease in his company, 'may I introduce Lady Alynna.'

The knight bowed respectfully over Alynna's hand. 'Meraud tells me you did much to help her recovery.'

'You are too kind, Sir John. I did little,' she replied, moved by the sincerity and obvious regard in which he held his betrothed. 'It was your faith and love that gave Meraud the strength to recover from her ordeal.'

The tender smile the two lovers exchanged lit up the room. To witness their happiness was both a joy and a pain, reminding Alynna that such intimacy was forever denied her with the Earl of Trevowan. Belatedly, as if finding it difficult to tear herself away from Sir John, Meraud introduced the rest of the guests. There was his younger brother, Sir Edmund, a rather shy man of twenty who had been knighted at Agincourt, and Lady Isabeau, Sir John's French mother, both of whom were to stay until the wedding.

Lady Isabeau's gaze flittered over Alynna. 'So this is Trevowan's ward.' The lightness of her tone did not hide its sting. 'A charity case, I believe. But then she is such a pretty creature, and Trevowan always had a discerning eye—though I thought he had put such indiscretions behind him.'

Alynna clenched her hands, fighting to control the urge to defend Lord Trevowan in his absence. Lady Isabeau was his guest and she could not be discourteous to her, no matter how unjust her words. Even at Higham she had heard of Trevowan's wild escapades, which were once the talk of the land. They had been in his early years, when, as the companion of the exuberant and headstrong Prince of Wales, it was to be expected he would follow the lusty pursuits of his friend. In recent years, especially since the prince had attained the throne, there had been no such gossip attached to either his Majesty or the earl.

An embarrassed silence hung over the room until Meraud, eyes flashing dangerously, said pointedly, 'Lady Isabeau, do you question the honour of my dearest friend and also that of your host?'

Two scarlet spots appeared on Lady Isabeau's pale cheeks, and she waved a hand in flustered denial, her brittle laugh that of a woman who could not resist gossip. 'Lord Trevowan was ever a law unto himself, yet now there is talk of his forthcoming marriage . . . Well, it is for Lady Celia to question his conduct. There is an understanding between her father and Lord Trevowan, is there not?'

'Take care of what you speak,' Meraud said firmly. 'Lord Trevowan has not announced any impending match.'

Alynna was careful to mask her pain at this reminder as she again found herself subjected to Lady Isabeau's gaze. She was spared further scrutiny by the chamberlain banging his rod several times on the tiled floor to claim everyone's attention.

'Sir Geoffrey Griswolde and his guests are below, my lady,' he announced.

'I had no idea Sir Geoffrey was coming!' Meraud exclaimed, looking anxiously at Alynna. 'And with guests! It is just like him to arrive without warning. I must see that the west wing is prepared.'

'Your place is with Sir John and his family, so would you rather I check that all is in readiness?' Alynna asked, needing to be away from Lady Isabeau's calculating stare.

Meraud gave her a grateful smile. 'I impose upon your friendship.'

'Nonsense! Besides, on your instructions the rooms have already been partially prepared. It will not take a moment to light the fires.'

Alynna excused herself from the company, but as she left, heard Lady Isabeau's voice drop warningly. 'Meraud, dear, you have such a trusting nature. Lady Alynna must be a delightful companion to be sure, but while Lord Trevowan remains unwed, he will be prey to any woman who thinks her pretty face will make her a countess.'

Is that what people will think of me? Alynna thought bleakly as she summoned servants to attend her in the west wing. This was going to be a far from peaceful Christmas. Not only would there be Lady Isabeau watching over everything, with an eye to reporting any gossip to the ladies at Court, but there would be the friction she always sensed between Lord Trevowan and Sir Geoffrey, whom she did not trust.

There was little to be done in the west wing. Her task completed and the servants dismissed, she was loath to return immediately to the guests and went up on to the battlements. She inhaled sharply, the icy air spiking her throat and lungs. Of late, Hester had caused her concern. Often in the middle of the night, from her truckle-bed at the foot of Alynna's own, she would cry out in terror, and sometimes it took an hour to comfort her, as she relived the horror of her burning at the stake. Troubled, Alynna walked along the battlements. For a long time she stared out across the sloping hills, savouring the rare moment of privacy, while the muffled sounds of the busy house drifted up to her. Then, from out of the wood behind the village, the blasting notes of a herald's trumpet proclaimed the Earl of Trevowan's return.

Dogs from both manor and village began to bark excitedly. The village across the moat, which until that moment had been virtually deserted, suddenly came alive. Doors were flung wide as whole families poured out to cheer and welcome him. It was a gesture so spontaneous that Alynna's heart swelled with pride. Although his duties kept him for weeks at Court, Meraud had told her that reports from all his lands and manors and any problems concerning his vassals had to be submitted to him weekly. It was an example many more of England's nobility would do well to heed. For although Trevowan had known every comfort and luxury from birth, he took his duties to his people seriously and was rewarded by a loyalty borne of love.

As the horsemen trotted through the village, her heart pounded as her gaze fixed on Lord Trevowan's tall figure astride a white charger. From her position on the parapet, unobserved by others, she could feast her eyes upon

him and allow her love to shine unguarded on her
face. Suddenly he looked up, and for a heartstopping
moment their gazes held—time briefly suspended—and
a pain, sharp with longing, went through her. Just for
an instant the barriers of restraint were down between
them. He raised his hand in acknowledgement, then
abruptly seemed to regret his action and brought it
down to stroke his horse's neck as he passed out of
sight.

Alynna leaned her brow against the cold stone of the
battlement wall. She had not imagined that fleeting
exchange, or the determined way Trevowan had re-
established the shield he meant to keep erected against
her. Of course, if he was intent on winning Lady Celia's
hand, he would want no hint to reach the Court that he
was romantically involved with another woman. The
setting sun had turned the sky saffron and crimson when
she left the battlements. She knew he was right. There
was no place in their lives for a sentiment that would
destroy honour. On the point of returning her cloak to
her room, Alynna was met by a page.

'My lady, Lord Trevowan craves audience with you in
the solar.'

Surprised by the summons, she quickly divested herself of her cloak and followed the page. Her pulse beat
fast. What did Trevowan want with her? Since before
their arrival at Thornbank, his moods had been unpredictable. The page stood back for her to enter a small
chamber, which appeared to be an anteroom to the
solar, saying, 'His lordship will attend you shortly, my
lady.' He bowed and left.

The minutes passed without further summons, and
her nerves became edgy. She straightened her spine.
Whatever the earl had to say to her, she would act with
calm dignity. Unexpectedly, from the far side of the
closed door, his voice rang out, sharp and questioning,
his anger barely suppressed. There was a sharp rejoinder, and she recognised Sir Geoffrey's tones. The
exchange became more heated until Trevowan's curt
command silenced his cousin, and then the dividing door

was wrenched open and the earl stooped to enter the ante-chamber.

For an instant the sight of his handsome countenance took her breath away. His hair was ruffled as though he had raked his fingers through its thickness, but there was no trace of tiredness in his lean face despite his having spent long hours in the saddle. A muscle throbbing in his neck, the only sign of his anger, caused her heart to tug in her breast. She longed in that moment for a return to their earlier relationship, where as a simple pilgrim she could reach out and teasingly soothe the rage eating at him. Fearful lest her eyes betray her love, she lowered her gaze to the gold pattern on the high collar of his black doublet.

'Lady Alynna, if you please.' Richard gestured for her to enter the solar, his voice more gentle than she had expected.

So he was not angry with her. With whom, then? Unaccountably she sensed a hidden menace waiting within the solar. Her glance sharpened, but his expression was guarded.

He said heavily, 'Sir Geoffrey has brought a guest whom I believe you would rather meet first in private.'

It was discomforting not to encounter the warm smile of the friend she had come to rely upon but this haughty visage and cool gaze, especially when he studied her with such unnerving intensity. Pride and defiance kept her head high as she moved past him to the room beyond. On the threshold her step faltered, and she stared in astonishment at the bejewelled, stout woman swathed in deepest mourning at Sir Geoffrey's side.

'Alynna! My darling child,' Lady Joan shrilled, a false smile creasing the fleshy folds of her face. She descended on Alynna, smothering her in a fierce embrace and a sickly perfume. 'I have been at my wits' end with fear ever since those brutes carried you off.'

Taken completely unawares, Alynna was momentarily speechless as she stiffly freed herself from Lady Joan's hold. If she had arrived with Sir Geoffrey, how had they met? And what lies had she been weaving to justify herself to Lord Trevowan?

Alynna looked at Griswolde, who was leaning against the fireplace, apparently unconcerned. Yet she had the distinct impression that he missed nothing. Why had he brought Lady Joan here? To spite Trevowan? That made no sense.

'Have you no words of greeting for your mother, dear child?' moaned Lady Joan.

Wondering what trickery she was planning, Alynna remained silent, trying to gauge Lady Joan's motives. Through her flimsy veil, Alynna could feel the warmth of Trevowan's breath on her neck as he stood directly behind her. Although he said nothing, he, too, appeared to be watching and waiting.

Had her stepmother's lies made him doubt her own story? Once Lady Joan had learned that he had given her his protection, she must have been out of her mind with fear. In a bid to save herself from imprisonment for what she had done, she would have devised a story to distort the truth.

'I should scold you, Alynna, for the worry you have caused me,' Lady Joan went on, regardless of the hostile silence in the room. 'What possessed you to journey halfway across England when you escaped those mercenary brutes? It was wrong of you to force yourself upon Lord Trevowan in that manner. And not a single word sent to me, your mother.'

'Stepmother!' Alynna burst out, unable to contain her outrage a moment longer. 'And an unnatural one at that! I have not forgotten our last meeting.'

'Words spoken in grief,' Lady Joan sobbed. 'With your poor father dead but a week—I did not know what I was saying. We were both upset.'

'Your sentiments were clear enough,' Alynna returned stonily. 'And what is this talk of mercenaries? You called the guards to throw me out!'

'Ungrateful creature!' Lady Joan retorted, turning to Trevowan as though seeking support. 'Did you ever hear such outrageous lies? I can only imagine the wild story she must have told you, my lord. She will say anything to win attention for herself.'

Trevowan stood as one carved from stone, his eyes flinty as his glance swept from Lady Joan to Sir Geoffrey. 'I have found Lady Alynna to be both courageous and honest.'

'You do not know the sly minx for what she is!' Lady Joan protested, undaunted.

Seeing Trevowan about to intervene further, Alynna put up a hand to stop him. She was overjoyed that his faith in her remained firm, but she did not need anyone to fight her battles with her stepmother. Drawing a long breath, she eyed Lady Joan coldly, noticing her changed appearance. Instead of the brightly coloured surcoat and oversized headdress she usually wore, she was dressed in black, with no paint or powder, her neck covered by a linen widow's wimple and over her hair a simple veil, held in place by a plain gold circlet. Obviously, for Lord Trevowan's benefit, she was acting the part of the grieving widow.

'You have not answered my question, Lady Joan,' Alynna challenged. 'You summoned the guards to cast me from my father's home!'

'That is a wicked lie!' Lady Joan countered with a swiftness that warned Alynna that this speech had been carefully rehearsed. 'I saw the mercenaries running into the hall behind you. That is why I screamed for the guards. To save us all.'

Alynna turned away, too disgusted and angry to trust herself to speak. Lady Joan had planned her story well—it sounded almost plausible.

'When I first came across Lady Alynna being attacked in the wood, there was no sign of mercenaries,' Trevowan cut in coldly.

'They were being pursued by my guards,' Lady Joan declared. 'After robbing Alynna, they threw her body into a ditch before escaping.'

Alynna whirled to face her stepmother. 'How is it that you know so much about these so-called mercenaries?'

A complacent smile dimpled Lady Joan's face.

'I explained everything to his lordship earlier. Sir Geoffrey's men captured three of them.'

Lady Joan moved to Griswolde's side, and there was nothing of the grieving widow in the way she coquettishly fluttered her lashes at him. Alynna chewed her lip to prevent her disgust showing on her face. In the past she had suspected her stepmother of taking lovers to arouse Sir Robert's jealousy, but now it seemed that she was set on winning Sir Geoffrey as a husband and becoming part of the powerful Dreux family.

'You owe Sir Geoffrey much, my dear,' Lady Joan simpered. 'When he heard your strange tale at Canterbury, he was moved to inform me of your whereabouts.'

Alynna eyed the knight, suspicion stirring in her mind. 'You have gone to a great deal of trouble, Sir Geoffrey.'

'I did no more than my Christian duty,' he replied smoothly, but there was an unsettling look in his eyes. 'Indeed, Trevowan—as I should have known—had already sent a message to Lady Joan that you were safe, but he was rather vague as to his intentions concerning your future.'

'Sir Geoffrey has been such a comfort,' Lady Joan intervened, her hand possessively touching the knight's arm. 'I can never repay my gratitude that his men routed those murderers and outlaws. For weeks the woods around Barkhurst were unsafe, as the band was constantly attacking travellers on the Canterbury road.'

Alynna faced Lord Trevowan, ready to refute every word, but although his expression remained impassive, she sensed, by the barely perceptible narrowing of his eyes as he looked directly at her, that he was warning her to say nothing.

'Christmas is the time of forgiveness and goodwill,' he astounded her by remarking. 'Families should be together at this time. Sir Geoffrey did right to bring you to Thornbank, Lady Joan.'

He picked up a handbell and rang it. When a page entered, he said courteously to the visitors, 'Rooms have been prepared for you. The boy will show you the way.'

Disheartened by his apparent acceptance of Lady
Joan's story, Alynna made to follow her stepmother
and Sir Geoffrey from the solar. Had she mistaken
Trevowan's look? She could not believe he meant the
matter to rest. Surely it was obvious that Lady Joan was
trying to twist this situation to her advantage.

'A moment, Lady Alynna,' Lord Trevowan
commanded.

Sir Geoffrey, who had stood back for her to pass
through the door, shot her a reflective look, his lips
tilting at the corners as he whispered. 'Until later, my
lady, when we shall renew our acquaintanceship.'

Griswolde's words startled her. His tone sounded
warm and friendly, yet he had brought Lady Joan here,
and her stepmother seemed to regard him as her own
suitor. With Lord Trevowan waiting to speak with
her, she could not question Sir Geoffrey on his actions.
When she turned back into the room she kept her eyes
lowered, too aware of the powerful pull of her attraction
towards Trevowan to risk meeting his gaze.

At Alynna's uncharacteristic humility, he contained
his amusement, knowing she was almost bursting at
having to control her own temper and not round on him.
Her shoulders squared, and he could see she was having
difficulty in curbing her need to speak without his having
given her permission. At that moment he would have
single-handedly fought a dozen men rather than cause
her further pain. He made his voice cool. 'It is best that
Lady Joan remain at Thornbank.'

'My lord, that scene was devised for your benefit, and
was all lies!' she burst out with a return of the spirit he
admired. 'You cannot believe . . .'

'Did I say I believed them?' he ground out, stung by
her censure. He was appalled to see her sapphire eyes
glistening with unshed tears, and instinctively he put out
his hand, only to check himself abruptly. He balanced
the weight of his body on the balls of his feet as though
preparing for combat.

He considered Griswolde's part in bringing Lady Joan

to his house. His cousin never did anything if it was not to his own advantage; too often he had seen the way he took bribes at court. Intrigue was second nature to him, and he ran roughshod over anyone who stood in his way. But why had he shown an interest in Alynna? It stemmed from something more than his inability to resist pursuing any beautiful woman. Trevowan's temper sparked at the image of him playing court to her. He passed his hand across his jaw, regarding her challenging glance in silence. He wanted to safeguard her from the worries that beset himself. There was already talk at Court about the two of them, but more disturbing still were the rumours that he had taken a Lollard into his household. A terse note from the king had arrived at Trevowan Castle commanding him to return to Court once Meraud was married.

Trevowan twisted the large seal ring on his finger, his thoughts bitter. Since he had been so outspoken on the carnage following Agincourt, his relationship with King Henry had been strained. Neither did he agree with the ruthlessness with which his Majesty persecuted the Lollards. And this summons was not the only message he had received at Trevowan. The information from Joel had been infuriatingly evasive. Unfortunately, the cold northern air had almost crippled his swollen joints, and he had been forced to stay on the Holy Island to be tended by the monks. What secret did Joel not even dare to commit to paper, or entrust to a third person to convey by word of mouth? There had been a note of warning too in the way the message ended. Joel had urged him to keep Alynna under his protection.

'My lord,' Alynna cut across his thoughts, her face flushed and accusing, 'why did you allow Lady Joan to stay?'

'I do not trust Sir Geoffrey,' he responded sharply, his anger returning. He could have throttled his cousin for bringing that female viper into his home with her shrill demands and sly insinuations, and had no intention of returning Alynna to the woman's clutches.

Alynna tensed, hurt by the chill hauteur in

Trevowan's voice, and not understanding it. 'What has Sir Geoffrey to do with this? It is Lady Joan you should guard against,' she flared. 'She is here because she fears imprisonment for what she has done . . . and you treat her like an honoured guest.'

'You forget yourself,' Richard warned. 'A lot has happened since your father died so tragically. Lady Joan's presence here changes nothing. I shall speak to the king as I promised.'

'Then, I beg you, my lord—order my stepmother to go!' she burst out, overcome by a deep unreasonable fear.

'Lady Joan is your guardian.' His eyes flashed with impatience. 'If she so chooses, she can order you to leave here. If I send her away and insist you stay under my protection, your reputation will be in shreds.'

'You would send me away!' Her shock unwittingly betrayed her dismay.

Thick lashes veiled Richard's eyes from her, his flat tone revealing nothing of his thoughts. 'I have not said that.'

A ball of icy misery lodged in her throat and her mouth moved, but no words came. How could she speak and not reveal her heartache? At last she managed to force out, 'Since the first moment we met I have been a burden to you, and now Lady Joan has thrust herself upon you. She is hungry for wealth, and tenacious as a leech if she thinks she can gain from it. I fear she will cause trouble for trouble's sake—and it is all my fault! I am sorry, my lord. You must curse the day you saved me from the ferryman.'

'What a heartless knave you think me!' The coldness in his voice shocked her as he walked across the room to gaze out of the window, saying over his shoulder, 'Better to have the devil on your doorstep, where you can see him . . . than have him hovering at your back. That is why Lady Joan stays. Griswolde is behind this mischief. He does nothing unless he believes there will be rich pickings in it for him. Therefore be on your guard against him, Alynna.'

CHAPTER TEN

DISMISSED FROM the earl's presence, Alynna returned to
the privy parlour, her thoughts confused. Trevowan's
formal manner disturbed her far more than his warning.
All that was female and free spirited in her rebelled,
urging her to fight to win his heart. Pride and honour
jousted against the age-old instinct to love and be loved
in return, while she reluctantly acknowledged that if he
intended to marry Lady Celia, far more than the barrier
of rank lay between herself and the earl.

In three weeks Meraud would be married. Then
she herself would be free of her obligations to Lord
Trevowan, and would find some way of leaving
Thornbank that did not leave her at the mercy of Lady
Joan.

Few of the guests were present when Alynna entered
the parlour. She smiled politely in acknowledgment of
Lady Isabeau's brief nod, and when the Frenchwoman
gave no sign of breaking off her conversation with Sir
Geoffrey, she withdrew to a quiet corner of the room.
Opposite her, Meraud and Sir John were seated, hands
entwined and heads close together as they laughed
softly, unaware of anyone else. Settling on a stool and
smoothing the folds of her surcoat over her knee, she
kept her head bent as Trevowan strode into the room,
his deep voice greeting his guests. There was a flurry of
questions as both Sir John and Lady Isabeau answered
their host, and during this a shadow fell across Alynna.
She looked up, disconcerted to find Sir Geoffrey smiling
down at her.

'God's greetings, Lady Alynna,' he said smoothly.
'Do I note a certain chillness in the air between you and
Trevowan?'

'How so?' she replied guardedly. 'His lordship is my
benefactor.'

'He made his interest in you at Canterbury plain enough—but then Trevowan is his own man.' Sir Geoffrey's smile broadened, his gaze openly appraising as he held her suspicious stare. 'It is several years since a beautiful face was enough to move my cousin to indiscretion, but of course he would do nothing to endanger his chances of winning Lady Celia.'

'You are insolent, sir!' Her eyes blazed, and with difficulty she kept her voice low.

He held up a hand in supplication. 'I meant no offence. I but paid tribute to your beauty, fair Alynna. Eyes such as yours . . . Their brilliance and colour is quite remarkable, and I have seen the like but once before.' He took her hand and raised it to his lips with the skill of a practised courtier. 'I am sad that their brightness is filled with scorn for so unworthy an admirer.'

'Keep your compliments for Lady Joan. They may impress her, but not me!' she said, pulling her hands from his.

If she had hoped to discourage him, she had failed. 'I fear I have displeased you by bringing Lady Joan here,' he said. 'That was not my intent.'

'What were your intentions, Sir Geoffrey?' She studied him warily.

'To see you again. Did I not promise I would come to Thornbank? I hoped I would win your favour by reuniting you with your family.'

'I remember well your words,' she said pointedly. 'You told me also you disliked mysteries. Did Lady Joan not supply you with the answers? Is that why she is here? You have put yourself to a great deal of trouble. The truth is very simple, and none of your concern.'

'Now I am more curious than before,' he chuckled, unrepentant. 'But with good reason. I fear, Lady Alynna, you have stolen my heart.' His heavy-lidded eyes sparkled with admiration. 'You are a very beautiful woman. I could not stay away.'

For an instant she was taken aback by his words. Although his persuasive charm had taken the sting from her anger towards him, she did not believe a word of his extravagant compliments, but she would have been less than human if she did not admit that his flattery had eased the pain of Trevowan's coldness.

'Your silence condemns me more soundly than any words.' He sounded contrite. 'I should not have allowed Lady Joan to come here. The poor woman was distraught when I told her you were at Canterbury, but the moment she began to make excuses to Trevowan, I saw my mistake . . . that all was not as I had been led to believe. Until then, I was convinced that there had been a misunderstanding between you.'

'There was no misunderstanding.' Alynna regarded him levelly. It was obvious from the frowning way Sir Geoffrey was looking at her that Lady Joan had not told him what had caused the rift.

'I thought I had acted in your best interest. I see I was wrong.'

He sounded sincere, and seeing his downcast expression, she overcame her resentment at his interference. Although not wholly won over, she could not believe he had acted out of spite, and her stepmother was an expert at twisting the truth. She relented. 'It is Christmas, the time of peace and goodwill, and the less said on the matter, the better.'

'You have a generous heart, Lady Alynna.' A fervent note crept into his soft voice.

At his extravagant manner she laughed softly. He was irrepressible! Out of the corner of her eye she saw Lord Trevowan and Lady Isabeau watching her. From the tautness of the earl's expression he did not look pleased. Remembering his warning, she wondered why he had been so adamant for her to be on her guard against his cousin. It certainly was not out of jealousy that he had spoken—not after the coldness of their reunion. She risked a glance, but he was now engrossed in conversation with Sir John and did not look in her direction. Another twinge of doubt entered her mind. He was an adept courtier who, over the years, had learned to guard his emotions from experienced intriguers. How much of himself had he really shown to her during the pilgrimage? Was that the true Richard Dreux, tender and caring, or had this noble warrior regarded his protection to a damsel in distress as part of his penance?

At that moment Lady Joan entered and came directly towards her. Alynna reluctantly stood up to greet her. She could hardly avoid her stepmother without seeming ill-mannered before Lord Trevowan's guests.

'Sweet daughter!' Lady Joan's overloud voice was falsely loving as she presented her cheek for Alynna to kiss. 'I am relieved to see you looking so well. How fortunate that Lord Trevowan was on hand to rescue you from those terrible mercenaries.'

Alynna barely touched her lips to her stepmother's cheek, guessing that she had rehearsed this scene, too, to perfection. Unless she was to bring discredit upon her father's name, she was forced to play Lady Joan's game. Despite that, she was not about to allow her to gain any advantage. She drew back, unsmiling, her voice heavy with meaning. 'Lord Trevowan saved my life.'

Lady Joan curtsied to the earl. 'Indeed, we are greatly indebted to his lordship.'

Lord Trevowan stiffly acknowledged Lady Joan's homage, but at the freezing hauteur in his eyes, she wisely said no more and a tense silence settled over the room, which was broken by Sir Geoffrey's cynical laugh.

'Since his pilgrimage, my cousin seems to have accumulated a variety of unlikely servants.' He had moved away from Alynna when Lady Joan entered the parlour, and was now regarding Trevowan mockingly. 'He has taken on a lame woman to be Lady Alynna's maid, and as for the jester . . .'

'What jester?' Lady Joan cried, looking agitated and ill at ease. 'You did not mention a jester, Sir Geoffrey.'

'Did I not, Lady Joan?' Sir Geoffrey shrugged, and spreading his hand before him, he admired the play of firelight over a large ruby ring on his finger, as though the matter was of no importance. Trevowan knew his cousin too well to be deceived. He doubted that Lady

Joan had told Griswolde the truth of Alynna's birth
—the woman was more interested in snaring his cousin
as a husband for that. Not that Griswolde would
succumb to her overblown charms—unless there
was a fortune at stake. Although partners, the two
obviously did not trust each other.

Trevowan fixed Lady Joan with a probing stare. 'This
jester interests you, Lady Joan?'

She paled and looked anxiously across at Sir
Geoffrey, who appeared to ignore her, being more
concerned with plucking some imaginary hairs from the
long trailing sleeves of his doublet. Clearing her throat,
she forced a smile, her voice deferential.

'My lord, there was a jester in my husband's service.
He disappeared the day the mercenaries attacked. If it is
the same man, I am concerned lest he impose upon your
generosity. He is a scoundrel, and quite unprincipled.'

'I have not found him so,' Richard said coolly. 'I was
impressed by his loyalty to Lady Alynna. Unfortunately
he is not with us at Thornbank. He has been troubled of
late by pains in his joints, and has gone to some priory in
Suffolk to be tended by the monks. I believe it is the one
endowed by Sir Robert Freston.' His grey eyes glistened
like polished steel. 'Joel was also deeply troubled. He
seemed convinced that the prior could guide him.'

At his words, Lady Joan looked about to suffer an
apoplexy; her face suffused with colour that faded like a
fiery sunset until her cheeks were ashen. Trevowan
smothered his disgust and anger. The woman was
frightened. What secret had Joel learned from the prior?
But it was the gleam in Griswolde's eyes, bright and
cunning as a fox, that worried him most.

At that moment, with a rustle of silk, Lady Isabeau,
clearly unable to contain herself at the hint of mystery
surrounding the guests, burst out, 'Lord Trevowan tells
me, Lady Joan, that you were married to Sir Robert
Freston. A charming man! I met him several times
at Court, but I cannot recall you accompanying your
husband.'

There was a pause, and Trevowan bent down casually

to ruffle the ears of a wolfhound bitch that had wandered in.

'It is some years since I have been to Court,' Lady Joan answered primly. 'It was there I met Sir Robert.'

'So you were not contracted to him from an early age?' Lady Isabeau seized upon the information with delight.

'No . . . That is . . .' Momentarily she floundered, then drew herself up, her expression smug. 'My betrothed died from the sweating sickness and, at the time, Sir Robert was contracted to wed another—a mere child of ten summers. When we fell in love, we married in secret. The king was angry, but eventually he forgave Sir Robert and allowed him to return to Court. For myself, I preferred to live quietly in Suffolk.'

Griswolde cut in. 'Lady Joan was married to Sir Robert in the same month you came to England for your own marriage. She was then lady-in-waiting to the late king's cousin, Lady Constance.'

Trevowan frowned. Griswolde, he realised, had deliberately turned the conversation and looked far too pleased with himself for his motives to be innocent. Lady Joan, too, looked taken aback, and he saw her give his cousin a frowning look as if displeased.

'I was in Burgundy this summer, where I met Lady Constance and her husband, the Count, who is, I believe, your cousin, Lady Isabeau?' Griswolde added with a wry smile. 'Lady Constance is still an acclaimed beauty—the toast of the French Court.

Lady Joan sniffed. 'I always thought her looks overrated.'

At the venom in her tone, Trevowan caught the triumphant glitter in his cousin's eyes, and in a voice light and full of mischief, Griswolde added, 'It is Lady Constance's eyes that captivate her admirers. They are unforgettable. Quite the most expressive and beautiful I have ever seen. Their colour is like . . .' He laughed. 'Your pardon, ladies! While at the Burgundian Court I fear I fell under Lady Constance's spell.'

Trevowan cursed his cousin for the devil's own intriguer. What was he up to? The most absurd notion was beginning to form in his mind, which he refused to dwell upon as being too foolish to consider. He must wait for Joel's report before leaping to wild conclusions. Deliberately he interrupted to change the subject. 'On several occasions, Lady Joan, I jousted against Sir Robert in the lists. His late Majesty, Henry IV, showed him special favour. Yet he was given no high office. Was that not rather strange?'

'Not everyone can be as fortunate as yourself, Lord Trevowan,' Lady Joan replied, failing to meet his gaze.

'Yet, despite his lack of office, I believe Lady Alynna was to become his Majesty's ward upon Freston's death,' Trevowan persisted. 'That is a singular honour for the daughter of a knight, would you not say, Lady Joan? Your two younger daughters were not mentioned in this wardship. That was rather remiss of our late Sovereign, was it not?

'Who am I, my lord, to question the decisions of Henry IV?' Lady Joan wrung her hands together in visible agitation. 'It was a long time ago. His Majesty's father is dead. The wardship no longer stands.'

'How so?' Richard contended. 'Henry V honours all the obligations of his father.'

'Alynna is no longer a child.' Lady Joan looked accusingly at her. 'She should have been married years ago, but Sir Robert would not have her leave his side. Already I have received an offer for her hand. I would not have her a burden to King Henry. She will be married within the year.'

Alynna jumped to her feet, her eyes blazing. With a slight movement of his hand, Trevowan warned her to remain silent, while with difficulty he contained his rising anger. Each word Lady Joan uttered condemned her further in his eyes. Did the creature think that by playing the innocent she could evade the law?

Although he had no proof, now that the ferryman was dead, he was convinced that Lady Joan had tried to have Alynna killed. If Alynna left his protection, he feared for her life. Had Sir Geoffrey and Lady Joan devised some scheme to divide the dowry between them?

According to Joel, it was more than substantial—it almost matched Meraud's. He was sure that Freston had not possessed such wealth. Was Alynna then not even his child—but the by-blow of a royal prince? From his discreet enquiries, he had learned that Freston had a sister, who had been at Court and had died unwed about eighteen years since. Was Alynna her daughter? It would not be the first time such a liaison had been concealed, and the child raised as another's. Would that not explain the mystery surrounding Alynna's birth? He moved to stand in front of Lady Joan, his voice, low with warning, for her ears alone. 'Any suitor would need his Majesty's permission before wedding Lady Alynna.'

'She is fortunate to have received an offer after her wild and immodest conduct.' Lady Joan retorted in an equally low tone, but not once did her gaze hold his. 'She is well past marriageable age, and has shown her wilful temperament by running off to tramp the highways like a common peasant. It was not easy to find a husband for her.'

'You forget in whose company she journeyed to Canterbury, Lady Joan,' Trevowan ground out, 'and that it was a holy pilgrimage to pray for Sir Robert's soul. His death was tragic. A hunting accident . . . ? And he a proficient swordsman in the lists!'

'Sir Robert's death was a great shock!' Her voice broke on a false-sounding sob, and she made a great show of dabbing at her eyes with the edge of her veil. 'Your pardon, my lord,' she sniffed, and continued after an effective pause. 'It is painful to speak of my husband.'

Unconvinced, Trevowan let the matter rest; too many curious glances were upon them. 'You have our sympathy, Lady Joan,' he said in normal tones. 'Should the Christmas festivities be abhorrent to you, I shall not be offended if you prefer to take your meals in your chamber.' He hid his grim amusement at the dismay twisting her face.

'Oh no, your lordship, I would not cast a gloomy note over your guests. Are you too not in mourning for your mother?'

Alynna clenched her hands at her side to control her mounting temper. She had no intention of marrying any suitor chosen for her by Lady Joan or the king. In fact, loving Trevowan as she did, she knew she could never marry anyone else. With Joel and Hester for company, she would be content to live simply and quietly. There must be some way in which she could gain control of the dowry set aside for her in her father's will and use it to start a new life.

The chamberlain entered the parlour and stood to one side, awaiting Lord Trevowan's order to announce the beginning of the feast. The earl bowed to Lady Isabeau, offering her his arm to escort her to the Great Hall. As the other guests were claimed by their partners—Sir John and Meraud, Sir Geoffrey and Lady Joan—Alynna found herself standing next to Sir Edmund. Not much older than herself, he blushed as he held out his arm. Taking their places behind Sir Geoffrey and Lady Joan, Alynna was able to study Trevowan's handsome profile as he spoke to Lady Isabeau while they walked through to the Great Hall. A blast upon the trumpets announced the arrival of the earl to the dozens of retainers, who stood behind their benches waiting for their lord to be seated before taking their own places at the tables. Halfway along the hall, Lady Isabeau halted abruptly and gave a scream, her body tense with horror as she pointed at Hester, standing amongst the other chamberwomen and maids.

'You have a squint-eyed woman in the hall, Lord Trevowan,' she cried. 'She will bring ill-fortune to us all. She must be removed for the duration of the Christmas celebrations.'

Hester cringed and pulled her veil across her scars, but as she made to scuttle away, Alynna ran to her side.

'Sit down, Hester,' Trevowan ordered loudly. He turned to Lady Isabeau, his tone gruff. 'The woman has proved her trust and loyalty. I will not banish her to a cheerless room because she has suffered a misfortune. The woman was scarred from a fire—she is not squint-eyed!'

'I had not realised that Lady Alynna's crippled maid was the Lollard who was set upon at Canterbury!' Sir Geoffrey exclaimed in astonishment. 'By the rood, coz! What is she doing here? Have you taken to employing heretics?'

'She is no heretic, but a good Christian.' Trevowan dismissed the matter.

Sir Geoffrey subjected Alynna to a hard stare, his gaze resting upon her hand, which was placed protectively upon Hester's shoulder. When he again faced Trevowan, his voice was low, clearly relishing his warning. 'You have often voiced your condemnation of the king's persecution of the Lollards. Take care, coz, that *you* are not suspected of heresy.'

Alynna felt her heart wrench. Could Trevowan truly be in danger? Surely he was too high in the king's favour.

'The king knows my mind on the matter.' Trevowan silenced his cousin with a glare. 'No more talk of heresy; it will distress the ladies.'

Hester's shoulders began to shake. 'Oh, my lady,' she murmured, 'I feared it would be thus!'

'Hush, Hester, you worry overmuch.' Alynna patted her shoulder and smiled reassuringly. 'Lord Trevowan is in no danger. Now enjoy the feast.'

The earl looked up at the gallery, indicating that the musicians should begin to play as he took his place at the centre of the dais.

Alynna, intercepting Lady Joan's smug expression as her stepmother nodded in acknowledgement of something Sir Geoffrey said, stifled a resurgence of her own fear. She did not trust either of them. Sir Geoffrey seemed to enjoy trying to provoke Lord Trevowan, not that the earl had shown any sign of rising to his bait.

She took her place at one end of the high table, relieved that Lady Joan had been placed at the far end and she would not have to endure her company during the lengthy meal.

'Wassail! Wassail!'

The cry from the people at the trestle tables drowned the fanfare of trumpets that had accompanied the Yule candle being carried in state to the dais table for all to admire. From her position at the far end, Alynna watched Trevowan ceremoniously light the multi-coloured candle with its twelve metal ornaments. This was the sign for the feasting to begin, and throughout the twelve days, the candle that had been carefully fashioned during the preceding twelve months would continue to burn. Another cheer went up as the huge Yule log was lit and another blast of trumpets announced the frumenty. Alynna made a pretence of eating, but it would have been easier to swallow burning embers. Even the outrageous capering of the Lord of Misrule—who had been chosen on All Saints' Day to reign until Twelfth Night, and now in his absolute rule played pranks upon noble and servant alike—could not lift her spirits. There was a tense air along the length of the dais table of which only Meraud and Sir John, in their new-found happiness, seemed unaware.

This was going to be nothing like the quiet Christmas planned. She could hear Trevowan's deep voice in conversation with those on either side of him, but could not share his laughter at the antics of the mummers. The space between them at the table was no more than a few feet, yet his exalted position and her lowly place at one end emphasised the gap between their ranks. Was it insurmountable? As he leaned forward to listen raptly to Lady Isabeau, his dark complexion and sharp profile were both formidable and handsome. Her heart betrayed her. Did she dare to let her love conquer her fears?

Early next morning, Trevowan summoned his steward and manor officers to hear their reports before he joined his guests for the hunt. He looked up from a closely written scroll of parchment, and was surprised to see Meraud put her head round the door.

'Oh, you are still busy,' she said, her disappointment obvious. 'I shall speak with you later.'

He stood up and dismissed his men. 'I have been studying the estate books for over an hour, so your interruption is welcome, dear sister.' He gestured for Meraud to sit on the stool he had just vacated, frowning at her worried expression. ''Tis not sisterly affection that brings you in search of me.'

She ignored the stool and paced the room. 'I am worried about Alynna. She is clearly unhappy. Have you quarrelled? You seem to be avoiding her.'

'She has Griswolde and Sir Edmund to keep her company,' he said more tersely than he intended, for it had been a strain to watch the two knights vying with each other for Alynna's attention.

'I suppose with Lady Isabeau being the gossip she is, you must take care that nothing untoward should reach Lady Celia's ears at Court. But your treatment is poor reward for Alynna, after all she has done.

'What the devil has Lady Celia to do with it?' Trevowan exploded.

'Oh, do not play the innocent with me, Dickon!' Meraud returned with more the old spirit than he would have wished at that moment. 'The whole Court is waiting for you to make your declaration known.'

Trevowan turned aside and drummed his fingers on the desk, unwilling to discuss even with Meraud the strange emotions Alynna aroused in him.

'Is it because you are undecided upon Lady Celia as a bride that you have become so withdrawn?' Meraud said sympathetically. 'It is time you were wed, Dickon. Now that Mother is dead, and I am soon to leave for Sir John's estate, you will need a wife to supervise the running of your houses.'

Trevowan's fingers stilled, and he stared unseeing at the parchments spread out before him. Since his return from France, he was uncomfortably aware that, despite all his wealth and power, something was lacking in his life. After his former betrothed, chosen by his father when he was still an infant, had died of the pesitilence six months before their wedding, he had been content to let the years run by without binding himself to another. 'Time enough for me to chose a bride once you are married,' he answered dismissively.

'Trevowan needs an heir.' Meraud would not be halted. 'It was Mother's wish to see you married and, hopefully a child conceived, before King Henry returned to France and war. You neglect your duty.'

'I am aware of my duty.' He eyed his sister sternly.

'I would see you happy, Dickon. Could Lady Alynna have anything to do with your indecision to choose a bride? She is beautiful, intelligent and spirited.'

His answering glower brought a shadow into his sister's black eyes. 'Lady Celia is the obvious choice as future Countess of Trevowan.' Meraud resumed her probing, undaunted. 'She will bring land, riches and power to our name—but would she bring you happiness? Having given me the chance to marry for love, do not deny yourself out of misplaced duty, dear bother.'

Exasperated, without knowing why, he took his sister's arm and led her to the door. 'The excitement of your own wedding has turned your wits! I shall marry when I choose—and whom I choose—for the good of the earldom and myself.'

He escorted Meraud to rejoin their guests, but made his excuses to the revellers, intending to visit the stables where an Arab mare had recently foaled. As he walked across the courtyard, the question of his marriage hung like a black canopy over him, his reluctance to think about it growing with each day. He had been fortunate in keeping his freedom for so long, but within the year he was resigned to marrying. Lady Celia, daughter of a duke and co-heiress to her father's estate, was an admirable match. He had enjoyed her company at Court. Why, then, did he feel no joy at the prospect of wedding her? Although she was pleasing enough to the eye, and possessed some measure of spirit and wit of her own, she was an insipid creature compared with the fire he was used to in Meraud and had glimpsed in Alynna. Yet he had been content enough with the idea before his pilgrimage.

If only Lady Celia were more like Alynna. He pulled his thoughts up sharply. What the devil was the matter with him? If he married Lady Celia, his income would double from the land and manors offered in her dowry. For what other reason would he marry? Certainly not because he was attracted to an indomitable free spirit, or a mystery surrounding a beautiful woman. Compressing his lips grimly, he resolved to defer his decision about a bride until after the Christmas celebrations.

Each of the lengthy banquets during the next twelve days became torture for Alynna. She was constantly in Trevowan's company, but the coolness in their relationship was markedly changed so that they were like strangers. Sometimes it seemed that she had dreamt those tender moments between them. She had lost her heart . . . but for him, had it been no more than a diversion? Now, as she heard the guests gasp in wonder at the performance of a fire-eater, the muscles of her face ached from the strain of forcing a smile. To cover her pain at Trevowan's indifference, she turned to Sir Edmund, who was shyly trying to draw her into conversation.

'Your pardon, sir,' she said, gathering her thoughts. 'The fire-eater quite held me enthralled. What were you saying?'

'That you look sad, Lady Alynna.' A flood of pink stained his pale cheeks. 'I fear I am poor company . . . I would wish to . . . more than anything to . . .' He broke off with embarrassment.

'It is I who am poor company, Sir Edmund,' she reassured him. She was aware that he was attracted to her, and although he battled against shyness, when he relaxed in her company he was witty and amusing. 'I cannot help remembering other Christmases when my father . . .'

At the far end of the table, Lady Joan's shrill laughter set Alynna's nerves jangling. Sir Geoffrey was leaning towards her attentively as on so many occasions during the feasting, and she felt a prick of disgust at the idea that Lady Joan might already be the knight's mistress. Clearly her stepmother had recovered from the shock of

Sir Robert's death. Alynna bit her lip, and her hand was hesitantly covered by Sir Edmund's.

'I understand what you must be feeling. I admire you above all women, Lady Alynna.' He withdrew his hand quickly, unable to hold her gaze.

She looked up and saw Trevowan watching them, but although his grey eyes seemed to impale her with their intensity, his expression was inscrutable. Her heart contracted painfully, but determined that none would guess her heartbreak, she sat back in her chair, her eyes misting as she stared ahead at the mummers now enacting the story of St George killing the dragon. When the Lord of Misrule leapt unceremoniously on to the dais, she forced herself to push aside her unhappiness, knowing that the sharp-eyed Master of Merry Disports would be quick to seize upon any sign of weakness and bring it to the attention of all present.

'It is time for our master and his guests to entertain us,' he cried. 'Clear the centre of the Hall. Make way for his lordship!'

Trevowan graciously rose, obeying the orders of the Lord of Misrule, as custom demanded. The servants and retainers cheered as he nodded for the younger guests, pages, squires and young waiting-women to join him. Only Lady Isabeau and Lady Joan were to be excluded from the boisterous games demanded by the Lord of Misrule. There was a burst of cheering and laughter as Sir Edmund and Alynna took their places. Looking up, she saw with embarrassment that they were standing beneath the kissing bush.

'A kiss! A kiss!' demanded the Lord of Misrule, his chant echoed by the servants at the trestle tables.

Dutifully she turned her face towards Sir Edmund, and his hot lips skimmed across her mouth.

'For shame on you, sir,' Griswolde chuckled from behind them. 'That's no way to kiss a beautiful woman.'

His arm slid about Alynna's waist, and she was swung round to meet the devilment in his eyes. Her protest was stifled by his lips swooping down upon hers, moist and masterly, but with none of the magic

Trevowan's kisses had evoked in her. When, instead of releasing her, his kiss deepened to seek a response, she stiffened and pulled back from him, angry at the liberty.

'Such fire, my dear, and such promise of passion,' he whispered, refusing to release her. 'My heart is yours, fair Alynna.'

Her cheeks burned with colour, and with an outraged gasp, she pushed him away as Sir Edmund stepped forward.

'You have insulted Lady Alynna,' he raged, his shyness and awkwardness disappearing. 'You will ask her forgiveness, sir.'

'Nonsense, man!' Griswolde was unrepentent. 'Lady Alynna took no offence. 'Tis Christmas. It was but harmless fun.'

The colour drained from Alynna's cheeks as the two men stood tense and hostile, their hands flexing in readiness for a fight. From the corner of her eye she saw Trevowan start towards them.

'Enough, Griswolde!' he snapped. 'You will show Lady Alynna due respect.'

'My lord,' Alynna broke in, 'I believe Sir Geoffrey has partaken too much of your excellent wine. He was caught up in the revelry of the moment. Has he not kissed all the serving-maids beneath the mistletoe already?' She attempted to make light of the situation and avoid a scene, but the look of scorn she received from Trevowan thrust like a halberd through her heart. He thought she was encouraging Griswolde! Her anger flared, and turning away, her fury deepened at seeing Lady Joan's narrowed glare upon Sir Geoffrey. Alynna knew that look only too well—Lady Joan was jealous! So her stepmother did see Sir Geoffrey as a future husband!

Unconcerned by the growing tension all round him, Griswolde raised a mocking brow. 'Perhaps my noble cousin wishes *he* had stolen that kiss?' he jeered. 'Or, mayhap, he has already tasted the sweet nectar of her lips.'

For an instant Trevowan's eyes were glacial, and Griswolde hastily took a step back.

'Not that for a moment I doubt your honour, coz,' he blustered. 'Nor the virtue of Lady Alynna.'

'Take care you do not, Griswolde!' Lord Trevowan threatened in an undertone.

Alynna's anger withered, to be replaced by anguish. It was his own honour as much as hers that Trevowan defended. She schooled her face to a serene mask, painfully aware of all eyes upon them: Lady Isabeau's sharp with interest, while Griswolde's stare was again bold and appraising. To her relief, Meraud's steady gaze carried no judgement, and she moved to her brother's side, her smile taunting.

'My lord brother, must you and Geoffrey always be at each other's throats? You know very well our cousin cannot resist a pretty face.' Meraud cast a speculative look in Alynna's direction before continuing, 'Why, Dickon, since you returned from Trevowan Castle, you have been as out of temper as a baited bear!'

Lord Trevowan bowed mockingly to his sister, his expression less harsh when he turned to face Sir Geoffrey. 'Lady Alynna is a young noblewoman under my protection. You would do well, cousin, to curb your weakness where a pretty face is concerned.'

The Lord of Misrule clapped his hands, and gestured for a page to bring forth a large mask shaped into a wolf's head.

'We shall spare Lady Alynna's blushes,' he quipped, presenting the mask to her. 'My lady, if you will put this on?' He turned away from her, calling out, 'Form a circle for Hoodman Blind. Musicians—a lively tune, if you please.'

A piper trilled a jaunty chorus, to be joined by tabor and lute, as Alynna placed the rather heavy mask over her head. It smelt musty, and the sudden blackness was disconcerting. Her shoulders were gripped and she was spun round three times. She could dimly hear the others circling her, and when a hand touched her shoulder, she whirled round, arms outstretched, but snatched at air as

Meraud's laughter drifted to her. Twice, other hands touched her, and she guessed a bolder one upon her hip was Griswolde's, but he, too, eluded her grasp. Then all at once a tingling awareness heated her body, and unaccountably she knew Trevowan was directly in front of her. Before even his hand touched her arm, she instinctively reached out and caught his sleeve. Cheers and laughter filled the hall, and suddenly she went cold with dread. Had she given herself away?

'Name your captive!' the Lord of Misrule demanded.

Her fingers trembled as they rested on the soft velvet of his sleeve. It was so long since they had been so close that she could not resist prolonging the moment. Slowly her hand moved up and sideways, feeling the strong rhythmic beat of his heart, and then, as her fingers moved on their way, the warmth of his freshly shaven cheek as she traced the line of his jaw. The rigid muscles under her touch almost unnerved her, and although her heart cried out to speak his name, she knew the others were watching—and possibly speculating on what might have passed between Lord Trevowan and herself during the pilgrimage.

'Sir Edmund!' she proclaimed.

A roar of laughter greeted her supposed mistake, but before she drew her hand away, she felt a muscle leap into life along Trevowan's cheek. The mask was lifted from her head, and the Lord of Misrule capered in front of them. His eyes alight with mischief, he appealed to those seated at the tables for advice.

'Lady Alynna does not know her own liege lord. What penance must she pay?'

'His lordship had best show Lady Alynna who is master here,' one of Trevowan's captains said, with a ribald laugh.

'And how will that be done?' the Lord of Misrule demanded.

'As any man shows a woman who is her master,' another soldier chuckled coarsely.

Alynna's throat dried as she caught a brittle gleam in Trevowan's eyes. He stepped towards her, forcing her to arch back her head to meet his challenging glare. When his arms pulled her against him, they were like clamps, hard and unyielding. His mouth grazed hers in a hot searing kiss that held no tenderness.

Keeping her lips tightly closed beneath his punishing assault, she clenched her hands against his chest, feeling his anger in the tense hardness of the muscles beneath her fingers. He was kissing her as though it was a penance he must perform and she a demon to be exorcised. When he abruptly released her, his eyes glittered with a light that told her more clearly than words that anything between them was over.

CHAPTER ELEVEN

THE NEXT few hours stretched Alynna's taut nerves unbearably. Unable to escape the revelries, she strove to present a carefree face to the Hall, but her heart felt as though it were being ground to dust. Griswolde found a stream of excuses to pass her chair, and he was at pains to make amends for his earlier conduct. The sharpness of his wit was such that she could not occasionally help laughing at his jests, but unfortunately he lost no opportunity to deride Sir Edmund, and the tension between the two knights heightened, until they were as antagonistic as fighting-cocks.

Alynna's heart lurched upon encountering the cutting glare of Lord Trevowan at the two knights vying for her attention. He blamed her for the growing hostility between them, yet she had taken pains not to encourage either.

When they all joined hands and slowly circled the hall to sing Christmas songs, Meraud, who was next to her, leaned closer to her to make herself heard above the chorus of the song.

'You look pale, Alynna. I fear I have neglected you these past days and have spent too much time in Sir John's company.'

'That is how it should be, since you are to be married in three days.'

'Yet you are not happy.' Meraud continued to frown. 'Have you and my brother quarrelled? He used to be relaxed in your company—now I think you avoid each other.'

The song came to an end, and Sir Geoffrey picked up a lute, the plucking cadences ornamenting his rich voice in a love song. Meraud's dark eyes sparkled with an impish light.

'Or is it my irrepressible cousin who has captured your

heart?' she teased. 'Sir Geoffrey seeks your company
often, especially if Lady Joan is not present. Take care
you do not give your heart lightly. Sir Geoffrey's conquests are legion! Now for a suitor who is worthy of you,
Sir Edmund would be . . .'

Alynna shook her head, swallowing against the pain
Meraud's words caused. 'I shall not marry!' She spoke
more sharply than she intended, deepening Meraud's
frown.

Meraud drew her into a quiet corner. 'It is Richard
you care for?' she said quietly. 'Oh, my dear friend, I am
so sorry. You know it can never be.'

'Yes, I know,' she said brokenly. 'Is it so obvious?'

'No, you have hidden it well. But Dickon, does
he . . . ?'

Alynna lifted her agonised gaze, silently beseeching
Meraud to say no more. They both looked to where
Trevowan was leaning against the wall, his arms folded
across his chest as he listened to Griswolde's singing.
The words of the song were passionate, and Alynna
blushed to discover that the singer was looking straight
at her. Abruptly Trevowan thrust himself from the
wall and strode to the dais, his expression dark and
forbidding.

An impish light sparkled in Meraud's eyes. 'So that is
the way of things! Richard dislikes the attention
Sir Geoffrey pays you. It seems you have dented the
armour which has for so long shielded my brother's
emotions.

Alynna shook her head. 'During the pilgrimage, I
thought there was a bond between us—not merely that
he had rescued me from the ferryman, but that there was
an affinity between two pilgrims. Of course, that was
before I learned who he was.'

'As the king's ward and under his protection, Richard
would have placed you out of reach,' Meraud emphasised. 'That does not mean he is impervious to your
charms—far from it.'

'It only makes it harder. I was raised no differently
from you with regard to honour and family position. My

father believed that honour was more important than happiness.'

'But if Richard loved you . . . ?'

'No, Meraud.' Alynna turned her head away, the bombardment of questions becoming too painful to discuss. 'I shall not listen to you.'

Meraud squeezed her hand, and added, 'Let me help you, my friend. You have your ghosts, which need exorcising as much as did mine. By making me face the reality that I was not to blame for the degradation to which the mercenaries submitted me, you saved my sanity and faith in humankind.'

'It was your strength of character which triumphed over adversity,' Alynna answered honestly. 'Lord Trevowan told me that you were a fighter. You healed yourself by coming to terms with your life.'

Meraud looked at her sharply. 'You, too, are a fighter. I would be a poor friend if I did less for you.'

'In this you can do nothing.' Alynna was emphatic. 'I cannot change my lowly status. No more can I bring shame upon my father's name and all he believed honourable, than I could bring trouble down on Lord Trevowan's head. Even his friendship with the king would not spare his Majesty's wrath should we become lovers. I am still the king's ward.'

'Then, to find happiness, you must come to terms with your life. As you made me come to terms with mine,' Meraud said with gentle insistence. 'I can guess something of what must have passed between you, but Richard will never forsake your cause. He does not trust Lady Joan, and will certainly speak to the king.'

Alynna nodded, too choked to speak, and scarcely noticed that Sir Geoffrey's song had come to an end. At that moment her dowry meant little to her, but it would be the means of starting a fresh life—a life where Lord Trevowan had no part.

'Sir Geoffrey comes this way,' Meraud went on more soberly. 'For all my cousin is charming and witty, he is ambitious and motivated by self-interest. Take care in your dealings with him. He is a delightful companion, but if thwarted, his temper can be terrifying.'

Sir John Holcombe claimed Meraud's attention and whisked her away, as Sir Geoffrey bowed to Alynna.

'Am I forgiven for stealing that kiss beneath the kissing bush, dear lady? In truth, I could not resist.'

'You were over bold, Sir Geoffrey,' she remonstrated, 'and it was wrong to taunt Sir Edmund as you did.'

He placed his hand over his heart, his eyes glowing with admiration, and despite Meraud's warning, Alynna found his attention soothing her pain. 'You are the fairest of all women, and I but a man, bedazzled by such beauty. I meant no disrespect, dear lady.'

'Then the matter is best forgotten, Sir Geoffrey.'

'Perhaps it was not I, but another, who has earned your displeasure. Trevowan did not seem amused when you failed to recognise him when we played Hoodman Blind—or did you?' Sir Geoffrey said with warm friendliness, but there was something about the narrowing of his eyes that warned her he was gently probing as to what lay behind Trevowan's change of manner towards her.

'I dare say you pricked his cursed pride,' he went on, when she refused to rise to his bait.

'I do not judge Lord Trevowan,' she countered stiffly. 'He offered me his protection, when many another in his position would just have tossed me a coin and thought their conscience well served. I am accorded every respect.'

'I envy Trevowan the loyalty you show him.' His eyes flashed boldly, making no secret of his admiration. 'Would that I were so fortunate as to be the champion of your cause!'

'I had thought it was Lady Joan's cause you were interested in,' she challenged, looking pointedly to where she was sitting at the high table. Even from this distance she could feel her stepmother's malice in the fixed gaze she turned upon Sir Geoffrey and herself. 'You escorted her here, and have been in attendance on her ever since.'

'Only because, as she persuaded me to bring her here,

Trevowan ordered me to keep her entertained.' His exasperation was obvious, and at the regret darkening his eyes, Alynna found the last of her antagonism towards him melting. Her arm was gripped possessively and he murmured in a husky tone, 'You must know that I hold you in the highest esteem.'

She shrugged his fingers from her sleeve, unwilling for him to misinterpret her feelings, and spoke sternly. 'You forget yourself, Sir Geoffrey.'

He smiled cynically. 'Trevowan has set you against me. I admit, to my shame, that until now my life has been spent in idle pursuits. Those days are over and done with.'

At his downcast expression, it was impossible to take seriously Trevowan's and Meraud's warnings. Surely she was not in any danger from this man? There was something of a lost boy in his angelic countenance, which was disarming, and although she suspected that he was aware of this and ruthlessly used it to his advantage, she did not see him as a threat.

Against her will, her gaze was drawn to the centre of the dais. Lord Trevowan was lounging back in his chair, drinking deeply from a goblet. Disparagingly his glance flickered over Griswolde and herself, causing her pain to gnaw deeper. At that moment a cheer went up from the end of the Hall, and eagerly seeking a diversion from his piercing glare, she watched a procession enter carrying a small tree in a tub.

'We must return to the dais,' she urged, unwilling to bring Lord Trevowan's further censure upon them. 'It is time for the wassailing of the fruit-tree that will ensure a goodly harvest next year. Already the pages are pouring the cider for the toast.'

'Should you have need of me, Lady Alynna, I am yours to command,' Sir Geoffrey said, walking at her side to their places on the dais.

For some time she did not trust herself to look in Lord Trevowan's direction, and fixed her stare upon the revellers. Their antics dispelled some of her unease at the building tension that had settled over the company since Lady Joan's arrival. In three days Meraud would be married. Then her own duty would be at an end.

At last Lord Trevowan rose from his chair, an indication that the celebrations were over for this day. Wearily, Alynna made her way to her chamber, her heart sinking as she saw the stout figure of Lady Joan waiting outside her room.

'I can see through your sordid schemes, Mistress Alynna Freston,' she hissed, following her into her chamber.

When the door was closed behind them, Alynna rounded on her stepmother. 'As I have seen through yours! You are here at Thornbank because you think you can gain from it, and because you fear imprisonment for your treatment of me.'

At the sound of their voices, Hester appeared from the bedchamber, but on seeing Lady Joan, she drew back nervously. Since Lady Joan had on several occasions mocked the maid's deformity, Alynna gestured for Hester to leave them.

Lady Joan sniffed disdainfully. 'For all your grand friends, I am your guardian. After the wedding, we return to Barkhurst, and in the meantime you will keep away from Sir Geoffrey.'

Alynna drew herself up, taking a moment to calm the indignation sweeping through her. 'I have no interest in Sir Geoffrey Griswolde! However, your intentions are all too obvious—and you supposedly a grieving widow!'

'I loved your father,' Lady Joan cried, but Alynna felt no pity for her. For too many years this woman's spite and jealousy had made her father's life a misery. 'Sir Robert scorned me. He married me only because he was ordered to by the king.'

Alynna frowned, the mystery of her birth returning to plague her. 'Why should the late king have taken such interest in a lowly knight? And I do not understand why I am his Majesty's ward . . . And what of my dowry? You lied about that! Did you also lie about my mother? Who was she?'

'She was a whore!'

'I do not believe that!' Alynna flared. 'She was a noblewoman.'

'I suppose that interfering jester told you so,' Lady Joan scoffed. 'He would say anything to ingratiate himself with you. I tell you that your mother was a whore! Why do you suppose Sir Robert never told you the truth? It was because he was ashamed of his conduct.'

'That is a lie!' Alynna sprang forward, gripping her stepmother's arm as her rage washed over her. 'I realise, now, that he loved my mother all his life. If he did not speak her name, it was to protect her!'

There was a blur of white before Alynna's eyes, and she reeled under the impact of her stepmother's slap. Hester ran from the bedchamber to her side, and as Alynna straightened, she tasted blood where Lady Joan's ring had caught the side of her mouth.

Lady Joan paused by the door, her lips curling into a sneer. 'If you are so clever—find out the whore's name! I shall never tell!' Her cruel glance settled upon Hester. 'How quickly the scarred cripple comes to your aid. A recanted Lollard, isn't she? A dangerous companion.'

'Hester, too, is under Lord Trevowan's protection,' Alynna declared. 'She is no Lollard now. Take care of what you speak!'

'From what I have seen, Lord Trevowan seems to have lost interest in your cause. He scarcely notices your presence. I warn you . . . Stay away from Sir Geoffrey, or you will regret it!'

'I am not afeared of you,' Alynna stressed. 'You have already done your best to be rid of me, and failed.'

'My dear child,' Lady Joan ground out sarcastically, 'I have not even begun!'

'Then you are a fool, Lady Joan. Lord Trevowan knows that you sent the ferryman after me. If you try to harm me again, he will have you clapped in irons.'

'First, your noble protector will have to prove I was involved! The ferryman was a mistake. Next time . . . !' Her words merged into a brittle laugh as she slammed out of the room.

*　　*　　*

On the morning of Meraud's wedding, Alynna rose early. She had been disturbed at dawn by Hester crying out in her sleep, and after comforting her, she had been uneasy and restless. Although she had dismissed Lady Joan's threat, Hester had remained troubled and her nightmares had become more frequent.

When she returned from morning prayers, Alynna ordered a bath for herself, but the heated, perfumed water did little to soothe her agony of mind. Lord Trevowan, as Lady Joan had taunted her, scarcely seemed to notice her existence. Since Twelfth Night, he had joined his guests only at mealtimes and spent long hours closeted with his estate officers. And yet she loved Richard Dreux . . . It was her misfortune that he was also the Earl of Trevowan, and so forever denied to her.

She schooled herself not to fidget while Hester braided her hair and pinned the veil over her high jewelled headdress. At last satisfied, Hester stepped back, beaming.

'Oh, my lady, you look lovely! A man's heart would have to be carved from ice not to be moved by your beauty this day.'

'I begin to suspect that his is!' she said quietly, but Hester caught her words, and frowned.

'You wrong his lordship! I have seen him looking at you when he believes himself unobserved. He is troubled—sometimes angry—but with himself, not with you.'

Alynna shook her head. 'I once thought there was some bond between us that was special—but it was no more than the foolish notion of an inexperienced maiden.'

She stood up and smoothed the pearl-encrusted bodice of her blue velvet surcoat, its sleeveless sides cut away to show the close-fitting saffron kirtle beneath. It was the finest of all the surcoats Trevowan had ordered for her at Canterbury, and until now she had not worn it, wishing to save it for Meraud's wedding. She smothered a sigh, recalling the tender moments during

the pilgrimage, and forced a practical note to her voice
to hide her torment. 'It is time we went to the chapel.'

The chapel was already crowded with servants and
retainers, and Alynna took her place at the front, where
spaces were reserved for Lord Trevowan's guests. There
was a stirring behind her. From the prickling of awareness down her spine she knew, without turning, that
Lord Trevowan was escorting his sister to stand at Sir
John's side.

When the chaplain began to intone a prayer, Lord
Trevowan stepped back a pace into the full light of the
candles. Alynna's heart stirred at the handsome sight he
presented. His doublet was wine red, and across his
shoulders hung a heavy gold chain from which hung his
lion device. His hair had been trimmed, the candles
highlighting the glossy black locks with a bluish sheen. A
wave of longing consumed her, and she dragged her eyes
away, not daring to look at him again.

The ceremony was brief, and throughout the banquet
and entertainment which followed, the sound of
Meraud's laughter was infectious, so that even over her
heartache Alynna felt the glow of her friend's happiness.
For Meraud's sake she was determined to enjoy her last
day at Thornbank. Several toasts were drunk to the
newly-married couple, and when Alynna stood up to
accompany Sir Edmund in a dance, she giggled, a little
shocked that the wine had made her light-headed and
rather reckless. Dance followed dance, her partners
alternating between Sir Edmund and Sir Geoffrey, and
once she danced with Sir John. Suddenly her partner
stiffened, and Lord Trevowan stood before them, the
steely glint of his eyes silencing her laughter.

He bowed to Alynna and held out his arm to lead her
back on the floor as the musicians struck up a stately
measure. To her dismay, she saw that the centre of the
hall was empty of dancers, as it had been earlier when he
had partnered Meraud. She realised that all eyes would
be upon them. He bowed—she curtsied—then their
hands linked as he led her forward and back. For such a
tall man, his step was light and graceful, and if it was not

for the frantic, almost smothering, beat of her heart, she could have fully enjoyed the pleasure of his touch and attention. The dance took them away from each other, and back again, before he spoke in a low voice.

'Am I such a dull fellow compared with Griswolde?' His piercing stare mocked her. 'You have been avoiding me these last days.'

His words astonished her, but aware of the glances turned upon them, she kept her expression blank. 'I have always enjoyed your company, my lord. You have other, more important, guests than I with whom to occupy your time.'

'So you deliberately chose not to heed my warning concerning my cousin?'

The dance took her beneath his upraised arm, and his lips curved back in a grim smile which did not reach his eyes. He was furious with her, not because he cared—as she had so foolishly begun to hope—but because she had defied him. Her eyes blazed. 'I choose my friends where I will, my lord!'

'And a strange band of strolling players they appear to be: a jester; a cripple, who could have us all condemned for favouring a Lollard; and an unscrupulous—not to say handsome—knight.'

'I once believed a humble pilgrim to be my friend,' she retorted, her voice as low and scathing as his. 'He, too, was not what he seemed.'

The whitening of the lines about his eyes showed her that her barb had hit its mark. 'You sound as though your pilgrim has proved a disappointment to you.'

She felt as though she was walking on quicksands. 'He proved to be other than he seemed, my lord.'

There was a disturbance from the back of the Hall, and as the dance took them in that direction, Lord Trevowan looked sharply at the travel-stained new-comer. The man shrugged off his cloak to reveal the king's livery. Trevowan halted, and the musicians ended on a discordant note. He excused himself to Alynna, and beckoning to his squire to follow, led the messenger out.

Alynna walked back to the dais, deep in thought, trying to fathom the train of Trevowan's questions. Absently she noted that her stepmother and Lady Isabeau had left the banquet. At least she would be spared one of Lady Joan's venomous comments on the abrupt manner in which Lord Trevowan had left her side. At that moment Sir Geoffrey, his countenance flushed, halted as he recognised Alynna.

'Has your partner deserted you so soon?' he commented. 'Forgive my cousin his rough manners. He is a soldier—not a gallant, though his valour at Agincourt and his skill in the joust has always made him the darling of the Court ladies.'

The jibe was deliberate, and despite her resolution to harden herself against Lord Trevowan, a sharp stab of jealousy contracted her heart. 'It was a messenger from the king,' she replied defensively. 'It must be important.'

'What could be more important than dancing with the most beautiful woman at Thornbank?' Sir Geoffrey favoured her with a winning smile. 'But I suppose even Trevowan must jump when his Majesty snaps his fingers. If Trevowan is too occupied with other matters—his forthcoming marriage to Lady Celia for instance— to take up your cause with his Majesty, I would be honoured to do so.'

For a moment the flickering torchlight dimmed before Alynna's eyes. She drew a steadying breath. Again his words had been deliberately baited, and although she knew she would betray something of her hidden emotions, nothing could stop the question tumbling out. 'Is Lord Trevowan to wed soon?'

Sir Geoffrey appeared not to notice the strained note in her voice. He shrugged. 'It is one of the reasons he must return to London. Although nothing has been announced—the duke, Lady Celia's father, grows impatient for the match.'

'Lady Celia would be an excellent choice for his lordship.' Alynna forced out through stiffened lips, praying that none of her pain showed in her voice.

'Indeed, there is no bride more worthy to bear the title of Countess of Trevowan,' Sir Geoffrey confirmed.

At that moment Hester appeared, clearing her throat nervously when Sir Geoffrey frowned impatiently at her. 'My lady, Lord Trevowan bids you attend him.'

'Ah! Perhaps my noble cousin is not so immune to your delectable charms as he would have us all believe,' he taunted.

Alynna cursed the blush stinging her cheeks, and subjected him to a freezing glare. Excusing herself, she followed Hester through the narrow corridors leading to the first floor, where she knew Trevowan had his rooms. She could not imagine why she had been summoned, but it would be a good opportunity to state her wish to leave Thornbank. At all costs, she must keep control of her wayward emotions!

When Hester stood aside for her to enter the chamber, her resolution almost crumbled. Trevowan stood by the fireplace, a hand resting on the lion's head of his device carved on the marble canopy, and one leg bent, his foot resting on the fire-dog as he stared down into the flames. The firelight threw the proud lines of his aquiline nose into relief, and there was a leashed power in his tall frame which caused her stomach to knot in apprehension. He seemed unaware of her presence, then his knuckles whitened. When he turned and saw Hester standing by the door, he barked out that she should wait outside. At the sharpness of his command, the puckered flesh of her scarred cheek became vivid purple against the draining pallor of her face, and she turned and fled.

'Did you have to scare Hester out of her wits?' Alynna flared, resorting to bravado to cover her own quaking, and quite forgetting the reverence due to the Earl of Trevowan.

'Guard your tongue, lady,' he warned, pacing the room in long strides. 'You forget to whom you speak.'

Alynna's head tilted defiantly. 'Your pardon, my lord,' she said coolly, causing his scowl to deepen.

He stopped to loom above her, his eyes brilliant with

rage. 'The king commands me to return to Court,' he said tersely. 'As for yourself, his Majesty . . .' He broke off angrily, twisting the ring on his finger for some moments. The look he shot her was bleak and condemning. 'Why did you ignore my warning?' he rasped, unexpectedly turning the subject. 'You have deliberately encouraged Griswolde's attentions. I had not thought you a heartless tease, but apparently I was wrong. You seem to delight in playing Sir Geoffrey off against Sir Edmund.'

The injustice of his words stung her. 'I have done nothing of the kind! I have accorded both no more than the politeness I would show to any of your guests, my lord.'

'That was not the impression I gained when Griswolde kissed you,' he retorted. 'How many times has he won such favour from you—or more?'

'How dare you accuse me of encouraging him, or that I would allow . . .' Her voice cracked with the force of her fury. She hated herself for the way the heat was rising from her neck to her face.

His gaze fastened upon her bodice, strained tightly across her rapidly rising and falling breasts as she fought to overcome her anger at his accusation. 'I know exactly what you are prepared to allow, lady!' his tone was insulting. 'While you remain under my protection, you will curb your wanton conduct.'

The words stabbed like an icicle through her heart, and she took an involuntary step back from him, only to find her wrist gripped as he jerked her hard against him. Her eyes widened as she caught the smell of wine upon his breath, but he was not drunk. He was deadly sober, and the more dangerous for that! There was a stubborn set to his jaw that warned her he would not listen to her pleas of innocence. Because she had responded so fervently to his kisses that night when he had come to her room, he believed her a wanton. Her pride rebelled. She would make no excuses for her conduct that night. How could she tell him she loved him, when he so clearly now despised her?

'I will burden you no longer with my presence. I shall leave Thornbank. Meraud is quite recovered and has no further need of me. Our debts are settled. You need trouble yourself no further as to my future, Lord Trevowan.'

'I never go back on my word!' he said savagely.

Undaunted by the glittering anger in his eyes, she regarded him steadily, her voice equally cutting, 'Then I release you from it!'

'I suppose Griswolde has offered you his help? You two are well suited! You will remain here, and will act with the discretion that becomes your rank.'

'What rank is that, my lord?' she bit out, too hurt to care what she was saying. 'As the daughter of Sir Robert Freston, or as some unknown whore's by-blow? What is the saying . . . As mother—like daughter?'

She turned away, angrily wiping at the angry tears scalding her eyes. Trevowan cut short a violent oath and caught her chin between his fingers, turning her round to meet his simmering gaze. She could feel the tension coiling within him. There was a tautness to the skin over the angular planes of his face, and the fine lines at the outer corners of his eyes were starkly etched, as they had been when she had first seen him on the pilgrimage. However he might try to hide it, he was troubled, and her presence at Thornbank, especially since the arrival of Lady Joan, must be adding to the burden of his responsibilities. Then, as though reading her thoughts, some of the bleakness left his eyes.

'Always the fire-cat, and double so when your pride has been hurt!' His lips twitched as though in amusement.

The gesture was such a poignant reminder of the way he so often looked at her during their time together on the road that she caught her breath. Her throat dried as he continued to gaze down at her, and she ran her tongue over her lips. Neither moved, or spoke, and for a breath-robbing moment she believed he was going to kiss her, then his long lashes shielded his eyes and he let her go.

'Do you care for Sir Geoffrey?' he asked gruffly.

'In what way, my lord?' she evaded, unsure of his line of questioning. He still stood very close to her, bedevilling her thoughts by his nearness. She pulled herself together with an effort. 'Sir Geoffrey is witty and charming . . .' The words were forced out from her arid throat. 'He takes pains to cheer me . . . when the pain of my grief for my father is sometimes more than I can bear.'

When her voice faltered, Trevowan rubbed his hand over his jaw, and his brows drew thunderously together. 'That was not what I asked you!'

She swallowed painfully. Why was he putting her through this torture? He did not want her for himself, and was treating her as though she was a felon! She would not be judged by him. 'I am not answerable to you, Lord Trevowan. Nor would I presume to question you regarding Lady Celia.'

His head shot up, and his hands dropped to the jewelled belt about his slim hips as he regarded her sardonically. 'What has Lady Celia to do with this?'

At the coldness of his tone, she turned her gaze from him to the fire, her voice splintering with suppressed emotion. 'Your pardon, my lord. I was impertinent.'

Trevowan put up a hand to touch her shoulder, and hesitated. The message from the king had been terse. Clearly his Majesty was still displeased with him, but the fact that it had been written in Henry's own hand was encouraging.

'The king has accepted your wardship and made his wishes known to me.' He fought down his returning anger at the orders he had received.

'Am I to go to London?' she said without turning, a strange catch to her voice.

'No. His Majesty is considering sending you to a convent on the Welsh borders.'

Her throat worked convulsively, but the expected refusal did not come. Instead, she lowered her head, and entwining her fingers, she brought them to her lips in a fierce gesture to master her shock. Her silence disturbed him more than her anger. His hand moved of its own volition to her shoulder, feeling the trembling that shook her body.

Suddenly he knew he could not condemn her to be shut away in a convent for the rest of her life, and his curiosity surrounding her birth intensified. He strongly suspected her to be the child of a royal duke, but such offspring were not usually hidden away. But, then, who knew King Henry's mind of late? His Majesty was becoming increasingly pious and bigoted. Trevowan turned Alynna to face him. Once he knew the truth of her birth, he could do more to help her. If only there had been further word from Joel!

'I shall speak to the king myself. Convent life is not for you.'

'What other choice is there?' she answered hollowly, and when she refused to meet his stare, he sensed a deep torment eating away at her. 'I am an embarrassment to his Majesty.'

It was not just the prospect of virtual imprisonment in a convent that had quenched the spirit he so admired. Something else troubled her. Did she care for Griswolde? She deserved better than that scoundrel! He studied her pale heartshaped face, and somehow his hands slid beneath her veil to touch the warm skin above the scooped neckline of her surcoat. A light seductive perfume wafted over him from her body, causing a fever to rage through his blood. What was Griswolde to her? The thought that she might prefer that posturing peacock . . .

'Is it Griswolde you want?' he demanded huskily.

Stricken, Alynna stared into his smouldering gaze. 'I want Griswolde even less than the prospect of life in a convent.'

After a long moment a smile tilted his lips, making her heart pound wildly. His fingers moved in slow circles upon her bare skin, and the seductive play of the firelight softened the angular lines of his rugged face, shattering her fragile guard. His arms tightened, pressing her against him as his mouth hovered tantalisingly above her own. She knew she should pull free, but her limbs had no strength against the entrancing force of his will. Feather-like, his lips brushed hers, then more hungrily, and he kissed her with measured thoroughness until her senses spiralled chaotically, her belated protest drowned by a wave of excitement. With a supreme effort she forced it down. She must not surrender! But her lips were besieged with masterly skill, and reason fled. He kissed her with leisurely delight, savouring the sweetness of each lingering moment. She closed her eyes, tasting the faint tang of wine on his breath, and breathing in the musky masculine scent of him. The searing persuasion of his lips rekindled a yearning that seemed incapable of quenching or denying. He wanted her. All sense of propriety was vanquished by the need for this moment to last for eternity. Ardently she responded to his passion, her arms winding about his neck as she bound him closer.

She gasped when his hand caught in her veil, inadvertently tugging at the pins securing her headdress. His mouth remained firm and insistent upon her own, as with a dexterity and gentleness, the envy of any tiring-woman, he drew the pins from the jewelled headdress and lifted it from her head. Then his hands were releasing the pins holding her braided hair. When its weight tumbled about her shoulders, she threw back her head, shaking it to loosen the restraining plaits. The gesture had been instinctive, but seeing the growing hunger in his eyes, she was startled and pleased that her impulse had such an effect.

He buried his head in the dark coppery tresses, murmuring huskily against her ear, 'Dear heart, you cannot know the torment I have endured—wanting you . . . needing you!'

Then his mouth returned to hers, his tongue moving over her parted lips languidly to possess the softness within. She rose on tiptoe as his hand moved down to the hollow of her back, moulding her body to his, until they fused from chest to knee. Somehow, and she could not recall when, he had slipped the narrow shoulder-bands of her surcoat down over her arms. When his hand slid lower to cup her breast, she momentarily stiffened. Her hand covered his, intending to push it away, but his fingers, gently stroking the taut, tingling peak beneath the flimsy silk, caused a quaking to begin in the pit of her stomach, demanding surcease from the need building within her, and strangely she felt no shame.

A low moan of pleasure rose to her throat. She clung to him, her hands spreading across the flexing muscles of his back. Consumed by a primeval hunger, she guilelessly moved against him, wanting to feel the hardness of his body more completely against hers. The thickness of his doublet frustrated her. The need to feel the heat of his skin—to caress him as he caressed her—rose to a fever. Hesitantly at first, she began to unfasten the row of buttons down the front of his doublet. He drew in his breath sharply, his kisses becoming more urgent. When her hand moved over the silk of his shirt, feeling the exciting warmth and quickening beat of his heart, she experienced the thrill and wonder that her touch could bring such pleasure to another. He raised his head to gaze down at her.

'You are mine, Alynna,' he murmured hoarsely. 'No one, not even the king, will keep us apart.'

For a wondrous moment she clung to his declaration. His hands grew bolder, sliding beneath the low neckline of her kirtle to caress her naked breast, but when his lips touched her ear and, ever conscious of the devil's mark she bore, she flinched—sanity returned to mock her. She had been carried away—lured by the tender memories of the pilgrimage. Trevowan was a devil, luring her to damnation. In his arms she had forgotten her vow to uphold her father's honour. She pushed back from him, her hands shaking as she fumbled to adjust her surcoat. 'No, my lord! Not this way!'

Steel splinters flashed in his eyes, and incapable of holding his accusing gaze, she turned away to retrieve her headdress from the coffer where he had thrown it. 'The king will never allow . . .' Her voice broke at the narrowness of their escape from risking the king's wrath. She was the king's ward, and even the Earl of Trevowan could not seduce her with impunity.

Trevowan curbed his rising temper, unable to believe that she had refused him. Stiff and defiant, she picked up the butterfly headdress and held it close to her chest like a shield, the overbrightness of her eyes unexpectedly unnerving him.

'I want you, Alynna . . . as you want me.' He drew her back into his arms, his voice low and insistent. 'Dear heart, I am offering you freedom. The king will be displeased, but . . .'

Her body was stiff and unyielding to his touch, and he cursed the rigid headdress that stopped him gathering her close.

'I will not be the instrument of your downfall, my lord. Neither have I yet come to terms with my own changed status. The lessons my father instilled in me are too deeply ingrained. However misplaced my pride may be when I am no more than a . . . Sir Robert's by-blow, I was brought up to uphold honour above all things. It is not something you cast aside because fate has been cruel. And, to my shame, at times I still think of you as Richard the pilgrim.'

The words were torn from her heart, but that did not excuse her stubborness. Trevowan regarded her icily. Had she actually implied that it was the Earl of Trevowan she was rejecting, not Richard Dreux the pilgrim? That was absurd! What could the pilgrim give her that the earl could not? Nothing! Then insidiously a glimmer of understanding filtered through his anger.

'It is obvious that I cannot remain here.' Her soft voice pierced his angry thoughts. 'I shall leave on the morrow.'

'Is it from me, or yourself, you would run?' Keeping a firm grip on his slipping temper, he taunted her. 'I leave for London in two days. You will remain here until I receive orders from his Majesty.'

He folded his arms across his chest as he watched her twist her dark hair into a braid and start to push it beneath the frame of her headdress. Wanting her with an obsession which defied reason, he spun on his heel and marched from the room, no longer trusting himself

to remember that she was supposed to be under his
protection. His thoughts were bleak.

No one had defied him as Alynna had dared. He had
offered her a life of ease and comfort, and despite all that
had happened to her, she had chosen honour instead of
shame. He rubbed his hand wearily across his chin.
Would that he should be so fortunate that Lady Celia
possessed such qualities. He stamped down his
thoughts. Lady Celia was the daughter of a duke, and
would be above reproach. His eyes narrowed. He had
numbered several high-born ladies among his mis-
tresses. None had cared that she had shamed her husband and family by her own wanton conduct—all had
greedily accepted jewels as a token of his favour. He
frowned, not wanting to be reminded of the intrigue at
Court or the veiled hints in the king's letter.

King Henry was disturbed by the rumours that were
circulating about the earl—that he was sheltering Lollards. They were serious allegations, for which, did his
Majesty not know him so well, Trevowan knew he would
now be mouldering in the Tower of London for suspected heresy. Even so, he could not entirely dispel a
twinge of unease. He had been away from the Court for
some months, and there were many who sought to take
his place as the king's close confidant. He must reply
immediately to his Majesty's letter, but it was not the
threat of heresy that troubled him. He must risk the
king's further displeasure by questioning his decision
concerning Alynna.

He scowled, recalling her obstinacy. During the pilgrimage, her company had eased the torment of his
guilt, and at her side he had experienced an inner peace
he had thought forever denied him. Stubborn and
proud, she was different from any woman he had met. A
bitter, mirthless smile twisted his lips. She cared nothing
for his wealth and position.

Devil take the bewitching jade! He alone would tame
her wildness. And when he returned from London . . .
by St George, he would have her!

CHAPTER TWELVE

ALYNNA FLED from the chamber as though the devil himself were after her. Ignoring Hester's plea for her to wait, as she tried vainly to keep up, she ran along the corridor. Half-blinded by tears, she cried out in dismay when she collided with a man's solid figure.

'Not so fast, my pretty!' Sir Geoffrey chuckled in her ear as he swung her into an alcove.

Breathless from running, Alynna was caught unawares as his hot lips covered hers. For an instant she froze, then her temper exploded. First Trevowan treated her like a whore—and now Griswolde! She punched his chest and tore her mouth from his.

'How dare you treat me like a common doxy!' she fumed, forced to break off her tirade as her unpinned headdress slipped from her head.

'Your pardon, my lady.' His eyes flashed coldly in the late afternoon light, his stare missing nothing of her dishevelled state. 'It would seem that I was not the first to make merry sport with you this day.'

Surprisingly, he stepped aside, and with a disdainful flick of her skirts she hurried past him, shuddering at the way his insolent gaze had travelled over her. Once in the privacy of her chambers, she paced the room like an enraged tigress, refusing to give into the tears that scalded the back of her eyes. By the time Hester shuffled in, looking drawn and worried, she was seated on her stool, her face cast into the rigid mask she must present to the guests during the remainder of the wedding feast.

In silence Hester repinned her hair and set the headdress back in position. The task done, she squeezed Alynna's shoulder in understanding. 'Be strong, my lady. No one will guess that your heart is breaking. The path of fate cannot be denied.'

'Then fate means to destroy us,' Alynna said darkly. 'I

will not always have the strength to resist him. How do
you think the king would view the seduction of his ward?
Lord Trevowan would be disgraced.'

'But his lordship is the king's friend!' Hester
observed.

'As were many others before they fell from grace.'

Alynna stood up to return to the Hall. There she
would have to face Trevowan again, but in a short while
Meraud would be led away to prepare for her wedding
night, and her duty was to be at her friend's side. When
Meraud was led by the ladies to her chamber, and sat
propped up on the pillows of the bed, the tiring-women
were dismissed. At a loud knock on the door, Alynna
opened it to admit the bridegroom, accompanied by
Lord Trevowan and the other male guests. She kept her
eyes lowered as the men filed into the room, and to avoid
any further contact with either Trevowan or Griswolde,
she stepped back into the shadows. Over the bawdy
comments Griswolde spoke to encourage the groom,
she heard a harsh whisper from directly behind.

'Whore!' Lady Joan wheezed, snatching at her sleeve
and pulling her aside. 'I saw you with Sir Geoffrey in the
corridor. So you think to steal him from me! He will
never have you. Never!'

How dared her stepmother so accuse her! Cold fury
whipped through Alynna at the absurdity of her
jealousy. But more than that, her conduct was an insult
to her father's memory. 'Is it the man you fear to lose, or
your claim to my dowry should I marry?' Alynna
observed icily, over her shoulder. 'The dowry will soon
be out of your reach. I dare say some of it will go to swell
the royal coffers, for I doubt the convent to which his
Majesty intends to banish me will be given so vast a
sum.'

A spasm of fury crossed Lady Joan's face. 'I will not
lose what is mine!' she fumed, shooting her a look of pure
hatred. 'Not now—not after I have risked so much!'

Alynna was unsure whether she referred to the dowry
or to Sir Geoffrey. She looked away disgusted, but her
disquiet at her stepmother's behaviour was overridden

when she saw the intentness of Lord Trevowan's stare upon her.

She had expected that their next encounter would be difficult—that he would still be angry at her rejection of his advances. She was not prepared for the challenge blazing from his grey eyes. His lips turned up in a self-assured smile to tell her that he would never let her go. She wanted him as she had never wanted anything so desperately in her life. For her, he was prepared to risk the king's displeasure, and that frightened her. By one means or another she knew she must sever the invisible bonds drawing them deeper into a web of self-destruction.

Somehow she uttered the appropriate good wishes to Meraud, and was the first to leave the bridal chamber to flee to the sanctuary of her room. To her surprise, she found Hester curled on her truckle-bed sound asleep. She hesitated to wake her; for the past two nights she had been plagued by nightmares, and instead she rang for another chamber-woman to help her to disrobe. The woman came in with fresh wine and honey-cakes, should Alynna require them in the night. After the woman had tended to her and left, she wrapped her silk robe tightly round her and sat by the fire.

Troubled and confused by a host of conflicting emotions, she absently sipped the wine, but finding it unusually bitter, put it aside after only a few mouthfuls. Soon the flames curling round the logs began to blur, and the leaden weight which had settled over her heart seemed to be spreading through her entire body. She rose, surprised to find herself so weary. Too tired to divest herself of her robe, she slipped beneath the silk sheets and fell asleep the moment her head touched the pillow.

Later she stirred, raising her hand sleepily to push against a heaviness pressed against her face. The pressure increased, and she came awake all at once, her heart hammering in panic. She could not breathe. Someone was holding a pillow over her face! Arching her body, she blindly raked at the fleshy arms of her attacker, but her limbs were heavy and seemed to have no strength. A cruel laugh reached her through the muffling pillow.

'I said he would not have you!' Lady Joan jeered. 'Die, bitch! As you should have died at Barkhurst with Sir Robert.'

Alynna's lungs began to burn as the air was denied them, and even as she twisted and writhed, she knew that her strength was giving out. The wine must have been drugged! She struggled frantically, but her kicking legs became tangled in the bed-covers. Suddenly, through her fear, she knew for certain that her stepmother had ordered the murder of Sir Robert—as cold-bloodiedly as she meant to murder her now!

Her nails her only defence, Alynna scratched and clawed at the hands pressing the pillow over her. Her lungs were on fire and her brain dizzy, but still disjointed thoughts sped through her mind. Hester, too, had been drugged . . . no doubt also the page who slept outside her door . . . Was there no one to raise the alarm? She heard a grunt as her nails gouged deeper—then a fist rammed into her stomach and the pain robbed her of the last of her breath.

The next she knew, there was a roaring in her ears, and bright lights seemed to be flashing about her closed eyes. At first her mind refused to focus on what was happening. Then memory returned, leaving her bathed in a cold stinging sweat. She was not dead! She must have only fainted. Had Lady Joan been disturbed by a servant? Her head throbbed with the concentration needed to summon her thoughts and open her eyes. Suddenly her nose and throat stung with acrid bitterness, and a bout of coughing left her dizzy. Wrinkling her nose, she ran her tongue over her dry lips, grimacing at the taste of smoke. When her eyes flew open, orange tongues of fire rose up before her, and instinctively she rolled on her side and scrambled from the bed. The bed-hangings were ablaze, and so was a tapestry on the far side of the room.

She screamed for help again, the smoke stinging her

eyes and making her cough violently. This was deliberate! Lady Joan had planned her murder cold-bloodedly, so that it would look like an accident. In her hatred, she had given no thought to the others who could perish. As she stumbled forward in the rapidly increasing smoke, her foot caught against the truckle-bed and she heard a groan.

Hester! Hester was still unconscious. She bent over and tried to rouse her, but it was useless. Angrily tearing the wide sash from her waist, she tied it over her nose and mouth. Spurred by urgency, she put her arms round Hester's body and began to drag her towards the door.

'Fire! Fire!' A cry went up from the corridor, and she heard the sound of stamping feet. The door to her outer chamber was flung wide, so that the flames snaking up the bed-hangings were fanned into greater fury. Then the rushes caught alight and the fire crept steadily nearer.

At that moment Hester regained consciousness, and her screams added to the horror. Sparks flew up to singe Alynna's hair as she staggered under the weight of her burden. Voices came from the ante-chamber, but Alynna had no strength left to answer or to reassure her maid, as the poor creature thrashed wildly. The fire snapped at the hems of their robes. Her knees buckled, and she gasped at the shock of freezing water thrown over her to douse the smouldering material of her robe.

Gruff voices shouted orders all around her, and suddenly Hester was wrenched from her arms. Strong hands caught her swaying figure, and she felt the cold steel plates of half-armour digging into her as a guard carried her from the burning chamber. As though from a great distance, Hester's screams gradually subsided to loud sobs. A human chain was already passing along buckets of water brought from the well.

'Praise God, you are safe, Alynna!' Lord Trevowan's strained voice echoed through the corridor. 'Here, give Lady Alynna to me, Sergeant—and make sure the fire is out.'

Alynna felt the familiar strength of his arms carrying

her, and her shivering body was wrapped in the folds of
the cloak he had thrown over his half-clad figure. The
heat of his body through the silk of his shirt warmed her,
and safe in the harbour of his arms she fought to overcome
the effects of the smoke.

'Lady Joan . . .' Her throat hurt, but she swallowed,
struggling to warn him of the danger. 'She started the fire
. . . She tried to kill me!'

Lord Trevowan halted, and swung round to shout
back at the guards. 'Put Lady Joan under guard. I will
speak with her later.'

'And Hester?' she asked worriedly. 'How is she?'

'Your maid has taken no harm. My physician will
attend her.'

As he carried her, she heard several voices, and
startled faces and guests briefly passed by her vision.

'Go back to your rooms!' Lord Trevowan commanded. 'There was a fire, but it has been dealt with. Lady
Alynna is safe and will be tended to.'

A part of her mind was repelled at the sight she must
present, but the drugged wine still clung to the corners of
her brain, making everything seem unreal. The soaking
material of her robe clung uncomfortably, and she began
to shake. And not just from the shock or reaction to the
fire; for, once they were away from the glances of the
curious, Trevowan's lips brushed her brow. A wave of
longing swept over her, her whole being smarting with
awareness of the strength and virility of his body again
pressed against hers. His arms tightened, and she
nestled deeper into the fold of his embrace.

Trevowan kicked open a door and ordered a page to
summon a chamber-woman. Then she was carried
through into a second room and laid reverently upon the
soft mattress of a vast bed covered in wolfskins. Without
being told, she knew this was the earl's bedchamber. She
struggled to rise, saying anxiously, 'My lord, I cannot
stay here!'

She was pushed firmly down on to the pillows, his
voice harsh and grating. 'Godswounds, woman, I have
no designs upon your virtue—tonight! Thornbank is not

large, and all the bedchambers are taken. You will remain here. Your women have been sent for and will attend you.'

A maid came in, and he left as she began to fuss around her. As she changed out of her wet robe to a warm dry one, she heard Trevowan giving orders to his men. Once she was snugly tucked beneath the animal skins and the maid had withdrawn, he returned, and sat on the edge of the bed. When he drew the wolfskin cover further up to her chin, she felt a fever burning through her mind and struggled to warn him of something—or had she warned him already? It was so difficult to remember.

'Lady Joan . . . She . . .'

'Hush, my sweet,' he soothed, stroking her cheek. 'Lady Joan will be questioned. I shall see she is punished for what she has done to you. You must try and sleep.'

'How can I sleep? This is all my fault. Your manor could have been burned down about your ears. You should have left me where you found me in the forest. I have caused you nothing but trouble!'

'You are too hard upon yourself, my dear. I could no more have left you then than I could now,' he answered so softly that she was not quite sure whether she had heard him aright. He brushed a lock of hair back behind her ear, but conscious of the imperfection there, she drew back. An impatient look crossed his face as the maid returned, accompanied by the physician.

Trevowan rose to leave. 'Tomorrow we shall talk.'

His parting words filled her with dread. What more was there to say? Each meeting made it harder for her to deny him, but if he believed his friendship with the king shielded him from his Majesty's wrath, she did not share his confidence. She would not be the cause of any rift between Lord Trevowan and the king. She must deny him—for both their sakes.

The physician applied a salve to the slight burns on her arms and feet. 'You had a fortunate escape, my lady. There will be no scars.' He looked long and hard at her, stroking his grey forked beard as he added, 'You are troubled, greatly troubled, and not just by the fire.'

He paused to sprinkle some powder into a posset handed to him by the maid and offered it, his voice edged with respect. 'You succeeded with Lady Meraud where I had failed. You have wisdom, courage and pride. Do not let pride be your undoing, my lady. It can be an uncomfortable and lonely companion. Now you must sleep.'

The honeyed warmth of the posset spread through her, but long after the physician had left, she still tossed. His words had the ring of truth, but he was Lord Trevowan's man. Had he spoken them at his master's command, to undermine her resistance? She dismissed the notion as unlikely—such was not Lord Trevowan's way—and that made the physician's words even more disturbing. She flung her arm over the pillow she had pulled down to her side. The bed carried Trevowan's scent, and whenever she closed her eyes, his image rose before her, the memory of his kisses and touch leaving her body aching for the surcease only he could give her.

After a fitful night, she arose looking hollow-eyed, and dreading the day ahead when she must confront Lord Trevowan. The maid who had attended her the previous evening helped her to dress. The heaviness of spirit which had settled over her remained when the physician was admitted.

'You should be resting, my lady,' he admonished, touching her forehead with his hand. 'You have a slight fever—which is to be expected after your ordeal.'

'I am just tired.' Alynna ignored his advice. 'Tell me how Hester is. She was almost out of her wits with fear.'

'The poor woman!' The physician shook his head. 'The fire affected her very badly. I have given her a sleeping potion, and she will be well enough to serve you tomorrow. But her mind . . .' He tugged at his beard, clearly reluctant to speak.

'I am aware that she is close to breaking-point.' Alynna guessed what he would say. 'I shall do all in my power to help her to overcome her fears.'

For some moments after he had left, she strove to

control her returning anger. Lady Joan had allowed her hatred, greed and jealousy to consume her. She was responsible for the harm done to Hester. It was time she answered for her crimes!

She stood up, knowing she could not stay in Trevowan's chamber and wait for him to seek her out. From the noise outside of snorting horses and rumbling wheels, the entourage must already be assembling to depart. She would face Lord Trevowan in the courtyard and ask him to take her to Court to petition the king in person.

CHAPTER THIRTEEN

THERE WAS no sign of Trevowan in the parlour or Great Hall, and as Alynna climbed the stairs to the solar, Meraud called out a greeting.

'Alynna! How are you?' Meraud led her to a window embrasure. 'Should you not be resting?'

Alynna stepped back from her embrace, her smile strained with sadness at their parting. 'How could I stay hidden away when you are about to leave? Are you happy, Meraud?'

Meraud smiled, her eyes sparkling with tears as well as joy. 'Oh yes, dear friend—but I cannot but feel anxious for you. Dickon told me of the king's decision. You know that there will always be a home for you with us, Alynna. It would be too cruel if he should banish you to a convent.'

'I pray it will not come to that, but I would not have you risk his Majesty's displeasure.'

'Lord Trevowan will not fail you.' Meraud hesitated. 'I know how it is between you. Were you to . . . well . . . If you and Richard became lovers, I would not condemn you. Nor would I wish it to change our friendship. Dickon does not wear his emotions on his sleeve, but the signs are there that he cares for you, more than he will admit even to himself. Lady Celia will never give him the peace and happiness that you can.'

Her friend's outspokenness was making it harder for Alynna to follow the dictates of her conscience. 'The king would never permit us to be lovers. The consequences of defying his Majesty are too terrible to think on,' she said forlornly. 'Yet I love him so. How can I bear to live without him?'

'I cannot advise you, but think on my words, dear friend.' Meraud lowered her voice to a conspiratorial whisper. 'If my brother has given you his protection, and is prepared to go against the king's wishes, it is not something he has considered lightly, or without good reason.'

The sound of wheels rumbling across the courtyard drew Alynna's attention through the window to the empty covered litter being brought from the stables. The score of armoured men moving towards it was a sobering reminder that her stepmother was to be taken to Winchester as a prisoner to await the king's arrival there to hold Court. Other horses were being led out from the stables, and from their emblazoned caparisons, she noted that both Sir Geoffrey and Lord Trevowan would be leaving Thornbank.

At that moment Sir John called to Meraud, and taking Alynna's arm, she led her down the stairs, saying, 'I have you to thank for my happiness. At Court I, too, shall speak with the king.'

As they reached the last step, Sir Geoffrey bowed to them.

'You ride with us only as far as Glastonbury, I believe, cousin?' Meraud looked askance at him.

'That is so. From there I shall visit my estate in the North.'

She frowned, looking at her cousin uncertainly, but upon catching sight of Sir John beckoning to her, she kissed Alynna's cheek. 'Farewell, my friend,' Her voice dropped to a warning whisper before she hurried to her husband's side. 'Trust Richard. Do not be swayed by others.'

'Lady Alynna,' Sir Geoffrey spoke softly, 'my heart lightens to see you so recovered from your ordeal. How can I express my regret at what happened?' She was discomfited by the ardour in his gaze. 'Lady Joan will be brought to trial. Be assured that I shall do all in my power to make amends for the grief I brought you by bringing that devil's handmaiden here.'

'You were not to know the extent of her evil, Sir Geoffrey,' she answered coolly, unwilling to give him any sign of encouragement. He took her hand, undaunted, and raising it to his lips, bowed low. 'My mind is set upon helping you. Indeed, from something Lady Joan once said, there might be someone who will know the truth of your birth.'

'Should you not tell Lord Trevowan of this?' she said. 'He has begun his own investigations.'

Sir Geoffrey grimaced, and released her hand. 'For you, dear lady, to discover all I can, I would ride myself—not send underlings.' He smiled at her startled expression. 'I told you at the inn that I mislike mysteries. Would you deny me the chance to play knight-errant to a beautiful woman who has been dealt a cruel blow by fate? Besides . . .' he smiled impishly at her, 'your dowry is substantial. If I discovered a way for you to win possession of it . . . I am sure you would reward me for my pains, Lady Alynna.'

She relaxed slightly. His motives were simply mercenary, and she could understand that.

'I have never yet disappointed a beautiful woman,' he added, and again a warning bell rang in her mind. 'I shall not fail you, dear lady.'

'You are very kind, Sir Geoffrey, but I would not put you to so much trouble on my account.'

'It is no trouble, I assure you. Besides, I do have some influence with his Majesty. Not so much as my noble cousin, and although Trevowan will present your case to the king . . .' Griswolde added slyly, 'he needs must pursue his betrothal to Lady Celia. The duke would not take it kindly should Trevowan speak too passionately in the cause of a woman whose name has already been linked with his.'

At that moment, with a bustle of confusion, several grim-faced men in Trevowan's livery were hustling a protesting Lady Joan through to the courtyard. She stared wildly about her, and seeing Alynna and Sir Geoffrey together, cried out vengefully for all to hear, 'You think you have won, but you gain nothing— neither of you!' Her glance flickered over Sir Geoffrey before the guards closed round her, the malicious tone of her laughter sending an icy shudder through Alynna. 'Your fine airs will not serve you now, bastard! You will be as much a prisoner as I. You do not know the devil you have roused.'

The threat drained all colour from Alynna's cheeks, and as Lady Joan was escorted outside to the waiting litter, she kept her head high, aware of Lady Isabeau and the other guests casting curious glances at her. Murmuring an excuse, she cut across Sir Geoffrey's parting words, and needing to escape the inquisitive eyes, left the hall. At the door, her path was barred by Lord Trevowan.

'I am glad to see you have recovered from the fire.' His voice was strained and worried. 'But you must not let Lady Joan upset you.'

When she kept her gaze lowered, hiding her tears of humiliation, he said more sternly, 'Look at me, Alynna!'

She lifted her gaze, and the jewelled brightness of the tears clinging to her lashes unfurled his guarded emotions—both desire and a fierce protectiveness—that no woman had hitherto aroused. For the first time he saw her as truly vulnerable. Three times she had escaped death, showing great courage. Now, the tears she was so valiantly striving to master almost unmanned him. Her pride was a shield she used against any who would degrade her—it was her greatest strength, but also it could be her downfall. Whatever her birth she deserved the right to live as . . . His eyes hardened as his thoughts rammed against an insurmountable barrier. Her birth was a stigma she would always carry. He wanted her . . . More than that—she was the only woman for him! In that one respect her pride would be conquered—but by him alone. No one, not even the king, would take her from him!

In the torchlit Hall, the sapphire blue of her eyes was shot through with amethyst lights—a strangely exotic combination. They had always entranced him, but there was again something about their unusual colour that nagged at the back of his mind. Unusual, yes—but not unique. Did not the French troubadours praise the beauty of such eyes belonging to the most perfect English rose? Then the noise of the restless horses and assembled people broke through his concentration. He was allowing his passion for Alynna to make him fanciful.

'We cannot talk here,' he said, taking her arm to lead her to the parlour, where he closed the door behind them. 'Pay no heed to Lady Joan's threats,' he said, moving closer. 'She cannot harm you now.'

Her head tilted defiantly. 'She can harm my father's good name, and shame us all!'

Again he was struck by the overbrightness of those sapphire depths, and as he studied the beautiful heart-shaped face more closely, another woman's face tugged at his memory. He had been a young page newly arrived at Court when he had last seen her, and she had spoken kindly to him, sympathising over the recent death of his father. There had been an air of sadness about her, and he had been so struck by her beauty that for years during his training to knighthood he had envisioned himself as her champion. It was so long ago that he had almost forgotten the incident, but all at once so many un-answered questions began to make sense.

'I leave for Court in a short while,' he said evasively. 'Lady Joan will accompany me to be judged by the king. She has denied your accusations, but the scratches on her hands and arms are proof that she tried to smother you. I will testify that the ferryman was in her pay, and that he tried to murder you at the mill and at Canterbury.'

'I believed she planned my father's murder. She said as much . . .' Her voice quivered with pain, and she lowered her gaze, anger battling with the need to avenge her father's death and the sensations aroused by the earl's hand upon her arm. 'Lady Joan brought the mercenaries to Barkhurst.'

'She will pay for her crimes, I promise.' His voice was gruff, and although his touch was one of sympathy and understanding, it still had the power to set her pulse racing. He tipped her chin up with his finger, forcing her to meet his gaze. 'I have confronted her with all this, yet still she shows no fear or remorse. And as to the identity

of your mother . . . the woman is so eaten up with hatred
that I believe, from sheer vindictiveness towards you,
she will die before she reveals it.'

'My father's silence was to protect my mother's name.
Lady Joan keeps quiet out of spite. It makes no sense!'

'Perhaps it does. I will explain it all to the king.'

'Take me to Court, my lord, that I may petition his
Majesty in person?' she pleaded.

He tensed, a shadow darkening his stormy eyes. 'I shall
do what is best. You will stay here, but when I return,
you will be mine, Alynna!'

'My lord, you know that can never be!' His impassioned tone diverted her thoughts and she tried to
pull back, but his hold upon her tightened and she
quaked at the fervour blazing in his eyes. His hand
moved over her throat to caress the base of her neck, its
slow seductive rhythm rousing a fever in her blood.

'I will have you, sweet temptress. You cannot deny
what is between us.'

'Would you have me go against everything I believe
in?' she forced out. She had to drive a wedge between
them before her will-power ebbed beneath the potency
of his touch. 'Marry Lady Celia, who is your equal, and
forget me. I am the king's ward. My honour is his
honour. I love you too well to bring about your downfall.'

He released her, and hooked his thumbs over his
sword-belt, studying her narrowly. 'Had you even a
small measure of affection for me, lady, there would be
no need for any of this!' he scoffed. 'Love! I doubt you
even know the meaning of the word.' A flicker of pain
clouded his eyes. 'If there was any other way . . .'

He broke off, frowning as he stared down into
her eyes. It was not Alynna's face he was seeing in his
mind's eye, but another. Again the long-ago scene in
Winchester Palace haunted him—a woman who was
Alynna's image when she had been the same age. The
resemblance was too strong for him to be mistaken. He
knew who her mother was, and the knowledge stunned
him.

'Dear God, I'll not be gainsaid! There is a way . . .'
He checked himself quickly. In fairness to her, he could
not voice his suspicions until they had been confirmed.
Anticipation gripped him, and he gathered her close.
'You cannot escape me, sweet Alynna, nor will I permit
you to.'

'I belong to no man!' She defied him, her cheeks
paling with anger.

'Remember to whom you speak, lady,' he cautioned,
the need to suppress the excitement of his discovery
making his temper fray at her obstinacy. 'I have been
patient enough. Do not let pride lead to a folly you will
regret. You are a true woman with a passion for life
—and more . . . so much more, that I will teach you!'

Captured in his arms, she struggled to combat the
desire raging through her at his touch. There was a fire in
his eyes, and the tender smile glowing in his face set her
heart somersaulting. Without the stiff lines of hauteur
etched upon his rugged contenance, he looked again to
be the pilgrim she had lost her heart to, and her senses
betrayed her. He was about to leave, and she did not
want them to part with anger in their hearts. He was
acclaimed among the flower of chivalry, and only the
king was his equal in the tourney lists. For years at Court
his sharp wit had made him the king's favourite. What
chance had she to triumph over such an adversary?

'You will be mine, Alynna.' It was a promise, not a
command.

For a wild moment the impulse to cry out: *I love you,
Richard! I will be yours and forget honour and shame*
sprang to her lips. She clamped them shut, but nothing
could stifle the traitorous arousal of her senses.

When he crushed her to him, she moaned softly at the
exquisite ache building low in her stomach. Her sigh of
pleasure was muffled by his lips as she responded to the
passion consuming her. Suddenly she found herself
abruptly released, the devil's own smile twisting Lord
Trevowan's lips. He had deliberately roused her passion
as a warning that she could not escape the destiny he
planned for her!

'I shall count the hours—and nights—until I return and make you my own, dear lady.'

She did not trust herself to answer. Not once had he spoken of his feelings for her—other than desire. Had she goaded his pride by refusing him? Was that why he was so determined to win her? How easily he had put aside her pleas to go to Court. A deeper fear filled her: would not—as Sir Geoffrey had intimated—her presence at Court be an embarrassment if he intended to win Lady Celia in marriage?

Of only one thing was she certain—she had to put a stop to his madness which threatened to destroy them both. Trevowan would be angry that she had disobeyed him, but he would soon forget her. She could not let him jeopardise his future. He should marry Lady Celia, who was his equal in rank. As for herself, she would love him always. Somehow she must find the strength, and the resources, to get away from Thornbank!

Next time she saw Richard—if she was still here when he returned, there would be no reprieve. But how could she leave alone? Her time on the highways had shown her the dangers awaiting any woman who journeyed unaccompanied, and there was not even Joel now to protect her. And she was the king's ward. However she might rage against his injustice if he decided to banish her to a convent, she must obey the king.

Three weeks passed without any word from Lord Trevowan. Yet that was hardly surprising. After the blizzard of a fortnight ago, the snow had begun to thaw only in the last three days and the tracks become passable again. She had felt isolated and safe, cut off by the snowdrifts. Even if she had been able to solve the problem of how to leave Thornbank, the weather had been so bad that she could not have done so.

The thought of being shut away in a convent horrified her. For her the breath of life came from wide open spaces, the thrill of the hunt, of discarding convention by casting aside the awkward side-saddle and feeling the power of a spirited horse beneath her legs. Encouraged by her father, she had enjoyed pitting her sharp mind against the learned men who had visited Higham Mote. He had taught her to question as a man, and not to be afraid to think or to act. Such freedom she relished. Convent life would be a slow death.

'My lady, you will hear word soon. You must not fret so!' Hester told her.

'Why can I not be free to lead my own life?' The frustration of the past weeks burst forth.

'No woman of gentle birth can live alone, especially an unmarried one,' Hester counselled. 'It was a pity that Sir Robert had no kinsman to protect you, but Lord Trevowan has your best interests at heart.'

'Lord Trevowan would use me to his own ends,' she responded heatedly.

'You wrong his lordship,' Hester said gently. 'He cares for you. But he is a man—an exceptional man —used to getting his own way. You would not love him if he were different.'

'That does not make it easier to bear.' With each passing day, as she missed Trevowan more and more, it became harder to stand by her convictions.

Joel had been adamant that her mother was a noble-woman—and apparently a woman whose dark secret must be kept. Perhaps it would have been better had she been a serving-woman, for then no one would have cared what happened to her child. The question of her birth was at the heart of all that had happened to her since her father's death.

'Come, Hester.' Alynna forced a brighter note to her voice. 'Did I not promise you I would teach you how to play chess? It will stop me dwelling upon the impossible.'

An hour later, a page knocked at the door and announced that Sir Geoffrey Griswolde was awaiting her in the parlour. Alynna rose to her feet, startled. She had not taken seriously Sir Geoffrey's impassioned vow to help her, but had dismissed it, as she did all his flattery, believing he was just trying to discredit Lord Trevowan in her eyes.

Calling Hester to attend her, she hurried to the parlour, then, at the door, she hesitated. Sir Geoffrey had made no secret of his admiration for her. Did he believe that, with Lord Trevowan absent, she would succumb to his advances? Perhaps, but it would take more than a woman's charms for a man as self-indulgent as he to endure the discomforts of travel over the snow-covered countryside, she reassured herself. Even so, she was prompted to whisper to Hester, 'Stay by me at all times.'

'Ay, my lady. I do not trust Sir Geoffrey. He should not be here without Lord Trevowan. I warrant he is up to no good, as he was when he brought your stepmother here!'

Alynna raised a rebuking brow to silence her. Calming her own disquiet at the knight's arrival, she was careful that nothing of her uncertainty showed on her face as she entered the parlour.

Sir Geoffrey turned from warming his hands by the fire, his eyes gleaming with pleasure as he bowed to her. 'Lady Alynna. Each time I see you, you are more beautiful!'

'And each time we meet, sir, your flattery becomes more outrageous,' she chided. 'What brings you back to Thornbank?'

'Who else but yourself, fair lady!' he continued suavely. 'Did I not say I would help you? I have discovered a woman who says she knows the truth about your birth.'

Excitement made Alynna forget her uneasiness at meeting Griswolde in Trevowan's absence, and she faced him, joy mingling with suspicion. 'I have heard nothing from Lord Trevowan. Who is this woman?'

His angelic countenance took on an air of affronted pride. 'I doubt that my cousin has learned of her existence. He has other matters which concern him at Court, and regaining his Majesty's favour is one of them. The king is said to have quarrelled with him.'

'That is terrible! I could not bear it if he lost favour with his Majesty because of me!'

'You have a generous heart, Lady Alynna,' Sir Geoffrey said stiffly, 'especially since Trevowan has been much occupied with Lady Celia . . . You know how important this marriage would be to him.'

Red-hot pincers squeezed at her heart, and with a dissimulation that was becoming second nature to her since her arrival at Thornbank, she forced a bright smile. 'Marriage to Lady Celia will make Lord Trevowan one of the most powerful men in England. She is a worthy bride.'

He threw her a calculating look, and she prayed that her expression revealed nothing of her turmoil. When he smiled, she knew she had succeeded.

'And such negotiations are likely to prove lengthy. But I am at your service, dear lady, and am determined to help you all I can.'

Alynna willed herself not to think of Trevowan playing court to Lady Celia, but concentrated on the news Sir Geoffrey had brought. There was a suppressed tension about him that pricked her curiosity. Crossing the room to sit by the fire, she curbed her impatience while she waited for him to seat himself opposite her. 'This woman you spoke of—what did she have to say?'

A pained expression creased his brow. 'There, I regret, I failed you. She is bound to an oath of secrecy, and will speak to no one but yourself, and then, only if she is convinced that you are who you say. The woman is sick and near to death. If you wish to learn more, I fear you will have to journey to a village near Huntington, where she now lives.'

'How can she claim to be a servant when my father had no land in Huntington? Who is she?'

'She was the midwife!' Sir Geoffrey declared triumphantly.

Alynna's eyes widened. He had done well, but despite her increasing excitement, she remained cautious. 'And how will I prove I am who I say?'

'She will know. The child she mentioned carries her mother's mark. She must mean your eyes. They are beautiful, and an unusual colour.'

Self-consciously she touched her ear with its imperfection, then lowering her hand from the devil's mark,
shifted uncomfortably. Griswolde sat back in in his
chair, watching her smugly.

'The midwife seems certain she will know you. There
is little time to lose, as she grows weaker daily. We must
leave at first light.'

'You are in a great hurry, Sir Geoffrey!' Alynna stilled
her growing excitement by voicing her nagging doubts.
'How can I leave Thornbank? It will place Lord
Trevowan in greater disfavour with the king.'

'If you stay, all could be lost,' he stressed, bending
forward as though to give added weight to his words.
'Did I not say the woman was near to death?'

'Lord Trevowan should be told!' Alynna persisted.
Something about Griswolde's eagerness troubled her.

'If the old woman dies, where does that leave you, my
lady?' he insinuated slyly. 'You may never learn the
truth!'

Alynna stared at him, torn between loyalty to
Trevowan and the need to know her true identity. There
was a fervent light in Griswolde's eyes, and Trevowan's
warning not to trust him sprang to her mind. Should she
heed his words? But Griswolde had sown the seeds of
hope, and they refused to wither. Studying his handsome face, she was reassured. There was nothing sinister
in his intentions—no more than his antagonism towards
his cousin, and his need to prove himself the better man.
She squashed a feeling of betrayal towards Trevowan.

'I believe you think you know who my mother is—am
I right?'

'I saw the resemblance at the inn,' he hedged. 'Others
could do the same. Perhaps that is what the king
fears.'

Alynna's heartbeat quickened. Sir Geoffrey was deliberately holding back. She would go nowhere with him
until he told her everything. 'Why should the king fear
anything from me? If my mother was well born, why did
Lord Trevowan not notice the resemblance?'

The gleam in his eye brightened as he caught the

anticipation in her voice. 'Because, as far as I am aware, Trevowan has never met her.'

Alynna's head whirled at the implication of his words. It was impossible, but yet—in a strange way—it made sense. A spark of rebellion stirred. She did not want to spend her life as a virtual prisoner in a convent; she had done nothing wrong! And if Griswolde was right, what then?

'Who is my mother?' she could not stop herself asking.

Sir Geoffrey lowered his gaze. 'If I were mistaken in this, I would be maligning a great and virtuous lady. The midwife must be the one to tell you.' She knew he was right, but his evasion raised her curiosity to fever pitch. 'My lady, I respect you too much to see you suffer unjustly,' he declared passionately. 'I would not see you wronged. Also . . .' his hesitation was brief, 'in recent years Trevowan and I have grown apart. Once we were close, and I would serve him by serving you in his absence, and so bring an end to our differences.'

His intentions were noble, not sinister as she first suspected. She glanced towards Hester, who sat quietly in a far corner. The maid looked worried at the conversation she had heard and very slightly she shook her head, her eyes large and pleading as she indicated that Alynna should remain at Thornbank.

Alynna was again torn by indecision. Though she might resent Trevowan trying to dominate her, she was none the less loath to leave the safety of Thornbank. But this was her only chance to learn the truth! Besides, it would give her time to think more clearly. At Thornbank there were too many memories of Trevowan. Each day she missed him more and felt herself weakening in her resolve to deny him.

'So be it!' She crushed the last of her doubts concerning Griswolde's interest in this matter. 'But word must be sent to Lord Trevowan.'

'But of course,' he agreed readily. 'Would it not be better for you to dictate a letter to a scribe explaining the urgency of the matter? A messenger will be sent immediately.'

She stood up, reassured by his consideration. 'I shall write that letter myself, and retire early so that we may make the greatest possible speed on the morrow.' Beckoning to Hester, she left the parlour.

'My lady, is it wise to place your trust in that man?' Hester cautioned as soon as they were out of Sir Geoffrey's hearing. 'I cannot rid myself of the notion that he is using you for his own ends.'

'He expects to be handsomely rewarded with gold for his trouble,' Alynna explained.

'That makes him no less a mercenary than the ferryman! Are you so certain that is all he wants from you?'

'I am still the king's ward and under his protection.' The overriding need to discover the truth of her birth was too great to pay heed to Hester's warning. 'There is another reason why I must leave Thornbank. I love Lord Trevowan too much to bring him down. You know that in the end I will not be able to resist him.'

'But Lord Trevowan loves you!'

Alynna's heart twisted, her voice shot through with agony. 'No, Hester, Lord Trevowan wants me. But it is not love that drives him! If it were . . .' She broke off, acknowledging at last her true dilemma. It was not enough merely to love, even to the depths of one's soul and beyond. Love must be infinite, unrestrained by the realms of convention, rank or status—as her parents' love had been. There was nothing more barren or unfulfilling than love unrequited. If she had won the accolade of Trevowan's love, she would have surrendered to his will gladly, casting aside all thoughts of honour.

'This way, at least, Hester, I can live with dignity. Once I have spoken with this woman, I shall go to the king and throw myself upon his mercy. Lord Trevowan means to marry Lady Celia, and I could never take second place in his life.'

'Then I pray you have made the right decision, my lady, and do not live to regret it!'

Though softly spoken, the maid's words had an ominous ring. Of course there would be regrets. She loved Richard too deeply not to mourn his absence from her life. As for Griswolde, was she wrong to trust him? But what other way was there if she was to learn the secret of her birth?

CHAPTER FOURTEEN

IN THE twilight of the fifth day of travelling, Alynna lifted her head and wearily scanned the road ahead. Mist distorted skeletal trees into sinister shapes. Most of the snow had disappeared, and the thick frost had hardened the rutted, muddy track, making their progress easier. It was hours since they had passed even a hamlet, and since midday Sir Geoffrey had hardly spoken. The change in his manner from the affable companion of the previous days was disquieting, especially as he seemed tense, and was short-tempered with his men. They were following the meandering bank of a river when out of the mist a partially ruined castle rose up.

'Behold Castle Clayton!' Griswolde proclaimed, as he rode back to her side. 'It is where I had the midwife brought to be cared for. The place is a near ruin, but some of the rooms have been restored. We shall travel to another of my castles, just ten miles from here, once the woman has spoken to you.'

'I thought the midwife was too ill to be moved?' Alynna said, the isolation of the place arousing her suspicions.

'Did I not say so earlier?' Griswolde shrugged, intimating that the matter was of no importance. 'The woman was taken ill on the way to Thornbank and could go no further.'

His explanation was reasonable enough, but suddenly Alynna was afraid. She felt hemmed in by the closely-packed escort, who oppressively echoed the manner of her arrival at Barkhurst all those weeks ago.

'Clayton is a bleak place, but you will find your room warm and comfortable.' Griswolde seemed at pains to reassure her. 'It will be but for a single night.'

As they neared the ruined castle, she saw it was built on an outcrop of rock, with only the circular Norman keep still intact. Its stonework still bore traces of the red paint that would have have made it an impressive landmark for miles around. They rode across the lowered drawbridge, several planks of which had been recently replaced. The chains and fitments, in contrast to the dilapidated condition of the rest of the castle, appeared new and were free from rust. When they rode under the gatehouse, she glanced up at the jagged spikes of the raised portcullis, inexplicably feeling like a prisoner.

The feeling stayed with her as they entered the inner bailey. Griswolde's description of the place as bleak was complimentary. It was grim and uninviting! The crumbling towers, with their sightless black sockets of window-openings, were devoid of life, and macabre in the mist-laden dusk. Forlorn in its neglect, the castle was ghostly, menacing, the haunt of lost souls and forgotten dreams. Alynna pulled herself together with a start, impatient with such superstitious nonsense. It was the dreary weather that was making everything look so depressing.

Apart from some livestock, the castle looked deserted. Where were the men-at-arms and the servants? When they halted before the stone steps leading up to the keep, several surly grooms wearing barbaric-looking fleece tunics appeared to hold the horses's bridles. The steps were slippery with ice, and she hesitated before dismounting.

Instantly Griswolde leapt to the ground. 'If you will permit me, my lady?' He held out his arms to catch her, his hands resting only briefly upon her waist as he steadied her before leading her up the steps.

That he had not taken advantage of her at such a moment was reassuring, but as they walked through the dim corridors lit by sparsely-placed flambeaux, she could not dispel a sense of foreboding.

'Your rooms occupy the whole of the second floor, Lady Alynna.' Sir Geoffrey paused by an open door on the first level of the keep. 'Some wine and food will be sent to you. Once you have refreshed yourself, and rested, we shall visit the midwife. If there is anything you need, do not hesitate to command a servant to fetch it for you.'

'My lady will want hot water to wash, and her coffers brought up,' Hester cut in, the tremor in her voice betraying her nervousness.

Sir Geoffrey glared coldly at her. Throughout the journey he had ignored her, and now he did not trouble to hide his distaste. 'It shall be done immediately.' With a curt bow to Alynna, he entered what appeared to be his quarters and disappeared from sight.

'Do not stay the night in this awful place, my lady,' Hester warned as they ascended the stairs. 'Demand to see the midwife at once, then leave!'

'I have stayed in more pleasant surroundings.' Alynna overcame her own misgivings to console her maid. 'It will be dark in an hour, so how can we leave?' She forced a more cheerful note. 'It is for just one night.'

They had come to the first open door on the second floor, and Alynna blinked several times, taken aback at the riot of garish colour that greeted her in the brightly-lit room. The painted walls of the ante-chamber were patterned with red and gold wavy lines that stunned the unsuspecting eye. The window shutters closed against the cold air were vivid green and decorated with paintings of peacocks, popinjays and other gaudy birds.

'This looks more cheerful,' she commented, without enthusiasm for what she considered to be vulgar and in bad taste. At the entrance to the bedchamber, a shocked gasp came to her lips, that was echoed by Hester. The walls were covered with painted hangings that depicted naked women being pursued by satyrs and other mythical beasts.

'My lady, where has Sir Geoffrey brought you?' Hester wailed. 'This is a . . .'

'A lovers' bower!' Alynna finished for her. 'Or so it would seem. Sir Geoffrey mentioned that this castle was but a few miles from another of his residences. As these rooms have recently been rescued from decay, I assume he entertained his women here—unbeknown to his late wife, poor creature.'

'Then you must leave at once!' Hester cried, aghast. 'You should never have trusted him, my lady. He is a lecher! Men like that never change.'

'Hester, be silent!' Alynna ordered, dreading that her maid would give way to hysterics. She was finding it hard enough to master her own growing alarm. If she had misjudged Griswolde, at least she was forewarned against him. She touched the slim knife she used for eating, which hung from the jewelled girdle at her waist. She would keep it with her at all times, especially when she slept.

There was a clatter of footsteps in the outer room; two men deposited her coffer on the floor with a bump and another placed an ewer of steaming water on a stand by a pewter bowl.

At Hester's worried expression, Alynna managed a weak smile. 'We are letting ourselves be frightened without cause,' she reasoned. 'Sir Geoffrey dare not harm me, for he would be answerable to Lord Trevowan —and to the king! It is this place which is upsetting you. As yet, Sir Geoffrey has given me no cause to doubt him.'

'I pray it remains so, my lady,' Hester said, moving to the coffer and selecting a change of clothing for her mistress.

Once Alynna had washed the travel dust from her face and body and donned a velvet fur-trimmed surcoat with two kirtles underneath for extra warmth in the draughty castle, she felt more able to overcome her doubts and fears. Hester rebraided her hair, looping the thick coils over her ears and covering them with a white linen veil and circlet. When Sir Geoffrey arrived to escort her to the midwife, she went eagerly with him up to the top floor. Upon entering a small shadowy room lit by a single candle, she strained her eyes to make out a grey-haired figure lying on a pallet-bed in the far corner.

'This is Lady Alynna,' Sir Geoffrey said to the woman. 'She is the one I spoke of.'

A frail hand beckoned Alynna to step closer, as the midwife struggled to sit up, but the effort left her gasping. 'Bring the light nearer, my lady,' she wheezed painfully. 'I must be certain to whom I speak.'

Before picking up the candle, Alynna rubbed her hands together to dispel the dampness forming on her palms. Holding the candlestick so that the light fell upon her face, she knelt by the bed, expectantly holding her breath as the old woman studied her and took her chin in a weak fluttering hold.

'You are very like her.' The midwife pushed aside her veil and hair. 'The eyes, too, are the same!' Briefly she touched her ear, and when she pulled back, conscious of the devil's mark, a light flared in the midwife's eyes. 'Yes, you have the mark! You are the child I delivered.'

She slumped back on the pillows, staring past Alynna to where Sir Geoffrey stood at the foot of the bed. Her expression hardened, her voice growing stronger. 'I shall talk to Lady Alynna alone, or not at all. Only she has the right to know the secret I have shielded these many years.'

The Earl of Trevowan crushed the parchment written by Alynna, rage sweeping through him as he questioned the messenger. 'You say Lady Alynna left Thornbank four days ago with Griswolde?'

At his nod of assent, Trevowan dismissed the messenger and turned to his sergeant-at-arms. 'Assemble the men. We ride within the hour.' He flung the crumpled parchment angrily into the fire. 'By Almighty God and St George, the woman gives me no peace!'

He had just come from a stormy interview with the duke, Lady Celia's father, where he had declined to accept Lady Celia as his bride. At the time, he had cursed himself as seven times a fool to allow the haunting image of sapphire eyes to cost him the chance of allying his house with the duke's. Yet once the deed was done, he had felt that a burden had been lifted from his shoulders. Until he received Alynna's letter.

Why could she not obey my orders? he thought savagely, raking his hand through his hair as he paced the empty room. I doubt whether Griswolde intends to take her to Huntington at all!

Pain lanced through him. If Griswolde had Alynna in his power, she was in grave danger. Why did the king refuse to discuss her? Trevowan's earlier suspicions returned, still unresolved. Until Joel confirmed his beliefs, he could do nothing. Now, it seemed, Griswolde had discovered the midwife. If his cousin learned the identity of Alynna's mother—and if it was the woman Trevowan himself believed—Griswolde would stop at nothing to use that information to his advantage. He snatched up his sword, and was buckling it on when a short, travel-grimed figure burst into the room.

'Thank God I reached you in time!' Joel brushed back his hood, his wizened face creased with worry. 'I heard from the sergeant that you are about to ride out. Is it true that Lady Alynna is with Griswolde? Does he suspect anything?' he laboured in agitation. 'If he does . . . Dear God! There is no time to lose. Everything was as you believed, my lord. But there is more! News that I had hoped would bring Lady Alynna joy. Instead . . .' He paused for breath. 'Can Griswolde be trusted? Otherwise—I fear if this information was in the wrong hands—it could be Lady Alynna's undoing!'

Trevowan strode to the door, his voice strained. 'Pray that we reach Alynna before it is too late. You had best tell me everything as we ride.' He gripped the jester's shoulder. 'Are you up to another long journey, man?'

'I could not fail my lady now!'

'It will take us three days' hard ride to reach Griswolde's lair—providing the weather holds.' An awesome dread scourged through him, and his voice was unsteady as he gruffly continued. 'Pray I am right as to my cousin's destination!'

Alynna walked dazedly back to her chamber. She had been aware that Sir Geoffrey was waiting outside the upper room, and that he had questioned her as she descended the stairs, but she was too overcome by what she had heard to do more than reply abstractedly.

Giving herself a mental shake as she approached her rooms, she collected her wits.

'Forgive me for not answering your questions, Sir Geoffrey,' she explained, 'but I gave my word to the midwife that I would speak to no one but his Majesty upon the subject.'

Sir Geoffrey smiled thinly, but even through the stupor which had settled over her, Alynna was aware of his heightened colour. 'Of course, my dear. You must be amazed at what you have learned.'

Alynna caught the odd note in his voice, and her heart clenched with returning alarm. How far could she trust him? In the light of what she had learned, had she been a fool to discount Trevowan's warning? She recalled her first impression of this isolated castle, and prickles of cold sweat broke out down her spine. From his hints, she knew Griswolde had guessed something of the truth. If that were so, her situation would indeed be perilous.

She forced a smile, sounding braver than she felt. 'The news has indeed shaken me. Will you forgive me if I retire early? Are we not to leave here tomorrow? You will be justly rewarded for all your trouble.'

'I am now, as always, your devoted servant, dear lady,' he replied silkily, but his expression was shielded from her by the shadows, and her doubts remained.

As she entered her room, Hester hurried out, her eyes anxiously searching Alynna's face for some sign of what had passed.

'All is well, Hester, but I cannot say more, even to you.'

'It was good news, my lady? Will it mean that the king cannot shut you away?'

'I pray so.' Alynna swallowed against a lump of emotion lodging in her throat, still dazed by the midwife's confession. 'We have to go to Court, where I must seek an audience with his Majesty.' She sat down on a stool. 'I would prove I want no further claim upon him, only what is mine by right—my freedom!'

Hester removed Alynna's veil and unpinned her plaits, before venturing further, 'How will this affect your relationship with Lord Trevowan, my lady?'

Strangely, the shock of learning her true parentage had been so great that she had been too numbed to analyse what it meant. Now, as she reflected upon it, a giant weight seemed to crush her heart and soul. 'It changes nothing.'

The sound of a disturbance by the door of the outer chamber made her whirl round, her hand seeking the reassurance of the knife in her girdle as she looked through the opening. Griswolde entered, resplendent in a doublet and hose of pale gold, followed by a host of servants bearing silver platters laden with food.

'I bid you join me, dear lady,' he invited her, while he gestured for the food to be laid out on a table being set up by the fireplace. 'I had the meal prepared in your honour. Although you must be tired from your hours in the saddle, you cannot retire without eating.'

Alynna tensed, her first impulse to order Sir Geoffrey from the room, but instinct cautioned her. Until now, he had been charming and courteous. Dared she risk angering him, especially as her position here was so vulnerable? Besides, there would be servants in attendance, and also Hester. Better to humour him, she reasoned, than antagonise him without due cause.

'You are most thoughtful, Sir Geoffrey,' she replied, gesturing for Hester to take a seat by the fireplace.

'I would be a poor host if I neglected the needs of my guests, particularly one as beautiful as yourself.'

Alynna hesitated before sitting at the table, disquieted that only a single servant remained in the room to attend upon them. 'You have a silver tongue, Sir Geoffrey, but I cannot dine with you if you continue in such a vein! I cast no slur upon your honour, but I must consider my reputation.'

'Not only beautiful, but wise!' He smiled ruefully. 'Your pardon, dear lady. Your reputation is my greatest concern, as I hope to prove to you. Tonight is cause for celebration, is it not?' He raised his large goblet, already filled with wine, in salute to her. 'I drink to your health and to your future.'

He drained the goblet, and to her dismay, beckoned the servant to refill it. When sober, he had shown his amorous nature, but if he became intoxicated . . . She shuddered. The gaudy colours of the room, and the erotic scenes on the tapestries in the bedchamber, were a disturbing reminder of how these rooms had once been used when Sir Geoffrey entertained a woman.

Throughout the meal he took pains to slice for her the choicest cuts of spiced game or honeyed pork. Often as he passed the meat to her on his knife their hands would touch, and she grew uncomfortable when his fingers seemed to linger deliberately upon her hand. Twice his thigh brushed hers beneath the table, but when she drew away, her eyes narrowing in warning, his expression did not change, and she wondered if she were being over-sensitive about an accidental contact. Despite her reservations, Sir Geoffrey was witty and charming, and she began to relax and enjoy his company as the meats and pies in their exotic sauces were presented to them one after the other. Yet she noticed that Hester scarcely touched her food, and that she fidgeted nervously on her stool by the fire.

Alynna drank sparingly, but as time passed and Griswolde's goblet was constantly refilled, her unease returned. With each new dish his compliments became bolder, occasionally edged with innuendo, and she was finding it more and more difficult to evade his wandering hands. When his thigh again pressed against her own and this time his hand lightly squeezed her knee, she leapt to her feet, spilling her goblet.

'The hour grows late, Sir Geoffrey,' she said coolly. 'It is time I retired.'

He stood up, his eyes heavy-lidded as his languid gaze travelled over her tense figure. 'I have kept you from your bed too long, my dear.' He moved to her side and, taking her hand, raised it to his lips, but instead of his mouth lightly touching her fingers, he turned her hand palm upwards and kissed it with an ardour that caused her stomach to knot in fear. When she tried to snatch it free, his hold tightened and he jerked her roughly to him.

'Release me at once!' she demanded, struggling against his chest.

His low chuckle of amusement was accompanied by a shocked gasp from Hester. The maid had risen to her feet and was looking uncertainly from Sir Geoffrey to the door, her indecision reflecting Alynna's own. Whom could she go to for help? The entire castle was garrisoned by Griswolde's men.

'A kiss, my dear. Is it so much to ask when I have taken such pains on your behalf?'

'Please leave, Sir Geoffrey!' Her tone was cuttingly polite, masking her growing fear.

'Nay, not until I have spoken.' His hands gripped her like iron talons. 'Why do you think I went to such pains to learn of your birth? It was for us—not just for you. Marry me, Alynna!'

'I cannot!' she gasped, momentarily stunned by the unexpectedness of his proposal.

'You are too modest, my dear. Your bastardy means nothing to me. I shall not allow it to be a barrier between us!'

'What you ask is impossible.' Her fear grew at the calculating glitter in his pale eyes. He did not want her—it was her dowry he sought.

'Nothing is impossible.' His voice dropped to a seductive whisper. 'I burn for you, my sweeting. Do not pretend false innocence with me; you have known all along I wanted you.'

'You go too far!' she raged, increasing her efforts to escape his hold. Seeing his eyes glaze with lust, her blood turned to ice. 'If you dare to lay a finger upon me,' she threatened, 'you will regret it!'

'Ah, such fire and fury—that is what I admire in you.' He caught her wrist as she lifted her hand to strike him, his grip bruising. 'We were meant for each other.'

'You are drunk and disgusting!' Alynna twisted, and strained away from his lips. 'Lord Trevowan will never pardon you for this. Nor the king . . .'

Her words were smothered by his lips grinding down upon hers with a savagery that nauseated her. From the corner of her eye she saw Hester move forward, holding an iron rod that was used to tend the fire. At that moment Alynna managed to wrench her lips free from Griswolde's plundering hold, but when she tried to push him away, his grip was merciless. She saw Hester pause, her scarred face twisted with fear as she waited to see if Alynna would yet reason with Griswolde. Rigid with revulsion, Alynna strained back from him, her eyes blazing with outrage as she saw his pale, greedy eyes mentally disrobing her. He ran his tongue over his lips as though savouring a treat, and her stomach writhed with sickening dread.

'You disgrace every code of chivalry upheld by a knight,' she seethed. 'Let me go at once!'

'Sweet Alynna, your beauty enflames me,' Griswolde murmured. 'I am not made of stone, but your virtue is a tribute to you. I admire that. When we are married . . .'

'Have I not made it clear . . . There will be no marriage between us!'

He scowled, his eyes pinpointed with rage. 'The priest will arrive in an hour. We shall be married this night.'

'No. Never!' She recoiled in horror, but his grip remained fast about her, his fingers like iron bands imprisoning her waist. 'I am not free to marry. The king will . . .'

His caustic laugh drowned her words. 'Naturally the king will be angry that I have wed without his consent, but your existence is an embarrassment to him, and he will be relieved that you have chosen to live a life of seclusion on my country estate. And do not fear; you are too bright a jewel for me to neglect. I shall visit you often, so that you will not be lonely.'

'Release me at once!' she fumed. 'I will listen to no more of this nonsense. I will not marry you.'

A sob broke from Hester. 'Lord Trevowan will hear of this. He will have your blood if you harm my lady!'

A feral glimmer lit Griswolde's eyes as he studied Alynna. 'So you do care for Trevowan! He was a fool to let you slip through his fingers. You will forget him soon enough in my arms. He is a coarse warrior . . . What does he know of love?'

His lips grazed hers brutally, with the need to inflict his will upon her. When his hands squeezed her breasts, she had to fight back rising waves of nausea. It was this lecherous, mincing fop who knew nothing of love! Love was the fusion of body and soul, the quickening of the pulses that sent her spirit floating into an ecstatic paradise whenever Trevowan caressed her. It was not this silent screaming terror and a crawling like grave-worms over her icy flesh! Something snapped, and she fought like a demented fury, scratching and kicking in her need to free herself from his noxious hold. Her heel razed down his shin, and he swore violently. When his hold loosened slightly, she slapped him hard across his cheek.

'Bitch!' he screeched.

Her own head snapped back as he returned her blow twice, both her cheeks stinging with pain and humiliation.

'Brute!' Hester screamed out. 'Leave my mistress be!'

Alynna saw her maid's arm raised, the iron rod turning gold as it briefly reflected the firelight before it thudded against Griswolde's shoulder.

With a yell, Griswolde flung Alynna away from him. Her foot caught in the trailing hem of her kirtle and she sprawled headlong on the rushes. Griswolde, meanwhile, had rounded on Hester, his hand blurred as he lashed out with a crack against her jaw. She staggered back two paces, then crumpled to the floor like a broken doll, and lay still. Unthinking of the danger threatening herself, Alynna lurched to her feet and darted across the room to see how seriously Hester had been hurt. She glimpsed the blood staining Hester's wimple and heard her low groan. Thank God, she was not dead! But then hands grabbed her from behind and spun her round. The scorn she was about to unleash upon Griswolde shrivelled on her lips as he lunged at her. His handsome face was contorted, no longer angelic—dusky red

staining his cheeks, a mixture of rage and passion that
made him resemble an avenging demon.

'So you think yourself too high and mighty to wed me!'
he snarled, dragging Alynna towards the bedchamber.
'You will be willing enough after tonight. There is but
one way to bring a woman to heel.'

'I will die before I submit to you!' Alynna choked out,
as she twisted and turned to escape his clutches.

'Brave words—but foolish ones! You cannot win.
There is no one to save you!'

He hauled her over to the bed and heaved her on to
the mattress, falling upon her before she could roll away.
She fought him like a mad, biting dog. Her teeth
snapped at his flesh, her long nails tearing as she slashed
at his face. As his weight pressed down upon her, she felt
the knife at her hip digging into her. Time and again he
knocked her hands aside whenever she tried to retrieve
it, slapping her almost senseless as lust and anger drove
him in an insane need to conquer her.

'Your skin is smooth, but as cold as marble,' he said
hoarsely, 'but I will make you burn for me—as I am on
fire for you!'

'You will burn in hell for this!' she gasped painfully,
her movements frenzied with desperation. 'The king will
see you punished. Have you forgotten that I am the
king's ward?'

Had she actually been able to draw her knife and
plunge it into his heart, the effect could not have been
more startling. Griswolde stiffened, his face turned a
sickly grey and he sat back on his heels.

Alynna flung herself off the bed, keeping its vast
expanse between them, and snatched the knife from her
belt to hold it before her. 'Come near me again, and I
shall use this!'

'You say you are the king's ward—I thought you were
Trevowan's!' he said in a dazed voice, and did not
appear to notice the knife threatening him. He rubbed a
shaking hand over his face, his voice strained. 'Was it on
his Majesty's orders you were to remain at Thornbank?
Had I known that . . .' He broke off, his eyes slitted with

cunning. He grinned down at the blade pointed at him. 'That will not stop me! This changes nothing. We shall wed. I may yet escape the king's wrath if I have you to bargain with.'

'Nothing you can say or do will make me marry you! I will denounce you to the priest and refuse to speak my vows.' She tossed back her head defiantly, but there was something about his stance, akin to a cornered wild boar, that alerted her to danger. Was he past listening to reason? She had to try. 'You have disgraced your knightly vows, but if you let us go, I shall not mention the incident to the king.'

'You should have spoken out at Thornbank,' he grunted. 'I have risked too much to back down now. After a few days as my prisoner, you will agree readily enough to our marriage. I can afford to be patient. No one will find you here.'

'There you are wrong!' Alynna returned hotly. 'Have you forgotten that I wrote to Lord Trevowan informing him we travelled to Huntington?'

His eyes glowed with triumph, the smug smile playing across his lips sending slivers of disgust through her rigid body. 'But we are nowhere near the place.' He gave a snort of wicked laughter. 'We are not even in the same county!'

There was a movement near the door, and seeing Hester watching Griswolde with undisguised horror, Alynna moved protectively towards her, and as much to reassure her as herself, burst out, 'You are a low, vile creature without honour or shame! I will never marry you.'

'You will eat those words, lady! I shall break your stubborn pride. I know your weakness.' Griswolde fumed, striding to the door and thrusting Hester roughly aside. 'Torture would not break that obstinate streak, but there is more than one way to gain my ends.'

The outer door rattled on its hinges as he slammed it behind him with a violence that made Alynna flinch.

'My lady, what are we to do?' Hester sobbed.

Alynna resheathed her knife and placed her arm around the frail shoulders of her maid, but before she could answer, four soldiers burst into the room.

'We are to escort you to other quarters,' the sergeant announced sharply.

At the sound of more soldiers running up the steps to the floor above, a chill foreboding settled over Alynna's heart. 'So I am to be treated as a prisoner, not an honoured guest!' she mocked. 'His Majesty will hear of this!'

None of the guards looked directly at her, but each wore a set implacable look, and Alynna knew that any protest she made would be ignored. She drew herself up proudly, striving to maintain what little dignity Griswolde had left her. Hester limped forward to gather Alynna's cloak, but was stopped by a guard.

'You are to take nothing.' He turned to Alynna. 'You have a knife, my lady. Give it to me!'

The insolence of his tone goaded her to refuse, but she had no wish to be subjected to the indignity of the man searching her, which from the harshness of his expression she judged he would do without hesitation, so she handed the knife to him. He stuck it into his belt and laid a hand on her arm to escort her from the room. She glared at his offending hand, refusing to move. He coughed uncomfortably, and dropped it to his side, his voice grudgingly respectful.

'My lady, if you please, accompany us.'

It was a minor victory that she would walk freely to her imprisonment. Head held high, she walked into the corridor, pausing only for Hester to fall into step beside her before nodding to the sergeant to proceed. They were taken to the upper floor, and as they passed the open door of the midwife's room, Alynna's step faltered. She glanced inside, and from the light of a single candle saw a man-servant stripping the bed of its covers. Icy fingers clamped her heart. The midwife was dead! Had she died naturally, or had Griswolde seen her as a threat and rid himself of her? He would not risk the woman talking of his foul deeds this day.

The guards halted outside a door at the far end of the corridor and stood aside for Alynna to enter. An icy blast of wind touched her face as she stepped inside. There were no shutters or glazing at the two narrow croslets that served as windows, and the dim moonlight filtering in showed that it was devoid of furniture except for a single stool and an indistinguishable bundle against one wall. The door rattled shut, the sound of heavy bolts being shot home echoing in the gloom.

'Oh, my lady, what is to happen to us?' Hester sobbed.

'You must be strong.' Alynna held her maid's arm, and strove to stop her own teeth from chattering as the cold bit into her flesh. 'Griswolde must see he cannot browbeat us.'

'But this room . . .' A shudder went through Hester. 'It's like the dungeon where . . . Merciful God, it's beginning again! Don't let this happen!'

'This has nothing to do with what happened to you before!' Alynna was alarmed at the hysteria in her maid's voice.

Hester drew a shaky breath, her body quivering as fear and cold took hold of her. 'I wish I could believe that. It's so cold—as if an icy devil were breathing over us.'

'You must not think that! It is me Griswolde is punishing, not you. Come, we must try and keep warm. Go and see what that bundle is by the wall.'

'It's a pile of sacks, my lady.'

'At least Griswolde does not intend us to freeze to death, but just to become as miserable as possible!' Alynna sat on the floor, pulled Hester down beside her, and spread the sacks over them. 'It could be worse.' She tried to sound optimistic. 'Listen, it is raining. At least there will not be any frost tonight.'

But as she listened to the hissing rain continuing for hour upon hour throughout the night, a deeper fear gripped her half-frozen body. The rain would turn the tracks into a quagmire. Even if Lord Trevown did suspect she was in danger and sent his men to search all

Griswolde's properties to find her, it could take weeks to travel the distance that they had covered in days over frost-hardened ground.

CHAPTER FIFTEEN

LORD TREVOWAN glowered at the churning torrent of flood-water that had swept away the wooden bridge which was the only river crossing for several miles. Tight-lipped, he wheeled his horse about and headed up-river. He scarcely noticed the rain, which was beginning to penetrate his thick cloak as he flexed his proud shoulders to ease the muscles knotted with tension. Every mile had been a battle against the elements, and he had pressed himself and his men relentlessly. They had already been four days on the road instead of the three he had planned, and Griswolde's lair was little more than two miles across the swollen river.

'Another delay,' Joel said, his voice gruff with anxiety. 'How much further, my lord?'

'Ten miles. We shall have to cross the river at the next town,' Trevowan answered grimly. 'In these conditions, that means another three or four hours.'

'Pray God we are in time!' Joel groaned. 'I doubt that Griswolde learned the whole truth from the midwife. But if he was desperate enough to risk the king's rage by bringing Lady Alynna here, I fear he is desperate enough to harm her, should she not fall in with his wishes. Sir Robert would never rest in his grave if he knew how fate had dealt with his beloved daughter. First Lady Joan, and now Griswolde! He feared she would become a pawn to some unscrupulous knave, which was why he kept her hidden away in Suffolk. Her beauty alone was enough to tempt any man, but her birth . . . !'

Trevowan looked away from the jester, whose creased face reflected his own deepening dread. 'At least Lady Alynna is safe from Lady Joan's spite and intrigue now that the king has placed her stepmother under guard in a castle on the Welsh coast. She can cause no further mischief.'

But Lady Joan was a harmless fledgling, Trevowan thought savagely, compared with Griswolde's cunning and malevolence when he saw wealth and power in his grasp. The vision of Alynna's face haunted him day and night.

On the verge of leaving Court, he had been summoned, together with Joel, to attend the king, who had somehow learned of the jester's visit to the priory. The interview had been at first stormy, the king incensed that Trevowan had meddled in the affairs of his ward. His fury had mounted at the request Trevowan had put to him, and he had remained adamant that Alynna be sent to a convent. Trevowan had refused to back down from his stand. Alynna was now more precious to him than life. He, who had never asked his Sovereign for anything, asked now, humbly beseeching him to change his mind. It took all his patience to keep his temper bridled. Already the king had delayed him an hour, and time was disastrously short!

Rage had clawed at his throat, but he conquered it. Since Agincourt, the king had been distant towards him. The friend of his youth was changing, the pious streak in him becoming obsessive.

'Yet I hear that the Lady Alynna is involved with a Lollard?' Henry confronted him.

Upon encountering the fanatical gleam in the king's eyes, Trevowan was warned that he, too, was under suspicion, and he felt the chill edge of the executioner's axe poised over him, since he knew his Majesty distrusted the Lollards since the attempt on his life. He himself had been emphatic in his denial, however. The drawn-out silence that greeted his words stretched Trevowan's patience almost to snapping-point.

'After all that has passed, Lady Alynna has a right to know the truth of her birth,' the king reluctantly admitted. 'Griswolde cannot escape the consequences of his abduction of my ward—if abduction it be! You will place him under arrest and bring him to London. With the exception of Lady Alynna, you will both swear an oath to speak to no one of what you have learned.'

When Trevowan and Joel readily agreed, the king had placed his arm about Trevowan's shoulders and granted his request out of respect and friendship.

Though all would be for nothing, if he arrived too late! It was that thought which plagued him still as he pressed the tired men and horses on through the pouring rain.

Alynna hugged her knees close to her chest to try to still the shivering in her body, but it proved impossible. At least the constant banging and shouting, which had drifted to them from the courtyard ever since the rain stopped, had now ceased. Above the distant stamp of heavy-footed sentries patrolling the battlements, an air of expectancy hung over the castle. Hester, who was over-sensitive to the change of atmosphere around them, began to sob. In the three days that they had been Griswolde's prisoners, Alynna had been unable to give any lasting comfort to her maid. Nothing she said could convince Hester that she was not awaiting torture and punishment as a Lollard.

She squeezed her arm. 'Come, Hester, be brave! Griswolde dare not harm us. Am I not under the king's protection?'

Her own nerves strung to breaking-point, she rose stiffly to pace the cold damp chamber. As always, when she gave her mind free rein, it turned upon thoughts of Trevowan. A wave of longing swept over her, and she closed her eyes against an onrush of pain. No torture Griswolde could devise would equal the torment of yearning for what could never be!

Deliberately she turned her thoughts from the earl. If there was ever to be a future for them together, she must first free herself from Griswolde's clutches. At least during the last days she had been spared his presence. For three days they had been denied food and given only brackish water. If he expected her to be cowed by her discomfort, or on the point of surrender because of lack of food, he was greatly mistaken. It would take more than the grinding pains of hunger, or even torture, to

break her into submission to his will. She was resolved to
die rather than become Griswolde's pawn.

A thin ray of sunlight warmed her chilled flesh, and
she circled her shoulders to relieve some of the stiffness
of her limbs. To her alarm, the roon spun crazily; from
lack of food even this slight exertion made her dizzy.
Panic seized her. How could she keep up her strength to
fight Griswolde if her body was showing signs of weakening already? She inhaled slowly and deeply, willing
herself to be calm. From the angle of the sunlight, it had
to be an hour after noon. She started when, with a
clatter, the door bolts were thrust back.

'Merciful St Winifred, save us!' Hester groaned,
flattening herself against the wall in the darkest corner.
'The guards have come. We shall be tortured, and we
shall burn. Burn!'

'No, Hester, those days are past,' Alynna soothed,
seeing her eyes round and starting with terror, she
hurried to her side.

The door was flung open and six men-at-arms stood
outside. At the grimness of their expressions, her flesh
crawled. The time had come! Griswolde was about to
show his hand. Composing her face to a serene mask,
she waited for the sergeant to address her.

He said nothing, merely indicating by a jerk of his
head that both women should follow him. His rudeness
almost stung Alynna into a rebuke, but she had to
remain calm and self-possessed. If she allowed her
temper to run away with her, she would lose any edge
she might have over Griswolde. When Hester hung
back, a guard grabbed her arm and dragged her forward.

Alynna's precarious control snapped at her terrified
wail, and she glared at the guard. 'Release my maid!'
The man dropped his hold, and she slipped her arm
through Hester's, lowering her voice to a whisper. 'It is
all right, Hester. I shall not let them harm you, I
promise. You must be strong, for my sake as well as your
own.'

With relief she saw understanding and hope register in
her maid's eyes.

'For you, my lady, I will try,' she said shakily.

Alynna held her head erect, her manner still proud despite her dishevelled appearance. Once in the narrow corridor, the guards pressed closely about them, a sign that Griswolde was still treating them as prisoners. When they walked past his rooms on the first floor, Alynna's stomach cramped at the aroma of spiced meats and freshly baked bread drifting from the open door, but she squared her shoulders. She refused to have her will undermined by Griswolde's sly trickery!

They moved on towards the great oak door leading into the courtyard just as Griswolde entered the tower. The guards fell back as he approached, and he bowed to Alynna. She glared at him haughtily, undeceived by his false courtesy.

'Your manners have not improved, dear lady,' he drawled.

'I pay homage only to those whom I respect!' she retorted. 'In that, as in all things, I will not be bullied into submission.'

'Everyone has their weaknesses—even you, my dear.' He gripped her arm, which she jerked away, as he led her to one side of the door while the guards ushered Hester through to the courtyard. 'I will have you as my bride, Alynna!'

'And I will deny you, sir, unto my dying breath.'

He laughed, a thin wheezing sound like the wind rustling leaves around a graveyard at night. 'I think not, my lady.' He insolently appraised her figure.

Alynna dug her nails into her palms, mastering her desire to strike the leer from his face. 'I shall never marry you. You are . . .' A demented scream, which set every nerve of her body on edge, cut short her scathing words. 'Hester!' she gasped, lifting the hem of her skirts to run out into the courtyard.

The bright sunlight after the darkness within momentarily blinded her. Blinking at the pain stabbing at her eyes, her throat dried as the screams continued and she beheld the scene before her. Hester, kicking and screaming, was being dragged by two guards to a huge pile of faggots, upon the top of which stood a large wooden stake.

'Stop! Stop at once!' she shouted, her voice quivering with outrage and a deepening terror at Griswolde's intentions for Hester. Her command was ignored. Shaking with anger, she started forward but found her way barred by Griswolde.

'There is but one way you can save your maid! Give me your answer.'

Alynna stared helplessly at Hester, who was now being tied to the stake.

'Well, my lady?' Griswolde urged harshly. 'Do we marry within the hour—or does the wench burn as a convicted Lollard?'

'Hester recanted!' Alynna protested. 'She was pardoned.'

'But I have witnesses who declare they have heard her speaking against the power of the church!'

Disgust and nausea writhing within her, Alynna flared, 'Then you have bribed them to speak your filth!'

Her wrist was gripped in a pinching hold as he leaned closer to make himself heard above Hester's screams. 'Choose your words carefully, lady. The fire is about to be lit!'

A black-robed priest holding aloft a large cross stepped forward, and Griswolde's guards were ringed about the stake. When the priest began reciting prayers and a captain advanced carrying a lighted flambeau, Hester's screams became demented.

'My lady, help me!'

Alynna's throat constricted. She could not let Hester die! Especially not in this way, which had filled her with terror for so long. She was prepared to sacrifice her own life, but not that of a dear and faithful friend whose loyalty had brought her to this end. Griswolde had won.

'Release Hester and have her tended to,' she said hollowly. 'It shall be as you say.'

Griswolde signalled for a guard to untie Hester from the stake, then declared triumphantly, 'The wedding shall take place at once.'

'No!' she burst out, overcome with panic.'

An ugly smile twisted Griswolde's face. 'Your word is given, my lady. Do you go back on it?'

An inner voice was ordering her to play for time. 'Would you shame me by wedding me while I still reek from the stench of my prison cell?'

'You are too proud! A little humility at such a time will do you no harm.' He beckoned to the priest and ordered him to await them at the village church, before turning back to Alynna. 'All is prepared. There is no need for delay.'

Hester was safe—but only as long as this repugnant bargain was kept with Griswolde. At the touch of his hand upon her arm, Alynna swayed, nausea sweeping through her.

'I warned you, lady. No trickery!' he snarled.

'Is it any wonder I am faint?' She seized upon this chance of delay. 'I have eaten nothing for three days. Would you have me swoon during the ceremony, sir, and be unable to say my vows?'

'There will be food and wine aplenty, once the service is over. I doubt you will faint, knowing that your maid's life depends on your compliance with my wishes! You have no hope of a rescue by Trevowan; he does not know of this place. Even if he did, the bridge was washed away in the floods yesterday.'

She knew then that she had clung to the foolish longing for Trevowan to rescue her. He was her knight —her champion—but it was an impossible dream. Griswolde and the threat of the stake were grim reality. Once Hester was safe, Griswolde's treachery could be exposed to the king. And Lord Trevowan . . . The hopelessness of her love buffeted her, leaving her wretched.

Dimly she was aware of Griswolde taking her arm and leading her through the castle precincts and over the drawbridge towards the village church. She saw everything through a haze, while all the time her thoughts concentrated on the Earl of Trevowan. Perhaps this way, at least, he would be free, she reasoned. It was not as though he loved her. The bond between them would be irrevocably broken. He would soon forget her and marry Lady Celia, who would bring him wealth and power—those were the reasons he must marry, to strengthen his house for the generations to come. No matter that she now knew her blood was as proud as his, nothing could erase the stigma of her bastardy. Was this how her mother had felt when she had been forced by the late king to set out for France where her chosen bridegroom awaited her? The knowledge of the truth of her own birth would be her downfall. Griswolde thought to save his skin by wedding her, the bastard daughter of Lady Constance, who was the late king's cousin.

Alynna's legs shook, not with fear, but with anger and humiliation, as they walked to the squat Norman church. Curious villagers, many looking puzzled as to what was happening, had come out of their cottages.

'Smile, my dear,' Griswolde commanded. 'Our people have come to see us married. There will be feasting and rejoicing this day.'

'Not by me!' she retorted fiercely.

'Your anger adds spice to the prospect of bedding you this night! You are a woman governed by her passions —you will not disappoint me.'

'It will be a hollow victory, sir, I promise.'

She turned away, her flesh cringing at the thought of Griswolde laying hands on her. When she saw their path to the church lined with Griswolde's men, she was seized with panic. There was no troop of galloping horsemen coming to save her! A wild impulse to run overcame her and was quickly stifled; even if she could break through the guards, she had given her word to save Hester. Her head tilted proudly. At that moment it would have been easier to walk to her execution; at least then she could have salvaged her honour with dignity. They halted in the porch, where the ceremony would be performed, before going into the church for the blessing. In a loud brash voice, Griswolde began to repeat his vows.

Alynna stood rigidly at his side, her hope fading as the priest turned to her and began to recite her vows. Every part of her rebelled at being forced to this act, but the sound of Hester's screams still echoed in her mind, and the words refused to form.

'Speak, woman!' Griswolde ordered. 'Or you know . . . !'

His words were drowned by a trumpet-blast from the ridge of the hill behind the church. Alynna's heart leapt, and the priest faltered. Unable to see what was happening, she strained her ears, and caught the thud of approaching hoofbeats.

'Get on with the ceremony!' Griswolde snapped at the priest's hesitation, his hand biting cruelly into Alynna's arm and preventing her from running outside. 'Marry us, damn you! Get on with it!'

In the churchyard, the peace was shattered by the noise of galloping, snorting horses sliding to a halt, accompanied by angry shouting. At the sound of steel resounding against steel Alynna spun round, but Griswolde grabbed her waist and held her back as Trevowan's tall figure filled the porch.

From outside, a voice rose above the others. 'Put away your arms. This is the king's business.' The sound of the fighting stopped.

'You are too late, Trevowan—the wench is mine!'

Sword poised ready to attack, the Earl of Trevowan froze in his tracks as he took in Alynna's dishevelled appearance. Then his glance settled on the priest in his vestments, and his colour drained.

'I arrest you in the king's name!' he said in a voice like splintered ice.

'On what charge?' Griswolde sneered.

'Abduction of the king's ward.'

'Lady Alynna came with me of her own free will,' Griswolde blustered, 'as she is about to become my willing bride.'

'That's not true, my lord!' Alynna cried. 'I had no choice. He was going to burn Hester at the stake.'

A muscle throbbed along Trevowan's jaw, and with a casual flick of his wrist he tossed the edge of his cloak over his shoulder, his voice low and dangerous. 'The

lady says she is not willing to marry you. Wise words, as
you do not have his Majesty's permission. Let her
go—now!'

Griswolde's hold tightened about Alynna, her
attempts to prise his arm free useless in her weakened
state.

'Of course she will marry me! What choice has the
wench?' Griswolde declared sanctimoniously. 'Her
reputation was lost the moment she left Thornbank.'

'With each word, you condemn yourself further,'
Trevowan said with lethal coldness. 'If you have harmed
Lady Alynna, this day will be your last.'

'At least I would marry her!' Griswolde sneered. 'You
would make her your whore!'

Alynna flinched at the cruelty of Griswolde's words.
Was he to spare her no shame? Trevowan's expression
was engimatic. He might have saved her from marriage
to Griswolde, but it changed nothing between them.
Behind the earl she saw Joel, his fool's stick stuck
incongruously in his belt, edge forward and look
expectantly at the earl.

'Do you intend to hide behind Lady Alynna's skirts,
Griswolde?' Trevowan provoked. 'Or are you man
enough to fight me for her?'

The effect of this challenge ran through the people
like heath-fire. Silence fell upon the churchyard as both
men glared at each other.

'This is God's house!' the priest declared, his voice
trembling. 'There will be no fighting here.'

Alynna could feel the tension coiling through
Griswolde's frame. Abruptly she was pushed towards
Trevowan with force, and he flung out his free arm to
catch her. Her heart beating wildly, she glanced up at
him, but his gaze was fixed upon his cousin. His sword
raised in readiness, he side-stepped, placing Alynna
protectively behind him. Joel appeared at her side and
drew her further back, but she was too much concerned
at the imminent duel to do more than acknowledge his
presence with a curt nod.

A gasp went up from the crowd when Griswolde drew

his sword, and with the tips of their blades touching, both men moved into the churchyard. Soldiers and villagers fell back as they circled each other. With an animal grunt, Griswolde lunged, his sword slashing viciously. Trevowan leapt aside, parrying the attack with lightning speed.

Joel sucked in his breath, and snatching the fool's stick from his belt, he shook it angrily at Griswolde. Beside him, Alynna was terrified that Trevowan would be injured. Her fears were groundless, for, despite his armour, it was obvious that he had the mastery over Griswolde.

'Lay down your arms!' Trevowan demanded. He was not even breathing heavily, while Griswolde was sweating profusely, his sword-thrusts erratic. 'Don't be a fool, man. You cannot win!'

'Damn you, Trevowan!' Griswolde panted. 'I'll see you in hell before I surrender. It was all within my grasp —riches . . . even a hold over the king. Do you know whose daughter the wench is? The king's cousin's! I would have had power, with her as my bride.'

'You would have won for yourself exile at the very least,' Trevowan rapped out above the clash of steel, as he forced Griswolde into retreat.

Sir Geoffrey's face worked with fury, his movements slowing. With a rush of pride, Alynna noted that Trevowan was deliberately holding back, unwilling, even after all Griswolde had done, to wound him. Griswolde began to slash wildly, and Alynna's heart lurched as his sword seemed about to cleave Trevowan's head, but with a deft turn of his wrist, he sent Griswolde's sword flying, and his own blade pressed against his cousin's heart.

Sir Geoffrey turned grey, but remained sullen-eyed as he held up his hands in a gesture of defeat. 'I yield —curse you!'

Alynna relaxed. Trevowan stepped back, resheathing his sword as he turned his attention to her. She felt Joel stiffen at the boldness of Lord Trevowan's gaze when he moved towards them. At the same time, from over Trevowan's shoulder, she saw Griswolde, his face contorting with hatred, spring forward.

A dagger poised in his hand, he shouted, 'Die, Trevowan! And may you rot in hell!'

Alynna screamed. Trevowan spun round, swiftly drawing his sword, but Joel had already started forward. With the dexterity of a tumbler, he leapt across the intervening space and brought his stick down hard across Griswolde's wrist. With a crack of snapping bone, the dagger fell to the ground. At the same time Joel's wiry body rammed against the knight, sending him sprawling back into a muddy puddle. Two of Trevowan's guards hauled Griswolde, dripping and spluttering, to his feet.

'Bind him, and take the cur from my sight!' Trevowan snapped. 'He will spend the night in his own dungeons. It is for the king to deal with his villainy.' He paused to speak to Joel. The jester nodded, and with an impish grin at Alynna, shambled off towards the castle. 'The fool goes to fetch Hester.' Trevowan answered her unspoken query, his hands reaching for hers and drawing her back into the porch before pulling her close. The priest coughed, disapproving of their conduct, but a glare from Trevowan silenced him, and he disappeared into the church.

'Praise God, I got here in time!' Trevowan's eyes blazed. 'Must I spend my life rescuing you from the folly of your reckless deeds?'

'You are relieved of such a burden. From now on my life is in his Majesty's hands,' she reminded him, the traitorous beat of her heart threatening to make her forget everything but the warmth of his hands covering hers.

'And if I should not want that freedom, would you deny me, Alynna?' he said huskily, his arms sliding about her waist.

His touch was destroying her control, but what he asked was madness. 'If you have learnt who my mother is,' she said heavily, 'you will know that what you ask is impossible. In my heart I shall never deny you, my lord—but bodily I must. The king would never countenance my becoming your mistress.'

'But I shall have you, Alynna.' He pulled her closer, his breath warm upon her upturned face, his lips devastatingly, temptingly, close. 'Did I not so vow at our last meeting? Nothing has changed.'

She reared back in his arms, her voice wretched. 'No! I love you too much for you to throw your life away because of a moment's passion. Even your friendship with the king will not save you from his wrath.'

Trevowan gazed down at her beautiful face, and brushed a stray tear from the corner of her eye, strangely humbled by the selflessness of her love. He could feel her resistance in the soft curves of her body as he drew her against him. 'Then, my dearest love,' he smiled, 'I shall have to marry you.'

Instead of the joy he expected, her eyes sparked with anger. 'Your jest is cruel, my lord, and unworthy of you. A family as proud, and ancient, as yours do not wed bastards—whether they be the king's cousin or no.'

'There is no woman in all England more fitting to be my bride!' He controlled his temper, and then realising that she knew only part of the truth, he relented. Did not her words prove her worth?

'Alynna, my beloved, you will be Countess of Trevowan with the king's blessing. Sir Robert and Lady Constance were young and recklessly in love. They made their vows before a priest—Father Dominic— but without the king's permission, the marriage was not legal. Lady Constance was pre-contracted to a Burgundian Count. The marriage to your father was annulled. You were born in secret, before Lady Constance left for France. It is a condition of the king's agreement to our marriage that the true circumstances of your birth remain a secret. Do you agree?'

Alynna's heart was too full to speak. She gazed adoringly into his eyes, her hands sliding over his broad chest to clasp his neck and draw his head down towards her lips in answer. The ardour of his response made her sway against him with a shiver of ecstasy, and his arms tightened until the unyielding steel of his armour bruising her hip made her wince. Instantly, he drew back.

'Curse this armour!' He grinned at her ruefully. 'In my need for you, I am thoughtless.'

'Never that, my lord.' She smiled wickedly up at him. 'This moment is too precious . . . Would that we were any place but here . . . for, to my shame, my lord, I want you!'

At the answering passion in his eyes, she drew back, blushing furiously, but, with a laugh, Trevowan led her into the church. 'Come, we shall find the priest. The king has decreed we shall be married in his presence at Court. But today we shall say our vows before the priest here. An hour's ride away I have a hunting-lodge. It will be our bridal chamber. Tonight you will be mine, my love. Truly mine.'

The crackling of the fire broke the silence of the cosy but sparsely furnished chamber when later that evening Alynna gazed raptly across the table. The half-eaten dishes were brushed aside as her husband drew her to her feet and into the circle of his arms. She was only dimly aware of Hester shooing the last of the servants from the room and closing the door behind all of them as they were left in privacy.

'My sweet, sweet, Alynna.' Trevowan's voice was low as he bent to kiss the throbbing pulse below her ear. 'I have waited too long for this moment. Would that tonight I could make you mine amid the grandeur and comfort of Trevowan—not this humble lodge.'

'I like the lodge well, my lord, for it was the pilgrim I fell in love with, not the noble earl. The setting is perfect. We are alone. This is all that matters.'

Gently he removed the circlet and flimsy veil covering her hair, running his fingers through the dark tresses, his eyes devouring her like silver fire—a fire that kindled an answering flame within her soul. Entranced, she touched his shaven cheek, his rugged handsomeness and the potent masculinity of his hard body rendering her breathless.

'My noble pilgrim,' she whispered. 'My love.'

His lips tilted provocatively. 'My pilgrimage taught me much—not least to value a rare and priceless gift when I hold it in my arms.'

She gazed at him wonderingly, cherishing his words, her heart full to overflowing. He kissed her deeply, and she felt her desire surging to match his. His hands moved to the sash at her waist, untying it, as he declared, 'From the first I wanted you—as I have wanted no other.' He slid the dressing-robe from her shoulders, his voice low with passion as his mouth travelled down her neck. 'When I left for Court, still ignorant of the truth, I had resolved to ask the king for permission to marry you.'

She arched against him as his mouth fastened over her breast. Her hands slid beneath his robe, delighting in the feel of the dark curling hair and the heat of his hard-muscled chest. She kissed a deep scar on his shoulder, restraining her desire to learn every secret of his powerful body.

'How I wronged you.' She purred contentedly as she nestled seductively against him. 'I wanted to hate you for the dishonour and shame I thought you would bring upon me, yet when you left, I was but half alive. I knew then that I would forsake honour rather than you lose you, my love.'

His exultant laugh set her cheeks aflame, and she was swung effortlessly into his arms and carried to the bed. 'My pilgrim countess!' The husky timbre of his voice gently rebuked her. 'I would show you how much I love you . . .'

The dominance of his lips silenced her, his hands and mouth causing a starbust of sensations as he explored and revered the soft curves and hollows of her body. And she answered him, kiss for kiss, touch for touch, lured by the mastery of his caresses until their bodies fused, in the fulfilment of everlasting love.